CHAPTER I

A bello returned to the computer room late in the evening. He had been for a longer than usual walk around the compound. He dialed the code and studied the readout covering the three hours of his absence. All robot supervisors of the either other compounds had reported at their programed hourly intervals and all was peaceful on Capernica. He left the room and walked softly across to the night rom removing his day robe as he went. By the turquoise light of one of the moons he could see his woman Eloni stretched out in the bed, her long black hair curling over her shoulders and hiding her superb breasts from him. He could feel the ache of love and desire in him. He shook his head impatiently and taking up his day robe again, he left. He returned to the computer room and sat staring at the variegated lights on the computers until he dropped asleep. He awoke in time to see the last of the five moons disappear below the horizon and the first outline of daylight was blurring the sky. In fact the five moons were each nothing more than large chunks of rock, the debris of some vast stellar catastrophe. Their turquoise light relieved the otherwise black nights. He stretched wearily and then bending forward examined the computer readouts for the rest of the night.

Xon compound again. Once more the robot supervisors had reported signs of vandalism. For the fifth week and for the fifth consecutive night of the fiftieth week. What had gone wrong, Abello asked himself again and again. As appointed Leader it was his responsibility to find out. He had been over to Xon compound countless times but could find no reason at all. Mattas, the compound's leader, was likewise as baffled as he. Other compounds had reported similar disturbances but these were apparently short lived. Why, thought Abello, after generations of peace and tranquility, should there now be a whole series of petty and so far apparently meaningless crimes? He was startled by a knock at the door.

"Come in," he said, and Eloni entered. "You did not sleep?" she queried.

"No, I stayed here."

She came and kissed the top of his head. "At least have the morning meal with me, it is all ready."

They both returned to the day room. After the meal Eloni asked him if he wanted to sleep but Abello shook his head. "I must get back to the computer room."

1

When he arrived the first thing he did was to feed in a series of computer codes and various different sets of coordinates. Simultaneously a different set of figures appeared on the screen giving a complete chronological pattern of disturbances. Abello gazed at them for a long time but the lists appeared meaningless. He aborted them in a fit of rage and strode across to the long square aperture and gazed out across the fields. Tiny plots of cultivation containing regimented rows of vegetables all tended by the robot workers. He reflected that they were fortunate that, although small, Capernica had extremely fertile soil in places enabling the population to live free from the threat of starvation. He could see little groups of robot workers walking up and down the rows carefully giving each plant an accurately measured rate of water for the morning. In the late afternoon they would do the same thing again.

This idle gazing was not doing any good, he thought. He must again return to Xon compound but first he would have a rest. He punched a button on the computer and the robot driver of the hovercraft answers. "Bring the hovercraft at 2 p.m.," he commanded.

He then sent a computerized message to the receiver set at Xon informing Mattas of his plans and then he went to rest. As he closed his eyes he wished that Eloni were with him but realized that it was too dangerous in the daylight.

Eloni woke him at one with some refreshment and watched him as he dressed. "Is there more trouble at Xon compound?" she asked.

"Yes, I'm afraid so," he replied and he drew her to him. They could feel their passions rising and it was Eloni who stepped back.

"No, no, not now, we may be caught." Abello reluctantly agreed.

"You must go and attend to Xon compound as you are the Leader," she continued. "I am merely your second woman."

"Be waiting when I return." "As ever."

Second woman. The words beat a tattoo in his brain. This staccato was interrupted by a rush of air which signaled the arrival of his hovercraft, gleaming in black and gold with the robot pilot in uniform of the same colors. Xon compound was barely an hour's flying time away and the hovercraft was an ideal way to travel. Capernica had no steep hills or anything resembling mountains and no tall buildings, just enclaves at the centers of various agricultural compounds. In deed the tallest group on the whole planet was the one containing the cluster of five water storage tanks. The terrain was mostly covered in orange sand but here and there a few acres of fertile land were to be found. Trees were sparsely scattered and rather small and squat. Scientists on the planet thought that this was the result of the high gravity and temperature with the combined effect of a thin atmosphere and little rainfall. Apparently in the past there had been very little volcanic activity and hence a dense atmosphere caused breathlessness after hard physical activity. However with the various robots doing most of the physical work the population rarely exerted themselves. Indeed they seemed indifferent to the gradual loss of physical prowess.

After about fifteen minutes of flying time Abello could see the complex astronomical installation that had been erected as part of Ishta compound. Although not as tall as the water tower its dish shaped aerial was an enormous saucer of finely tuned parts. It maintained a constant scan for evidence of other intelligent life forms which must, on a statistical basis alone, revolve around many of the stars which could be seen at night. It had long been proved by experiments that given the right conditions of radiation, chemical constituents, etc. molecules were formed which led to eventual reproductions of themselves. It was inconceivable to Abello and the leaders before him that the two thousand inhabitants of Capernica were the only intelligent life in the whole vastness of space. Another forty minutes or so and the craft whispered to the ground at the arched entrance to Xon compound. Abello descended to great the old man advancing towards him.

"Mattas! You are well?"

"Yes, for an old man. Come, let us go in and talk in the courtyard."

Each compound was built in a circle with a center courtyard. All main rooms had doors leading onto this and in the center were usually a few flowers and an ornamental fish pond. Mattas led the way and indicated the two seats by the pond. One of the women from the compound brought a cold drink for Abello.

"I am almost afraid to ask what has brought you to Xon again," said Mattas, "especially as you have not brought either of your wives, Arilyn or Eloni with you. I fear it is as our acknowledged leader that you are here."

"Too true," replied Abello. "Last night was the fifth night in succession that the robot supervisors reported vandalism here. I would like to see it."

'Over here."

Mattas led the way to his rooms. Inside the main hall lay broken chairs and tables and other pieces of furniture which looked as though they had been picked up and hurled to the ground in a fit of rage.

"Why?" murmured Abello. "We have such a tranquil life here."

Mattas shook his head. "Come and I will show you more."

Abello followed him to the farthest outside wall. It was painted in vivid colors with all sorts of obscenities. "I left it untouched in case you would like to have it examined by the scientists," Mattas said.

Abello nodded. "Did anyone hear or notice anything?" he questioned.

Mattas shook his head. "I have found no one."

3

"Well, I must see all in this compound," said Abello. "I am the leader and I will have our laws obeyed. This must come to an end. Mattas, have the order passed that I will inspect all homes in the compound in an hour."

"Yes." He disappeared and Abello returned to sit by the pond. Presently Mattas reappeared. "It is done," he said. It was cooling off by now but the atmosphere was very still. How nice it could be to have air blowing, thought Abello suddenly. He realized Mattas was talking to him. "Have you checked all this on the computer?"

"Yes, I have been dialing and redialing each night." Mattas was obviously very worried as due to his seniority he was responsible for life and the continuance of law and order within the compound. "It is the very pettiness of it that worries me. I am afraid that whatever or whoever is behind it will get on to bigger and more danger ground."

"If necessary I will search every room in every compound," said Abello.

"But you cannot. That is breaking the rule of privacy."

"I can and I will. I am the Leader. This has not happened before and I must therefore make fresh decisions on this. Of course I will consult with the other members of the Council before taking such a step."

"Is it possible that some of the robots' circuits have become tangled and they are responsible?" queried Mattas.

"No, I can rule that out because they are programmed to obey us in positive commands only and such negative destructive orders would have no meaning for them. However, enough of this subject. How is your family, Mattas?"

The old man smiled. "My daughter Rester, who is married to Arabus the woodcarver, is due to have a child shortly. As you know, I had practically given up hope of ever seeing any grandchildren. My wife is long gone and Rester is my one joy. And how are your wives?"

"They are both fine," Abello said.

Immediately a picture of Eloni appeared in his mind. Each leader was allowed two wives in order that all his needs may be satisfied and that the chance of the qualities of his leadership would be carried through should either of them have a child. Unfortunately neither of his were pregnant although it was hardly Arilyn's fault as he seldom went to her, preferring Eloni instead.

At the end of the term of the leader's office – about two years – the women went to Eus compound which housed the old, barren and former leaders' women. There they helped with the children and prepared two more girls for the next leader.

By this time the two assistants came to tell Abello that all rooms were ready for inspection and that each family was within its own rooms in the

4

compound. Accompanied by Mattas he inspected each room for signs of anything unusual or different but found nothing. Neither could he elicit any information from any of the people there. The process took about an hour.

At the finish Abello clasped Mattas' hand. "Don't worry, old friend, I will take care of this for you. Go and rest, as I know you must be tired. I will return to my compound, and thank you for your help."

They embraced. Abello left, the hovercraft kicking up a fine spray of orange sand. On the way back to his compound the computer flashed a message that some petty vandalism had just taken place over at Zin compound. Abello ordered the hovercraft over there but he could learn nothing upon arrival.

Returning to his compound he found Eloni waiting with the evening meal. He told her of his day. Afterwards they lay on the night couch which was about three feet off the floor, attached to the ceiling by woven golden chains. This gave the bed a gentle rocking motion and took advantage of any night breezes which might happen to pass. Eloni started to massage him as she could sense that he was in a disturbed and restless frame of mind. Soon she began kissing and touching him gently. He gradually responded and the caresses on both sides became firmer. Shortly they began to fondle each other in the warm and private places of their bodies. From being limp and yield the bodies became hard and suffused with desire. Their breathing became shallower and he could see that Eloni's eyes were glazed and withdrawn and knew that his were likewise. Finally the need to dominate and to be dominated overcame them both. She opened her legs and he plunged joyfully in and the moment of orgasmic triumph was as a split second of true unity. Afterwards they lay side by side in a mutual spirit of warm contentment and drowsiness and Abello, marveling yet again at her peach soft skin and almond shaped blue eyes wondered again how he could part with her. They fell asleep.

Next morning after breakfast Abello again returned to the computer room. This time he reran all the readouts from the memory bank concentrating on statistical evidence. While this was being done he contacted the other members of the Council and informed them of his visit to Xon yesterday. He also informed them of this decision to carry out simultaneous searches of all compounds if he had their agreement. One or two of them were flatly against the idea but most of them thought it was the right idea after they had mulled it over. Abello said that he would bring the matter up at the next Council meeting which was a month away. Little did he realize that the spinners of fate had woven a different pattern.

As Abello glanced over the now complete sheets of information he noticed a disturbing trend running through the population trends. There was a distinct decline in the birthrate. How odd, he thought, that I was never aware of it. He was used to seeing small groups of children at play and on his walks he could hear their young voices chanting the replies to the teachers. He recalled Mattas' words of yesterday that he had almost given up hope of seeing any grandchildren, and he realized too that neither of his wives was pregnant. Indeed it appeared quite a while since any leader had gotten one of his wives with child. He read on. The women normally had a child breeding expectancy of ten years during which they had two periods a year. They could at a maximum produce five children. However, over the last few generations it would appear that this had declined and in fact it was now usually one in that time or two at the most. He redialed these figures into the computer and it showed before his eyes that on these calculations the population would decline to a handful of people within a short period of time. He immediately wondered why this had happened and if anything could be done to alter the trend. He resolved to talk to one of the doctors who dealt with the women.

Three successive shrieks of the alarm jarred his ears. This was the emergency call. Grabbing the speech communication switch he yelled, "Abello here – what is it?"

"Abello – quickly, it is the water tanks," a voice shouted. "At least one of the tanks has been holed."

"I am coming, and try to get hold of something to catch the liquid in," he said.

Quickly he gave the command for the hovercraft to be brought around. He tore outside and as he strapped himself in he ordered the robot driver to take him to the water tanks at maximum speed. Upon arrival he found everyone running about and shouting. Quickly he gave instructions for a hole to be dug to see if any of the water could be caught. One of the men came running up to him.

"The robot workers have had all their instruction tapes nullified and they are quite useless." Abello nodded. He went and checked the level of the water in the tank. Almost three-quarters empty. The precious liquid which would take years to replace. He realized that it would mean rationing for both domestic and agricultural use. Just then one of the fellow Councilors came rushing around the corner.

"Abello, I have found a hole in the tank. Come and see."

They ran around the corner and he indicated an opening in the outer wall of the tank. Abello squeezed through and stood up. The inner wall looked solid enough. Cautiously he squeezed around and after he reached halfway he saw the hole – not very big but distinct enough. So this damage had been done willfully. Abello felt almost physically sick at the thought of it. That anyone on Capernica might even contemplate such a thing was beyond his mind and at the back of his conscious thought he realized that he was afraid it may be someone he knew, even a friend. He squeezed back again and out through the hole. The fellow Councilman was still standing staring.

"Get some samples of the water to the laboratory for analysis," he said.

He kept the awful knowledge of the sabotage to himself. By this time the men had dug a large hole and sprayed it with plastic foam which hardened into a waterproof seal. They hastily dug a channel and it looked as though they would save the remainder of the water. Abello checked each robot worker and reprogrammed their tapes. He then made sure that there was no damage to the other two tanks. Finally all was restored to normality and he was left alone with the workers. He returned to his hovercraft. He was going to return to his compound and Eloni when impulsively he decided to go and visit Mattas again. He felt the need to talk over what he had discovered with the old man. When he arrived he discovered that Mattas was out. He was about to leave when a voice called to him through the gathering night.

"Abello, are you not at least going to spend a few moments with me?"

He turned and looked. "Is it Rester?" he queried. "Mattas' daughter? How are you?"

"I am fine," she smiled. "I have been sitting here watching the pale light from the moons make dancing patterns on the sand. My father has gone to visit some friends and my husband is still working on a carving down at the shop. This is the most peaceful time of day for me when I can sit outside and gaze into the distance. But come, sit down beside me." She indicated the ground beside here.

"I did not realize you lived next door to your father," said Abello.

"I do not. I live at the other end of the compound, but when Arabus notified me that he would not be home until much later I decided to walk down here and keep father company. I should have checked first to see if he was here."

"I had not realized that they were so busy at the carving shop. Has he often been working late?"

"Yes, for many weeks, now, although every once in a while he is home early for a whole week. Did you come straight from your compound, and where is Eloni?"

"No, I have been out." He was reluctant to tell her about the water tanks. "Eloni stayed behind tonight."

"Would you like some refreshment? You must be thirsty," Rester inquired.

"If you have a cool drink ready, please."

She rose clumsily and as she turned to go into the house the aqua light from the moons threw her outline in sharp relief. Abello was astonished to see how enormous she was. He could not recollect of all the women he had seen that had been pregnant that any of them had been anything like the size that Rester was. She fetched their drinks and they sat in sociable silence for a while.

"I should leave," said Abello eventually, "Would you like a ride home in the hovercraft?"

"No, thank you, I will wait a bit longer."

"Abello, what are you doing here?" It was the irritable voice of Arabus. "I came to find Rester and take her home, as she shouldn't stay so far from our home in her condition."

"I came to see Mattas and I found Rester here, so I was just keeping her company until he returned."

"One of my fellow workers told me about the accident at the water tanks. Did you lose much water?"

"Almost one tank full," replied Abello.

"Wat is this about the water?" questioned Rester. Abello explained that one of the water tanks had sprung a leak. More than that he did not divulge.

"Well, I think I should take you home, Rester," said Arabus. He was obviously ill at ease for some reason and anxious to be off. They walked off into the dark. Abello went to get into his hovercraft when he heard a cry of pain. Dashing up to them he found Rester clutching her stomach.

"What is it?"

"My labor pains," she gasped.

"Come, let us get her into the hovercraft and I can take you all home."

"No, no," protested Arabus, "we can manage." They continued walking but soon Rester bent double with more pain. Arabus turned and called to Abello, "You had better get Mattas' bed ready. I don't think she will be able to travel at all."

Abello dashed into the house and pulled back the cover on the bed. He ran outside and the two men carefully carried Rester into the night room and gently laid her on the bed. She was moaning to herself now and clawing at her body. Arabus left to call the doctor. He went into the living room to use the small computer which acted as a communications instrument as well as controlling the cooking, heating, lighting and the functions of the servant robots. Abello tried to calm Rester and endeavored to cover her body with her night robe as she had ripped off her day robe. When Arabus returned to stand by the bed Abello left and quickly called up Eloni on the speech channel.

"Abello, what is it? You have been gone so long," her worried tones echoed in his ear.

8

"Never mind, have my spare hovercraft bring you to Xon compound. Rester is here and her pains have started. I don't know how long the doctor will be but he will need trained help."

"I'll be there," she said.

Abello paced the living room checking on Rester every once in a while. Most of the time Arabus stood by the bed staring down at her. After a while the doctor arrived. He was a young man called Oah. He explained that he had just replaced Arias as the chief physician for women. He went straight into the bedroom, first removing Arabus and drawing the curtain over the doorway. Soon after Eloni arrived and joined Oah in the bedroom. Abello attempted a few words of comfort but Arabus seemed to prefer to stare moodily out of the window. From time to time jagged screams rent the air and then all would be quiet. Of Mattas there was no sign. Suddenly the screening curtain was pulled aside and there stood Oah, drenched in blood. He looked grim.

"What is it? What is it?" Arabus yelled at him. "You are father to three."

"Three!" Arabus and Abello chorused.

"Yes, your wife delivered three, but one of the boys died soon after. However, you have a boy and a girl."

Arabus knocked aside Oah and charged in to see Rester. Eloni came flying out of the room.

"Come the both of you and wash up." Abello turned, it was Mattas. "I heard," he said in response to their unspoken questions. He looked old and weary. Oah and Eloni went to wash up and Mattas and Abello sat down.

"Never can I remember two births at the same time, let alone three," commented Abello.

"My poor daughter," said Mattas.

"Cursed you are, accursed, and you have brought death to me," they heard Rester yell. "Get out. I don't even want to look at you."

They heard racking sobs. Arabus appeared and Oah returned to the bedroom. Abello told Eloni that she had better go in and see if she could assist the doctor. He crossed the room and put his arm around Arabus. "Come, let us toast your son and daughter. You have been fortunate indeed."

"Fortunate indeed, you blind fool, Abello, I am as Rester says, accursed. It would be better if I died."

"But you have two children."

"Two. Two more brought into life for what? To be carvers or teachers or maybe bring the girl up to be the Leader's woman. You cannot mean it. There is nothing, nothing here for them or me. Abello, you are so blinkered you cannot turn your head and know what is growing beside you. I despise you, my wife and this planet. If I could only escape."

"Arabus, Mattas, come quickly," interrupted Oah. The men disappeared into the room.

Eloni came out and rushed into Abello's arms. "She is dying and she is not even trying to live. It is as though she fully accepts it. And Abello, Arabus seems indifferent to her and he has not even looked at the children."

Just then Oah reappeared. "She is dead. She died in Mattas' arms."

Arabus rushed out of the night room and tore outside. They heard him start up his hovercraft and accelerate into the night. Mattas came out, and Abello went to comfort him. Eloni went to another house in the compound to make arrangements for Mattas to spend the night there.

Oah came out of the bedroom with the two babies, all freshly scrubbed and wrapped in new cloth, one under each arm. Abello looked at them asleep, unaware of the tragedy surrounding them. "Will you send for two of the women from Eus compound to come down and take care of these babies here for the time being? Ask them to bring emergency supplies of food."

"I will, and I will also organize some robot watchers to stand guard over Rester's body until it is time for it to be prepared for the funeral pyre," responded Abello.

While he was doing this Eloni returned with Anice who lived a few doors away. Mattas left with her to spend the night, his steps faltering with the weight of his grief. Abello and Eloni waited silently, each holding a child, until the women arrived from Eus. After Oah had settled them and the babies for the night he explained that he would sleep there as well so as to be on call in case of an emergency. Abello and Eloni boarded the hovercraft and returned to their compound.

Abello recorded the night's events on the computer tape and went wearily to the night room. They lay silently together as the bed rocked to and fro. Both were aware of the night's happenings and Abello was troubled by events. They fell asleep. Eloni was already up when Abello awoke.

"You have slept long, my love," she whispered as she bent to kiss him, her embraces soft and gentle.

Abello smiled at her. "I thank the moons and the sun that I awake to you," he said.

"You do not have but five more months," she mocked.

"Do not mock me so," he protested. "I must dress and go and find the latest news of Mattas and his family. And do we know where Arabus has gone?"

He dressed rapidly and went to the control room. He ordered a robot guard to stand outside and admit no one. The first thing he did was to check on the babies. Oah reported that all was well there. "Has Arabus returned?"

he asked.

"No, there has been no sign of him here. Anice has been in to say that Mattas had shut himself in her night room but I told her to leave him alone."

"Thank you, Oah."

Abello then checked all around for the latest reports. Several robot workers were busily repairing the water tank. No one had seen Arabus and on such a small planet it looked as though somebody was hiding him. After he had received the last reports Abello walked to the left-hand corner of the room. He pressed a spot on the wall known only to each successive chosen leader. A small panel slid open to reveal an intricately carved box. Carefully he took it and carried it to a table. Placing it on the table he opened it and lifted out the ancient document it contained. This was the Great Charter by whom all lives were governed. It was brought by their ancestors and had been handed down from generation to generation. At one time the Council had considered having it microfilmed and stored in the computer memory bank but it was felt that it would be better to keep it in its original form. He began to read. An hour passed. He made some notes as he went along. He finished and returned the document to the box and to the wall. He rejoined Eloni for lunch. Afterwards he went again to the control room and worked on the report of the water tank incident for the Council. He checked the readouts once again and noted that as yet Arabus was still in hiding. The day passed. That night his need of Eloni was so great that she had barely time to climb into the bed before he was upon her. Afterwards they fell asleep holding each other closely.

"Leader, Leader, come at once," a voice yelled over the alarm loudspeaker system.

Abello pressed the communications switch beside the bed. "Abello, what is it and where is it?" he asked.

"It is Oah, Arabus has returned. He had grabbed the boy child by the neck and is threatening to kill him. I have had one of the women fetch Mattas but you must come."

"I will be there."

Immediately he ordered the hovercraft and while waiting for it to arrive he dressed and ordered Eloni to stay where she was. Soon he was on his way, ordering the robot driver to maximum speed with little regard for safety. All the same it seemed to take too long to get to Mattas' house. He ordered the robot to follow him inside. A terrible scene met his eyes. Arabus was holding the boy child in the air. Dead. Blood pouring everywhere. Mattas was crouched on the floor, his body shielding the girl baby. Oah was unconscious on the floor. The two women from Eus were huddling in the corner.

"Put him down," commanded Abello.

"No, I will not. I have killed him and I am going to kill myself, but I will kill you first if necessary."

"No, you will not. Put the child down," commanded Abello, and he advanced towards Arabus. Arabus dropped the child and stared at Abello. "I will kill you," he threatened.

"No you will not, I am your Leader and I will be obeyed."

Abello put out his hand and gripped Arabus' arm. Noticing that Oah had regained consciousness he said, "Give Arabus a draught of some kind," and he held Arabus' arm as he drank. He then ordered the robot to take him back to the compound and to be placed under guard. Abello then went and helped Mattas to his feet and picked up the baby. "Take Mattas and the child back to Eus with you," he ordered the women.

"But no men allowed in Eau compound," protested one.

"I am ordering you to take him and his grandchild. It is all he has left now and give him shelter until I have decided what to do." Finally he turned to Oah. "What happened?" he asked.

"We were attending to the boy baby and Mattas was rocking the girl baby when Arabus burst in. He was shouting about his guilt and berating himself and Rester and Mattas. He seemed suddenly to notice us in the corner and he charged over here. He tore the baby from my grasp and as I went to take it back he hit me and I remember nothing more."

"Oh my heavens," said Abello. "How much more will happen? Murder. Never before have we ever had violence. All forms of it are anathema to us. And now, vandalism, sabotage and murder. It is like an enveloping cloak of darkness drawing ever tighter around our tiny planet. And I must decide the punishment. I alone have the responsibility."

"I must go," said Oah abruptly. "The women and Mattas and the child are ready."

Slowly Abello followed them to the door. He watched them disappear into the distance before returning to the room. He called for another hovercraft from his compound to collect him and then sat silently recalling each horrifying event. When he arrived at his compound he found the place in an uproar. He was informed that Arabus was asleep and that two robots were assigned to watch over him. Many of the Council members were demanding information. Abello finally sent a message to all of them to say that a full Council meeting would be held at noon the following day. He then went to the night room to rejoin Eloni, who was joined by Arilyn. Both seemed unable to comprehend the enormity of the night's happenings. Finally Abello sent them both to check on Arabus and the arrangements for the Council meeting.

As the dawn broke Abello went to see Arabus. He was awake and sitting moodily in the corner. "Leave us, women," he ordered and went and stood by Arabus. "I have come to hear from you what has driven you to this deed. I am to meet the Council at noon and I shall need to give them a full report. I need to come to a decision with compassion rather than with anger and disgust. Tell me."

Arabus raised his head. "What can I explain?" What will my noble leader understand of my torments? I was never content. I did not realize this until I grew to be a man. I am not interested in science or music or art, and I disliked the thought of teaching even more. I would have liked to be a farmer but whoever heard of a Capernican being a farmer. It is all controlled by the scientists and the harder work is done by the robot workers. I think that is why I started pulling up the flowers. It was so frustrating to see them growing in all their glory and not have participated in any part of the planting or care. I confided to nobody but settled on becoming a carver. At least I felt I was allowed a certain amount of freedom of design there. I could select what I wanted to carve and take my time."

"It was while I was working in metal that I fell in love. No, not with Rester but another. She was already married. Still is, for that matter. She did not know of my feelings although she found out later." He stopped speaking and stared at the wall. Abello waited for him to continue. "I married but I could not settle. One day I hurled the piece I was working on against the wall and then I deliberately picked up the pieces and smashed them. To my surprise two or three of my fellow workers came and told me they understood my feelings. We then used to meet at the break times to discuss our feelings. I also told them about the flowers, and several of them revealed their inner frustrations. We all felt we would never be found out because although we have sophisticated computer equipment for making tables, records, etc. they cannot gauge the human element. It was another who suggested that we should do something more positive. Maybe we basically wanted to draw attention to ourselves – I am not sure. It was a while before we hit on the idea of the water tanks. At first we were rather scared of the idea, the sheer magnitude of it awed us but as we kept niggling at the idea it became more exciting. I stole some of the chemicals from the laboratory next door to where I was working. It was all very easy as no one kept any checks, as everyone was supposed to trust everyone else. I started experimenting with them at home to find out just what each of them did, and Rester came in unexpectedly. She was curious as to what I was doing but I would not tell her. She picked up one of the bottles and recognized the labeling from the time when she used to help Mattas in the science department. Naturally this made her even more curious as she knew that I, Arabus, was just a simple carver. I refused to tell her and as she stood there her face flushed with anger, her eyes sparkling and her body taut and her breasts pushed against her day robe I was driven to violence and desire for her. I grabbed her and dragged her to the floor beneath me. Tearing off her robe I rode her savagely until I was almost too weak to stand up. Our children were conceived in that moment. I could not touch her after that. When Oah told me that she had given birth to three I was in torment. They all entered this world, not as a result of warmth of feeling but of a savage lust. The o ne boy died, but I realized that I had to kill the other so that his evil should not survive. Even then I returned to the house I had not finally made up my mind. More I cannot explain." He fell back exhausted on his bed. Abello stood looking down at him.

"Arabus, I have known some torment, but I cannot touch the iniquity of your soul. As Leader I must report this all to the Council. I can only hope that whatever their decision it will be made with compassion, as mine will be. I can offer no explanation as to why you are cast in such a different mold. I will leave you now, but I will return later for the names of the others."

Arabus looked surprised.

"Oh yes, I must know who they are, as they will all be punished, but of course your crime is the most hideous."

"Abello, I believe I have misjudged you," said Arabus. "I thought you were just like all the rest, a simple and kind Capernican."

Abello smiled at him. "I will be back for the names, Arabus," he said and left.

There was just an hour to go before it was time for the Council meeting. As he passed the long aperture Abello could see that a crown was gathering already. News travels fast, he thought, faster even than electromagnetic tapes when it is bad. He stopped in at the computer room and ran a series of coordinates through the machine. Satisfied with the answers he returned to his night chamber. Eloni was there laying out the ceremonial robe of gold thread, together with the Rood which symbolized the office.

"Draw me a bath, please," he said and she went to do so. He watched her slinky movements and felt again the familiar ache in his body. Not now, he told himself angrily.

"It is ready," she said, and he stripped off his day robe and undergarment and stepped into the bath. Eloni washed him, caressing him at the same time, until they could both contained themselves no longer and he jumped out of the bath and they made love on the floor. As he lay there looking down at her when all was finished he thought of Arabus and Rester.

"What is it, my darling?"

"Noting, just that I love you so much and I marvel each day how

14

fortunate we are."

"You must get ready, it is almost noon,"

"You are right."

She dressed him and with a last embrace Abello left. He went to see Arabus and found that he had obtained a sheet of paper and pencil from the robot and had already written the names upon it. Abello read them in silence. Twenty-five in all.

"Are they all equally guilty of all the crimes?" Abello asked.

"They would not wish to be treated any differently," Arabus replied.

"Very well. I am going to the Council to make my report and then we shall pass judgment upon them and you. I suggest you give a thought to your daughter and your late wife who is to be buried tomorrow."

Abello left and strode to the large chamber which served as the Council's meeting place. All the members were there, and looking around he could see Mattas, Eloni, Arilyn and Anice there as well. The meeting began with the ritual opening and after the last choruses had died down Abello stood before them.

"Fellow Council members and people, as you are fully aware we are convened to discuss the heinous crime of murder unknown to us in the entire history of our planet. We also have several other crimes to attend to, and I have here a complete list of names which Arabus has given to me. It is my duty as your chosen Leader to inform you of all the facts and in the final analysis to pass sentence. I will therefore begin my part by repeating to you the conversation which I have held with Arabus, and when you have heard it I will allow you some time to discuss it amongst yourselves and to come to a solution if you can."

He then went on to repeat what Arabus had told him in the stark, white room. As he spoke he watched the expressions of all before him and he realized that all the Council members, despite the undeniable horror of the crimes, showed no flicker of sympathy.

He concluded by saying, "As you know, the taking of life is anathema to us, s therefore we cannot punish Arabus by taking his life. I leave you to ponder this and the rest as I said I would, and I will return in thirty minutes."

He left the chamber. He stood waiting and wondering and watching the people outside. How involved were they, he wondered, and how many of them carried secret guilt. He read again Arabus' list and marveled that he could have been so blind. A messenger came to say that they were all ready for him.

"Do any of you have any questions?" Stony silence. "I have made my decision and as Leader you will abide by it. As I told you, the killing is without precedent and the punishment will be as well. There are also the others to consider, and I consider it unwise to keep them all locked up in a compound by themselves. I feel that this evil must be eradicated once and for all. Accordingly Arabus and his band of discontents will be dispatched on a space ship as soon as it is ready." A gasp rippled through the crowd. "Until the ship is ready they will be kept in isolation under the supervision of the robots. I see no reason why like our ancestors we cannot build and successfully launch a space ship, and after that their fate is in their own hands, which is apparently what they wanted. The whole planet will be involved in the building and training and equipping of the ship and every possible aid will be incorporated. That is my decision."

Pandemonium broke out in the chamber, with everyone clamoring to be heard, but Abello left. He went directly to see Arabus and to tell him of his decision. Arabus looked at him and then started to laugh.

"I have indeed misjudged you, Leader. You have as much steel in you as I have. I look forward to this challenge. I hope the rest of them do. I know the names on the list and that it includes Anice. I would also take my daughter along with me in order that she may comfort me in my old age, should I live that long. Indeed, all traces of us will vanish and you may go back to your calm orderly life and Eloni." Still mocking him he left with the robot guard who had come to take him into isolation with the rest.

Abello returned to his day room. He felt incredibly weary. Eloni came in. "You cannot mean it, she cried.

"I do, woman, I do," he said angrily, "and he is to take his daughter as well."

"I would not have believed it of you," she said and left.

Mattas came to see him. "I understand your decision, Abello. I am an old man or else I would go, too. I have nothing here. I understand that my granddaughter is to go, too. I wish that I had never seen the light of day and I repeat that I understand your decision. You are a brave man." He left.

Abello set about organizing work on a continuous basis. The sound of machinery echoed day and night throughout the tiny planet. It did seem as though everyone was involved. Various members of the families involved came to plead with Abello to change his mind in their case, but he was adamant. He had a visit from Anice who said she was glad to be going. Abello guessed that it was she whom Arabus had been in love with. Eloni had taken the task of looking after Arabus' daughter on herself. She had not spent any nights with him since the decision, and when he thought about it it wrenched at his feelings.

One night she came to him. "Abello, I too have come to a decision. I am going with Arabus and his people. I have his daughter to care for and I cannot bear the thought of living apart from you in Eus compound and still be on the same planet. I know that it is contrary to the rules of the Great Charter for us to stay together and therefore we must part, but I will not stay here and see you and not be able to touch you or stoop to a secretive affair. It would be different if I were carrying your child. I would be allowed to stay, but I am not."

"Eloni, my love," said Abello and put his arms around her. "I understand your feelings but you cannot do it. You may die out there."

"So be it," she said and walked away from him.

The ship was gradually taking shape, a huge orange mushroom which seemed to dominate the landscape for miles around. Abello drove the workers even hard. He checked and rechecked all the equipment. He did not tell anyone but he made sure that they would have no external communication. Whatever happened it would be unknown on Capernica. Finally after many months, the ship was ready, and the day of the launch dawned. Abello was first out to the ship and stood waiting as the twenty-five, Eloni and Arabus' daughter filed before him.

"My friends," he recalled. "The time is at hand. The ship is ready for launch. We should all be proud that we built her. She is the symbol of our finest scientific, electronic and navigational efforts. All knowledge that anyone holds has been made available for this epic undertaking. Eloni has chosen to go in order to look after Arabus' daughter. Now farewells must be said and the people get on board." He watched as they climbed up the hatchway. He then then turned and raised his hand. "This is my farewell, too." A great cry of protest arose. "No, I am going too, for I have as much guilt as they do. I cannot give up my woman Eloni. I nominate Ohn as my successor. I bid you farewell."

He went onto the ship. He saw the look of radiant amazement on Eloni's face. He looked around at the peaceful, still world of Capernica for the last time and slammed the doors of the exit compartments. Upon reaching his seat he ordered all to strap themselves in for the preparation of the aerodynamic flight.

"Start engines and ascend to ten miles," he ordered Omas the engineer.

A muffled noise was heard and a hard vibration felt throughout the body of the mushroom shaped space ship as the eight contra-rotating rotors gathered speed. Everyone held their breath. The vibration died as the ship rose slowly from the surface creating an enormous dust storm, the fine aqua sand being blown in all directions by the down draught created by the blades. Thus Ohn and the rest of them rapidly lost sight of them and by the time the dust had settled they were no longer visible.

While they were gaining altitude Arabus asked the one question which everyone wanted to know the answer to. "Where are you taking us?"

Abello did not answer him immediately, instead he unlocked a small drawer in the console in front of him and took out a small piece of writing which he gave to Ain, the navigation officer.

"Feed these Galactic coordinates into the directional computer."

Ain looked at what he had been handed in disbelief but proceeded to dial without comment the forty-seven digits which Abello had written down. The rest of them watched this operation with mounting horror as they counted the number of times the keys of the computer were punched. None of them were well versed in computer technology but even they could realize from the complexity of numbers that their destination was farther away than any journey that had ever been undertaken before.

There was a sudden lurch in the craft brought on by a change in altitude which caught them all unawares, followed immediately by a sudden acceleration as the main nuclear engines fired and they left the vicinity of the planet with ever increasing velocity. Speech, even breathing, was almost impossible for a moment, but then the acceleration settled to a steady force of ten times their gravity. Arabus looked at him and gasped, "Well, madman, where are you taking all of us now?"

"We are on course for the golden sun of Benu," Abello replied.

CHAPTER II

For the space of several minutes there was only the very faint hum of the motors and the life support system. Expressions in all eyes faded as each person inwardly digested the enormity of Abello's statement. Suddenly everyone was yelling and screaming questions and protests and it was quite a time before order was restored. Arabus asked him – he had evidently been appointed spokesman for the entire assembly – "You must be fully aware that Benu is over fifty light years away from here."

"It is fifty-four-point-eight-six light years, as far as the most recent calculations show," Abello retorted, "and I most certainly realize the risk that is involved. But consider what would have happened if I had not come with you. You would have flown all over the place and probably died as you hurtled through space. What would you have done, Arabus?"

He scratched absently at his chin. Then he looked at him straight and said, "I would not have known what to do. I can see you are right and for the duration of this journey I will continue to accept you as the Leader."

Abello leaned towards him as far as his seat straps would permit and touched his shoulder with his fingertips. Abello knew that this was a difficult admission for Arabus to make and he also realized that, for the time being, the threat to his leadership had been shelved.

"Now I shall explain the plans to you as far as I am able. I realize that your minds are full of doubts. Know then that I have in recent months experienced many strong and strange feelings, particularly with regard to Eloni. My mind has been dominated by strong emotions emanation from my purely physical being, and this has disturbed me as I feel that I have been tainted by the same mutant genes as you, Arabus."

"With these thoughts in mind and having decided the punishment of famishment I made my own plans, in secret. I was aware that this was in conflict but I felt that as Leader I had no choice. That is why I directed an intense astronomical investigation on the two hundred stars nearest to our three planet system and I found that it was Benu which had the largest and most erratic motion, indicating that it has a large number of planets or dark bodies revolving around it. As this looked the most promising from the point of view of being able to support life this should be our destination. Now you should all attend to your personal comfort and prepare your space couches for the most difficult part of the journey. You must all eat and refresh yourselves in preparation for the adjustments that Oah, the doctor, must carry out on each of you."

Abello turned back to his control console and noted with satisfaction that while he had been talking and discussing the speed had built up as planned and was now passing the one hundred miles per second mark. He kept the information to himself as this was only to be a very small fraction of what the maximum speed would be.

"We have completed the first part of the journey. I do not mean in distance or in time, but in function. There has been preliminary acceleration to be followed by major acceleration, coasting, major deceleration and finally slowing to move within the confines of the planetary system which it is almost certain Benu has. After this we will survey all the planets individually to ascertain if any are suitable for us to inhabit. I am sure that most of you realize that to accomplish this journey of fifty light years we need to travel very, very much faster than any speed that has been attempted before, as far as we know; in fact, to make the journey possible at all a speed comparable to light has to be achieved. At such speed we will take full advantage of the time dilation effect and the journey will seem to us to be tolerably short, although still taking fifty-five years to any outside observer. To achieve this speed in reasonable time the acceleration has to be about three times that of the initial boost and will continue at this rate for about forty days and nights. Such tremendous accelerations would render you all incapable of any movement, so I had installed lids which are above you and which can be lowered to make a seal around you. There are also a number of electrodes and connectors which Oah, the doctor, with help will connect to everyone before sealing. These electrodes will reduce your entire metabolism to a very low order so that the energy inside you from the meal you have just eaten will provide all the functional momentum your bodies will need during the time."

"The electrical system is connected to the computer which will automatically restore your body functions as soon as the acceleration ceases. Your circulation system will also be supplied by pressure systems and to ensure that your brains do not suffer damage through lack of blood reaching certain portions you are each to have an additional operation. Oah will open an artery to the brain and insert a small tablet. This will slowly disintegrate and provide controlled boosts of oxygen to the brain in the correct form. This is also programmed to last for the forty days and nights. One final point – you may all have severe headaches when regaining consciousness but these should disappear within an hour or two upon resumption of physical activity. There is no time for any questions, and I know that Oah is already at work in the stern of the ship. You are all to use the toilets and then return to your bunks."

Abello then went aft to check that Oah was managing and then returned. Soon all except Oah and he were in a comatose state. Oah then operated on Abello and Abello on him, following Oah's precise instructions. Just before sinking into oblivion Abello rechecked the course and computerized settings for the automatic implantation of the programs. Soon, too, his mind was a black void and he knew nothing.

Complete silence enveloped the ship for about ten minutes and then a soft whining note echoed throughout as the nuclear motors switched to maximum thrust and the tiny universe hurtled ever faster through the Stygian space with its precious crew of barely living beings.

*   *   *   *   *

Looking back on that first awakening, Abello could not decide how much time passed from becoming vaguely aware of lights, shapes and faint noises. It seemed that suddenly he became aware that he was aware of these things and then the pain and distress started. He kept his eyes tight shut, sucked in his breath and momentarily went rigid with the pain in the optic nerves. Luckily, those that had received their capsules first had recovered from this stage and some rushed forward to assist breaking the seal of the couch lid noiselessly and gently lifting the sufferer into a sitting position. Abello let out his breath slowly with the relief, however slight, that his movement afforded. A hand offered a glass containing a small quantity of sweet brown liquid which Abello downed eagerly, knowing that complete relief would soon follow. Indeed, in less than an hour all had recovered from their ordeal and were busy taking up conversations with their neighbors as though they had only interrupted themselves for a matter of moments.

After taking refreshment and drinking a considerable amount, the entire crew turned in a somewhat casual fashion to their various duties involved in the running of the space vessel. Abello carefully studied all the information which the playback of the readouts from the main computer had accumulated during the period of major acceleration and noted with satisfaction that all had proceeded according to the predetermined program. It appeared that the nuclear drive had slightly overheated towards the end of the acceleration but the computed conclusion was that this was not serious. Abello became impressed by the complete lack of any vibration or movement within the body of the ship: it was as though everything was at rest rather than hurtling through space at close to the velocity of light. Abello swiveled his chair through ninety degrees and reaching down between his legs took out the heavy metal boot soles with the built-in permanent magnets. Strapping them on his own feet he stood up carefully and for a few minutes walked cautiously up and down the narrow space between the flight couches. Now that the ship was in a state of zero acceleration all things were weightless but he quickly learned to compensate for the tendency of his body to continue forward motion after each step when his feet were held firmly on the floor by the attraction of the magnets: it was tiring at first.

He turned to Arabus and said, "Put on your soles and we will both go up into the observation dome to see what no other living creature has seen." After much grunting and puffing both reached the vertical ladder which led to the observation dome on the uppermost section of the space craft.

Abello reached up and seized one of the high rungs: he then pulled his feet free from the floor and using his hands only, effortlessly pulled himself up. Indeed, he had some difficulty in stopping his motion before hitting his head on the transparent top surface of the dome. Arabus joined him immediately. Once they had steadied themselves they looked back along the direction of their flight and could see – nothing. As the dome was in darkness there was no illumination of the upper surface of the craft, nor were there any stars visible whatsoever. This was not surprising as the frequency of the electromagnet waves from the stars passing them was now so slow as to be in a range to which their eyes were totally unresponsive. Looking forward, the firmament contained but a very few stars which were bluish white in color. Arabus scratched his head with surprise.

"I did not know there were stars in places of those magnitudes."

"No, I think they should normally appear to us as a very dull red, that is if we were back on Capernica," was Abello's reply, "but at our velocity the frequency has been halved and so they now appear as we see them. The rest of the stars which we would normally see having higher frequencies than the red are now invisible as our eyes are again not sensitive to such frequencies."

"Ha," Arabus grunted. "The whole spectacle is a bit of a letdown if you ask me – hardly worth the effort with the magnets and the struggle to get up here."

Before descending the ladder again, Abello had one last look around. He sensed rather than saw that there seemed to be a ring of white light at exactly ninety degrees to the direction of flight and that this seemed to go right around the craft. He had this impression when he looked slightly to one side of this direction and when he looked at this impression it vanished and he could see absolutely nothing again. He could not make up his mind whether the light was near him or right out in space. "How odd," he thought.

Once back in the control area, Abello was surprised how quickly all became used to the monotonous routine of the ship. In fact, the only flicker of notice was to observe the time dial. Abello had already explained to the crew that at their speed time itself moved very much slower. Their routine was set, they awoke, they ate, they attended to the ship and they retired to rest, the days seeming quite normal to them all. The computer itself registered the passage of time in similar normal days but in addition it had been programmed to register the passage of time as experienced by an outside observer. This was accomplished by a back-extrapolation factor which varies with their speed. It was exciting to note that every two days the computer registered the passage of a whole year.

Thus the voyagers passed one hundred and eight days routinely, speculating on their chances of ultimate survival. That they had not this far was considered nothing short of miraculous: that they would arrive within the influence of the star Benu was now a certainty. That Benu had a large planet or a number of small planets was of a very high order of probability. The only question to be answered was whether a planet could be found upon which they could breathe and live and multiply. Much amusement was caused among the crew by competitions to see who could conjure up the most bizarre and unlikely environment they could think of. But it was noticeable that during the last two or three days of this part of their journey the speculation and amusement died and each crew member became preoccupied with his or her own hopes and fears.

On the last day with the crew all sitting quietly in their places, Abello told them that the small operation treatment would have to be repeated so that they could withstand the equally great pressures upon their bodies as the space ship decelerated to the speed of interplanetary travel: this deceleration period would likewise last for forty of their days, those days being as they knew on Capernica.

Abello then went on to say, "Member of the crew, please give me your individual attention for a little while longer as I wish to give you my decision as to how we will organize ourselves should we make a successful landing. It is imperative that we should adopt most of the clauses given in our Great Charter, although I recognize that our new unknown conditions may impose some modifications to those rules. There could be a lot of trouble between us because there are only five women, ignoring Arabus' daughter who is only an infant as yet, and twenty-one males. We may have to agree, for the sake of the community, that the females will have to act as common wives to several males. The idea of sharing Eloni with others is totally repugnant to me at the moment but it may become a question of our very survival. Most of the other clauses of the Charter should be quite acceptable and workable. Such as those of sharing out the work and the proceeds of our labor equally. We must not kill or steal: we will set up a small Council of three to act as a decision making body and tribunal of appeal should disputes arise. At all times each individual must make the prime concern of thought and action the well-being and advancement of our tiny colony: indeed, we are far too few in numbers to permit quarrelling factions to develop. Think about these matters for the next few hours and we will have discussions on the proposals during our exploration of the planets of Benu."

Having been through the preparations for a period of coma there was no anxiety as Oah and his assistant began their rounds of medical work. The crew members one by one fell deeply asleep with cheery words about next seeing their companions in a new life on a new world, and once again a complete silence descended upon the ship. This lasted for about an hour and then the ship very slowly started to turn one hundred and eighty degrees through its flight axis, this movement being controlled by the release of gas through some small nozzles on the vertical face of the ship. When this operation was complete, the computer checked the flight altitude and then the nuclear engines fired up once more, weight returned to the ship and all it carried and the long process of deceleration started.

Upon wakening, all agreed that once again there was no appreciation of the time that they had been asleep: there was no impression that they had been asleep a long time, nor could they say that it seemed to be but an instant. It was just a complete blank. Because the speed of the ship was once again constant Abello and Arabus were forced to struggle with the magnetic soles before they were able to ascend to the observation dome once more. A very different sight greeted them as they went up, for they noticed a very faint illumination and when they were in the dome and looked towards the rear there were all the stars that they knew so well shining with familiar brilliance. Arabus released the tension in his body by blowing all the air out of his lungs quite suddenly, and turning to Abello took him by the shoulders and shook him in a silent embrace. Although neither would have admitted it, both were very pent up with emotion at that moment.

There were shouts for information from the main cabin below and so Abello said, "We are looking back along the way we have come and we can see all the familiar stars shining as we know them – some that were especially bright from Capernica do not seem so bright now, but there are a few others which are now much brighter. We have the impression that both types are somewhat displaced from the usual positions but we would need instruments to determine by how much. This is to be expected for the journey we have made is large in comparison with the distance such stars are from us."

Arabus and Abello turned towards the front of the craft and reported a similar situation. He then drew the attention of Abello to a faint iridescence which appeared at the edge of the craft towards the end of the plug nozzle where the charged particles were discharged and which caused the acceleration or deceleration depending on the altitude of the craft. Abello studied the phenomenon for a few seconds and then pressed a switch holding it down for a fraction of a second. This cause a small tangential jet of compressed gas to be ejected and very slowly the spacecraft rotated on its fight axis. The light gradually grew brighter and then quite suddenly a very bright star appeared. Both observers could scarcely believe that their luck could have been so great, for here shone the gold sun call Benu and it presented a small but very definite disc. They stood motionless for such a long time that the rest of the crew began to fear that something was wrong and they grew restless. Eventually they could contain their impatience no longer.

"What is it you see up there?" called a nervous voice. Both moved to the head of the ladder and smiled won reassuringly.

"Nothing is wrong, my friends," call Arabus, descending into the main cabin. Abello followed and when he reached the bottom he said, "We will show you what we were looking at so intently," and he pressed another button on the nearby wall which caused the darkened portion of the observing hatch to fall away. A golden glow immediately filled the whole of the observation capsule, the light cascading down the ladder and brightly illuminating the faces of the crew members nearest to the opening. Complete silence reigned for several seconds and then, suddenly, everybody was on his or her feet, waving their arms in the air and shouting themselves hoarse. Their eyes filled with tears, tears that were a mixture of profound relief and at the same time of immense pride in the fact that they had achieved the impossible. Chaos continued in this fashion for a very long time but eventually the emotions ran their course and quietness and order returned.

One of the crewmen in charge of the stores suddenly stood up and called everybody to order. "Comrades all," he cried, "let us all express our heartfelt thanks to Abello for bringing us thus safely through to our goal just as he said he would. Never let any of us forget that without his foresight and careful planning we could never have made such a journey. Indeed we would have ceased to exist years ago. So I say Long Life to our Elected Leader, and may he enjoy many years of happiness with his chosen partner, Eloni."

There was a renewal of the cheering and arm saluting in which Arabus joined with a rather fixed small smile on his face.

Oah clapped him on his back and shouted above the din, "It will be a long time before we have to elect a new leader, I think."

Oah was disturbed to see the smile vanish; Arabus' face growing dark with anger as his brows knit together. The doctor's hand was roughly shaken off as Arabus turned his back without bothering to reply. Abello held up his hands to restore order.

"My friends, I understand your wild enthusiasm as you realize how lucky we have been. But you must accept this luck with humility for we have not yet found a home where we can live in freedom and establish another Capernica. If we do, who knows but that one day our own people will venture forth and find our colony, or rather our descendants. But you must realize that although the most lengthy part of our journey in distance is now over, the difficult task of exploring a whole system of planets now lies before us and this will be very time consuming. First of all, we have to find the planets, then examine each one in turn to find if it is suitable for us. There may be a dozen or more such bodies and we will have to travel to all parts of the system of Benu as the planets are not likely to be neatly lined up just for our benefit. Remember, too, that we are down to interplanetary speed now and the distances are likely to seem immense. But let us get to our tasks without further talk. Where is Aqa, our astronomer?"

Some distance away, Abello could just see a figure reach out and punch a switch on a small control panel. A soft voice sounded in Abello's ear. "Yes? What are your instructions?"

Abello ordered, "Go up into the observation capsule and focus our large telescope on the surface of Benu. I want you to see if you can see any surface details – there should be dark areas similar to t hose which appeared on our two suns. Take measurements to see what angle is subtended between the plane of rotation of Benu and our present flight path and also the direction of rotation relative to our direction of flight in space. We down here will set up the magnet wave recorders to obtain confirmation of results by measuring the same phenomenon at different electromagnetic wavelengths."

Scarcely had Abello finished speaking when all that could be seen of Aqa were two rather skinny legs disappearing into the observatory. The light faded as the screen was replaced.

Quite a while elapsed before Aqa reported through the intercommunication channel that he could see the surface quite clearly under very high magnification but if there were any dark patches present they were below the limit of resolution of his eyes. This meant that they would be very small and probably unreliable for measurement. Using an occulting bar he examined the edge of Benu very closely and he could see that there were violent disturbances taking place but again too small for reliable measurement.

Abello, said, "That confirms the instrument readings I am getting down here for magnetic waves. The disturbances are too generally spread over the entire surface to be of any use in determining the direction of rotation. We will hold our present course and direction. In the meantime, feed the image of Benu into the main computer so that it will keep constant watch for us and let us know when a suitable black spot appears." Sometime later Aqa reappeared down the ladder and returned to his seat. Arabus switched the astronomer's console directly into the main computer so that he also would be immediately alerted as soon as anything appeared.

After Abello had retired to his couch for a well-earned rest and had sunk into a deep sleep, Arabus called up to Aqa and said, "Why does the leader wish to know the angle and direction of rotation?"

"So that our course may be altered in such a way that we will encounter the maximum number of planets in the minimum journey time and distance."

"How's that?"

"Well, all the stars we have examined from Capernica were rotating and their erratic motions against the background of the very distant stars were consistent with planets revolving not only in the plane of rotation of the primary but also in the same direction of spin."

"Where does knowing that get us?"

"We will then alter course so that we will spiral down towards Benu in the plane of rotation but in the opposite direction to the rotation of the planets around Benu. In this way, we will add their speed to our own and be able to locate any planets the more quickly." Arabus grunted his thanks for this explanation.

The crew then settled back to an unhurried routine as they all waited for the dark spots to appear on the surface of Benu, day following uneventful day. Abello spent a large part of his waking hours in the observation capsule with Eloni at his side, but the space up there was too crowded with instruments to do more than make love to one another with their eyes and the touch of their fingertips. Nonetheless, Abello began to suspect that two of the very bright star-like objects he could see fairly close to Benu might be planets for they seemed to be moving rather too rapidly against the background to be distant stars. He ordered Aqa to take a series of observations over a period of ten days to quantify any movement and to work out their orbits should they prove to belong to Benu.

About six days later, the computer gave audible warning that an object had appeared on the surface of Benu. The warning came so suddenly that everybody jumped with fright, thinking that something was about to happen to the ship. Aqa got to the ladder just ahead of Abello and both went up with a rush. Disconnecting the computer for a short while they split the image from the telescope and both gazed at the small circle which seemed to swim in each eyepiece, and there towards one edge was the unmistakable black area which they so eagerly sought.

"Good," said Abello. "It's up to you now, Aqa. You should have sufficient measurements in two days' time to supply the information which will determine the next part of our journey."

Two days later to the hour, Aqa reported that there was an angle of thirty-two degrees between their flight path and the plane of rotation and, as luck would have it, they were already proceeding in the required contra-rotational direction. The spacecraft would pass through the plane of rotation in five days' time, which would enable very accurate measurement to be made on the bright objects. As Arabus said to al and sundry, "We may already have our fist planets in sight."

CHAPTER III

Some three days later the flight engineer, Omas, asked to have some few words with Abello in confidence. Abello could immediately sense that something must be wrong from the expression on Omas's face and the way he hunched his shoulders and with a nod of his head indicated that Omas should follow up into the observatory. It had proved an irresistible distraction to all the travelers to gaze at the sheer wonder of all the stars and the ever increasing size and brightness of the disc of Benu whenever they entered the hatch, and this occasion proved to be no exception.

"I bear bad news, Abello."

As the spacecraft was slowing rotating on its fight axis in order to keep the whole of the skin of the craft at a reasonably even temperature, within a short time the whole of the observable space had passed before their eyes.

"It seems to be," said the engineer after a gentle sigh, "that the arms of our Galaxy are much sharper here than they seemed to be from Capernica."

"Yes," said Abello, "although you cannot see any individual stars as such nonetheless the diffusing effect of an atmosphere is missing and so everything seems to present a sharp-edged image. But not, Omas, what is the bad news you have for me, for your whole attitude is one of impending troubles?"

"I have been very carefully examining by means of the main computer the status of everything on the ship which is capable of measurement and hence comparison with the start of the journey is possible," Omas replied, "and you will be very pleased and relieved to know that everything is in fine shape (and that includes each and every member of the crew). Everything, that is, with the exception of the most important item, and that is our nuclear drive. There would seem to be two things wrong here. Firstly, I suspect that both inner and outer walls of the plug nozzle have been badly damaged and probably holed. This would have occurred during the major acceleration and deceleration periods when this part of the ship would have been subject to the most enormous pressures at very high temperatures for eighty days on end. I think we should not be surprised that there is damage in that part but rather we should be grateful that there is anything left at all of the original structure. There must be holes and misshapen surfaces in a number of places for the direction of the thrust is now variable both in content and in direction. This means that we have lost about twenty percent of our maximum thrust which in itself may not be too critical. At the same time it is a comfort to know that you can count on the maximum response in times of emergency."

"Is it possible to effect repairs either from the inside of the engine housing or from outside the spacecraft?" enquired Abello.

"In theory, yes," was the reply, "if we had enough time to allow for the decline of the intense secondary radiation from the walls, and that we just do not have."

"Oh," said Abello somewhat gloomily, "but that is not the worst you have to tell me, is it?"

"No," said the engineer, "there is something very much more serious for us to worry about and that is the loss of our nuclear fuel through usage. Our calculations of this on Capernica were a little optimistic in the event but we should not be too gloomy of them mathematical exercise as there were imponderables in our calculations and we were reasonably right. What we now have to worry about is that we now have only about twenty-five percent of our original thrust left; that is a twenty percent loss due to damage and a further fifty-five percent loss due to usage."

"Thank you for telling me this in confidence," Abello said warmly. "I feel that had we discussed this in the presence of the others there would have been a lot of unnecessary anguish, particularly by those who do not appreciate the engineering side of our journey. I suggest that we keep this discussion strictly to ourselves for the time being and I trust I can rely on your secrecy in this."

"Without question," was the response.

"Right," continued Abello, "you have now given me the bare facts of the situation, the past and present of it so to speak, now what of the future?"

"According to my further calculations," replied Omas, "we have the capacity for about four descents to or ascent from a planet's surface that is assuming that the planets have the same surface gravity as Capernica. A higher gravity the fewer such operations, the lower the more."

"I understand", acknowledged Abello. "Remember we must keep this to ourselves as long as possible." Both descended the ladder pulling themselves down carefully with their hands.

A further two days passed without incident until Aqa announced that the craft was in the plane of rotation of Benu and the appropriate change of course was carried out so that the flight was now in the required direction. Some weeks then passed as the bright objects drew away from the vicinity of Benu and through the telescope the observers began to appreciate that the objects presented small discs and that the prophecy of Arabus had been true. Slowly the two objects which had been drawing apart began to draw together again and then eventually change their relative positions against the background of stars so that the object which was originally farther away from Benu now became the nearer and similarly the nearer became the farther.

Aqa explained this to the crew by saying that the planet which had first been seen farthest from Benu was in an orbit closer to the primary than the second although at the moment it was also very much closer to the ship. Later still Aqa was able to feed the telescopic image on to the video screen and the whole crew looked at the picture for a very long time in complete silence, for it the truth were known each individual was overwhelmed at the thought that for the first time they were seeing a planet other than their beloved Capernica which indeed none of them would ever see again.

What they saw was a flat shining disc, for they were too far away from the planet for the equipment to register a sense of sphericity. The disc was not a true circle, being noticeably flattened at the polar regions which were a blinding white. Aqa said that this flattening indicated that what they were looking at was not solid rock and that the mass was rotating very rapidly. His measurements indicated that the planet was over thirty times as large in diameter as Capernica and that the surface was very cold indeed, too cold for any living thing to survive. The image showed large bands alternating in color being largely shades of red, brown and orange. There were also many oval blotches on the bands which appeared to be nearly black by color contrast. Aqa then lowered the magnification and blotted out the glare of the planet by means of an occulting disc. He was then able to point to a number of points of light three to one side and seven to the other at varying distances from the planet's surface and in the same plane as the equator which he said were undoubtedly the planet's satellites, some of which were quite large.

In response to a question from Arabus, Aqa gave it as his opinion that they would not be able to support themselves either on the main body or on any of the moons, particularly as all showed strong spectroscopic evidence that the atmosphere consisted of hydrogen and hydrogen compounds with nitrogen and carbon. There was no evidence for the presence of oxygen or water vapor although it could not be ruled out that these might exist at lower levels in the dense atmosphere where the temperatures could be very much higher due to the radiation emanating from what could well be a small solid core to the planet.

"Right," said Abello, "we obviously cannot land there so let us proceed to our examination of the second object our computer has discovered. Have you formed any opinions about that one yet, Aqa?"

"Nothing very definite yet, I am sorry to say," replied the astronomer.

"You will have seen that we have passed reasonably close to the first planet, it being between Benu and ourselves. The second planet is in an orbit superior to our present course and therefore I would expect that the surface conditions will be even more inhospitable, particularly with regard to the surface temperature. Here you see the tiny image on the screen and you can all observe that the body itself seems to be misshapen with big bulges on each side of the equator. I have never observed anything like this before and frankly I have no explanation as the calculations of the computer indicate that such a shape could not result from just a very rapid spin. So we will have to wait for a number of weeks to pass in order to get much closer. Then we may resolve the mystery. In the meantime, I will be keeping a very close watch in the hemisphere around Benu towards which we are spiraling and it should not be very long before more planets are detected. I am sure you will all like to know that the computed momentum of the two planets so far observed does not completely account for the erratic motion originally observed from Capernica." Heads nodded in agreement that this was good news indeed.

Sometime later when all but Abello and Omas were fast asleep, the Leader seized the opportunity of re-opening the subject of the damaged engines by enquiring if Omas had had any change of opinion since their previous conversation. "Nothing has happened to make me alter my opinion," was the reply, "particularly if you are looking for an improvement in the overall picture. But by the same token I am bound to say that the situation has not deteriorated either, for our life support systems do not consume power in any significant quantities."

"I was afraid that that would be your answer," groaned Abello. "I am right in thinking that if we do not find a planet around Benu which we can colonize, then we will have sufficient power to get away from this part of space entirely?"

"Of course, that is so. But having done that, there will then be no power left with which to decelerate if we were lucky enough to reach another star with planets."

"True," acknowledged Abello. "in that case I will decide here and now that if the worst comes to the worst we will alter our course to a circular orbit around Benu. At least when our food and life support systems give out we will die in the light and not in the utter darkness of outer space like some poor animal in its hole when the roof caves in."

"There is no other decision you could make," and turning away Omas muttered his breath. "There just has to be an acceptable planet – we cannot have come all this way at such a cost just to end the venture in complete futility."

Omas was a very old fashioned being, for he believed in the adage of the ancients that every person's destiny was written out before he was born, and somehow he felt that his was to start a new life in a different part of the universe. He was not aware of any sense of impending doom but rather that he was on the threshold of a truly great adventure. But Omas kept these thoughts strictly to himself.

Eventually came the time when Aqa told the company that they were now well inside the orbit of the large planet which they had first observed and that he had detected two more planets which had emerged from behind the glare of Benu. They were still too far away for detailed measurements but he suspected that they were very much smaller than the first two; by the use of colored filters with the telescope image he estimated that one was of a reddish hue and the other mainly a bright blue. He was forced to admit that he again had no explanation for such a color but time would tell. Sufficient distance had now been covered to bring the planet with the bulges into proper telescopic view. Aqa threw the image on to the video screen and everybody was fascinated to discover that the side bulges were in fact three banded rings which encircled the entire planet. The planet proved to be even more flattened at the poles than the previous one and once again the surface presented a banded appearance but this time the bands were essentially brown and white. Aqa again demonstrated the presence of satellites but as a home the entire system was unacceptable.

And so the spaceship traveled on, slowly spiraling down towards the surface of Benu which it would undoubtedly approach very closely if the present course was not eventually corrected. But there was plenty of time in hand for a thorough examination of the intervening space before that eventuality had to be faced.

It was a week or so later that the frightening event happened which had their hearts in their mouths for what seemed to be an eternity of time. It was probably an inevitability that the alertness of the crew should fall as the journey went on week after weary week, cooped up as they were in a relatively small space, on top of one another all the time with no chance of real privacy. The routine of the waking period occupied so little of the time and far less of concentration that each individual grew somewhat lax. This coupled with a sense of invincibility because of what had been achieved so far was almost the undoing of the entire expedition.

Abello, too, fell into the trap of complacency in permitting an insufficient watch being kept during the normal sleep period. It thus happened that the entire crew was sleeping with the exception of Aqa, the astronomer, who remained in the observation dome later than usual attempting to obtain telescopic images of the two latest inner planets so that a preliminary investigation of their orbits could be carried out. This had meant observations in a forward direction. Suddenly Aqa felt his eyes become hot and itchy and he took his eye from the telescope eyepiece and screwing up his fist, rubbed vigorously with is knuckles. Feeling better for this he was about to bend to the eyepiece once again when his gaze fell upon a small misty patch at an angle of about one hundred and twenty degrees from the planets. He looked at the object for several minutes, muttering to himself how odd it was that he had not noticed the spectacle when he started working some hours previously. Suddenly a thought flashed through his mind, almost like a premonition, the object was quite small and not very far away. He swung the telescope around and looked into the instrument. He saw a mass of gas glowing white with three extra bright areas within the gas. The cloud was slightly elongated and from this it occurred to him that its motion was towards the spacecraft. He hurriedly made a few measurements and the computer told him almost instantly that it was on a collision course. Gliding to the hatchway he yelled, "Abello, up here at once if you want to land somewhere safely one day."

It took Abello a couple of seconds to gather his wits and another five to join Aqa in the hatch. Aqa silently pointed out of the window towards whatever it was and then to the readout from the computer with its nerve racking calculations. Abello reacted within a split second and put his down the hatch.

"Omas," he roared, "engine ignition sequence immediately."

Luckily, the engineer had been woken up by Aqa's yell for Abello and Abello noted with great satisfaction that response to his order was instantaneous, which was hardly surprising as he had been brought up in an old school which taught unquestioned obedience to a leader's orders.

"Up here when you have finished that," continued Abello.

Omas joined the other two within a few seconds. The somewhat pale and frightened face of Arabus appeared in the hatch. "What's gone wrong? What's all the excitement about?" he asked somewhat angrily, sleep still befuddling his brain.

"Not now, Arabus, we are in great danger, get below and get everybody firmly strapped down, and I mean firmly. Exceptions to be Oah and his assistant and those of the women trained as nurses. Get the exceptions to give the rest sedative injections for unconsciousness in two minutes. Duration of the coma to be thirty minutes."

Arabus looked as though he were about to argue or pose more questions. "Hurry," bellowed Abello, turning his back on Arabus.

In the cabin Arabus found that there was no need to repeat the orders as everyone had clearly heard the Captain's shouted words. Swiftly, Abello explained to Omas the situation while Aqa worked furiously at the computer.

"Right, Omas, tell me how long it will take for the engines to be working at maximum thrust from the time you initiated the firing sequence?"

"A few seconds over five minutes," was the immediate reply.

"Will there be any thrust available before then?"

"It's of no real advantage to fire the engines before maximum thrust is available, for the reason that as power it taken out so it will take longer to come to maximum," and looking out of the corner of his eye at the glowing mass of gas which was visibly coming nearer with every passing second, "we are going to need maximum thrust plus a bit extra if we are to avoid a collision with that thing."

"True, Omas," said Abello, "and thank you for your assessment. Return to your console now and send Ain, the navigator, up here, and fast." Omas didn't waste time acknowledging this order but dived headfirst down the hatchway yelling for Ain as he went.

Ain appeared. "How long have we got now, Aqa?" asked Abello, indicating that Ain should wait by a wave of his hand.

"About three and a half minutes." Another rapid explanation to Ain who, after looking at Aqa's computations, gave his opinion that they should turn away from Benu, ascending above the plane of planetary rotation as the object would be passing through this plane but in the opposite direction. A very sharp turn would be necessary to avoid a collision and passage through some of the outer parts of the gaseous envelope was inevitable, but such a course would minimize the time of contact and hence the effects of any hazardous radiation. Aqa chipped in, "There is just not time to make any assessment of that danger, Abello."

"We will just have to trust that the level is not so high that an exposure of a fraction of a second will prove lethal. Down to your couch now, Ain, and make sure you receive an injection immediately. Tell Oah to inject his assistant and two women who will serve as nurses now as their services will be needed if the rest of us are not injected and do not survive the shock of maximum acceleration."

"Right."

"Aqa, how long now?"

"Just two minutes."

"Right, thirty seconds to clamp everything down here then to our couches the pair of us."

Abello glanced at the ball of white hot gas as he shot down the hatchway. It now filled almost the whole view from one side of the observatory. Back in the cabin, Abello found that approximately half the crew had received their injection in time, including Arabus and his daughter, and they lay as if dead. Abello coordinate his console with that of Ain and saw that the correct flight path data had already been fed into the machine. He had a sudden impression that not only he s crew who were still conscious but also the machine itself, indeed the whole spacecraft, was watching the second hand on the clock go around the dial so slowly but so irresistibly. As though the whole was a living entity, just praying that action would take place in time to avoid annihilation.

"Thirty seconds," call Abello. "Is everybody well secured?"

Muttered "Ayes" came from various parts of the cabin.

"Good luck to us all then, and may we all live to see our..." Abello did not finish his sentence, for he felt as though he was suddenly hit in the head with a sledgehammer as the motors fired on full thrust. The acceleration drained so much blood from his brain that he blacked out immediately.

Gradually, the black void in his brain grew less impenetrable and he became aware of his surroundings. But thinking was a very slow process for he found he would slip into darkness for an unknown time and then back again. It took him a long time, or so it seemed, to work out why his body still seemed as though he had an enormous weight pressing on it, but eventually inspiration came. In all the excitement both he and the engineer had failed to tell the computer how long the thrust should have been maintained, and it was still operating. Luckily the necessary switches on the console were only a few inches from Abello's fingers and he was so familiar with their relative positions he did not need to try to open his eyelids as well. But what a time it took for his arm and fingers to travel those few inches, and all the time the fierce acceleration went on and on, taking them farther and farther away from their goal. He didn't dare wonder how long he had been blacked out or what the drain on the nuclear fuel would be as a consequence. Time enough to worry about that when and if he could stop the infernal acceleration. Slowly, so slowly his fingers walked forward rather like a slow motion study of the leg movements of the large spiders on Capernica. But eventually, the task was done, the noise of the pumps died away and immediately the weight was lifted from his chest. Presently, the rest of the crew came out of their comas, groaning with their pains and mopping their faces where the blood had spurted from ruptured vessels in their noses. The child whimpered helplessly and called for her father in a weak voice, but no one could go to her aid for more than an hour.

"Lie still, everyone," called Oah. "As soon as I or my assistant are strong enough to move around we will visit every couch in turn for an examination. Only when we give medical approval will we permit anybody to leave his couch. Do we have your approval of that order, Abello?'

"Most certainly, Oah," agreed Abello. "Speaking for myself I will be

36

incapable of movement for hours yet."

But eventually, heads cleared and movement returned. Abello discovered that the maximum acceleration had continued for a total of four hours and twelve minutes and that a further two hours and twenty-seven minutes had passed since he had managed to turn off the nuclear drive. This was not as bad as he had at first feared but it did represent a further draining of the ship's capabilities. Aqa and Ain once more disappeared into the observation hatch for several h ours of observation to determine their position and current speed and hence the necessary course corrections to bring them back to the plane of rotation. Once more the craft had to be slowly rotated through its flight axis and then the engines restarted to gradually bring them back to their original speed and orbit. The effect of this loop in the journey was to advance them by many millions of miles towards the first of the two smaller planets that Aqa had seen a little before there narrow escape. At last they were near enough for measurements to be made and the image of the object to be thrown on to the large screen in the main cabin. The planet proved to be of an essentially red color with darker blotches. There were two white caps at the axis of rotation which did not seem to be water. Although the planet was the same size, approximately, as that of Capernica it was by no means as dense. Hence the gravity was much lower and there was consequently no atmosphere to speak of.

"Another disappointment," was all the comment Arabus seemed prepared to make.

At about this time, Aqa was able to pinpoint the positions of a number of bodies all revolving around Benu in the plane and as they traversed towards the innermost orbits, he plotted the positions of some twenty-two of these objects, ranging in size from just large lumps of rock to little planets about a sixth of the diameter of Capernica. They seemed quite dead and obviously without atmospheres, but Aqa was puzzled when he reported that even quite small ones showed evidence of craters.

There was a general discussion of these phenomena one day when Aqa said, "As you know, I have recorded the positions of some twenty-two of the objects over a very small part of their orbits around Benu and a simple calculation shows that there must be thousands of such bodies in total. Adding up all their masses would indicate a single body half to two-thirds the diameter of Capernica. But why such a planet should have broken up I have no idea. If this did happen then it must have been in the remote past because the pieces left seem to form an entire orbit around Benu. Thinking along these lines I am wondering if the ringed planet we passed obtained its rings by some of this debris approaching that planet very closely and being disintegrated under the enormous forces generated. Alternatively, the rings could have been formed by the disintegration of a satellite which got too close. I have no sure knowledge that such phenomena have been observed by Capernican astronomers before. It is regrettable that we cannot interrupt our journey to land on one of these tiny planets to see if the craters are volcanic or meteoritic in origin. It is impossible that the smaller ones would have volcanic action on account of their size but it is just possible that the volcanoes were present on the original large body and what we see today are survivors from the disintegration. We will probably never know."

The spacecraft swept through the orbit of the small red planet, gradually but inexorably drawing nearer to Benu whose disc was now very much larger. Calculations showed that in terms of the immensity of space they were beginning to run out of distance before they would have to alter their course because of the radiation hazards from Benu which made a closer approach impossible. All began to wonder if they would find a new home, and some of the crew began to mutter among themselves that maybe Abello had not been so clever after all. The more rational members were quick to point out that no one could have known beforehand if they would find a planet suitable to be their new home but at least the leader had been right in saying that Benu probably had several planets around it for they had already inspected three. And now they were on their way to number four which seemed to be the most mysterious of all in that it was a bright blue color with irregular flashes of the most brilliant white light. It was almost as though the planet was signaling to the ship telling them to hurry along for on her lay salvation. This blue planet also had a large white satellite which swung from side to side of the central body on its orbit. All hopes were now on the blue planet as its path in space and that of the spacecraft drew them slowly together. It was obvious to Oah that the entire crew had long since ceased to enjoy the novelties of the voyage and that a dull nihilism was the general feeling. However, this almost despairing attitude did not last for very long as Aqa began to make his reports of his astronomical observations. His first announcement was that a spectroscopic examination of the white flashes showed them to be identical with the light from Benu itself. Therefore the light must be a mere reflection from some enormously large reflecting surface somewhere on or near the planet's surface. What this could be was argued about for a very long time but no really feasible suggestions were forthcoming. It could not be something which they had experienced. Time passed and they drew ever nearer. Then Aqa said that he could detect variations in the intensity of the reflected light which had nothing to do with the white flashes. It was suggested that this could be the effect of dry l and on the one hand which would be dark in color and not have a high reflection and the topes of white clouds on the other. Everyone marveled that the cloud cover must be very extensive and variable to produce such effects which could be observed from such a distance, for there had been very few clouds in the atmosphere of Capernica. A crew member suggested that this might mean that the blue planet had a lot of water vapor in its atmosphere, there being very little on Capernica, but Aqa cautioned that it was too early to say this. There were many other substances which could give the effect of reflective clouds. Much later still, when the planet showed an appreciably sized disc, Aqa projected the telescopic image on to the screen in the main cabin and all members were able to gaze at the image. What they saw was a bright blue surface with whirls of white clouds in places and towards each of the poles these whirls coalesced into very large masses. That the white areas were clouds was shown by their constantly changing shapes and positions and the blue area must lie beneath the white clouds.

Closer still and Aqa determined that there was water vapor in the atmosphere and that the blue color was due to large areas of deep water. The greens and browns of land masses began to show, their outlines being constant in shape. And so with the passage of time and distance Aqa's reports continued to be favorable and it came to be realized that they were indeed looking at their new home. Came the time when Abello summarized all the findings and confirmed that the necessary course corrections were being computed in order to affect a landing at the earliest moment. Abello stood up.

"My friends all," he cried, stretching out his arms to embrace symbolically the whole crew. "In about thirty more of our days we should have completed our monumental journey and made a safe landing in our new..." The rest of Abello's announcement was lost in a burst of shouting and cheering, both sexes embracing one another in small groups, with many a moist eye in evidence. Slowly calm was restored and everyone resumed their couches, all eyes being turned to the leader, Abello. No one moved for quite some time and then Oah stood u and signaled to Abello that he wished to say something.

"The floor is yours," said Abello.

"I think I speak the words which everyone would like to say when I say thanks to our leader for his unfailing attention to our welfare, for the miracle of our safe journey, for the wisdom of the chance of the planetary system of Benu..."

Abello interrupted Oah at this point by holding up his hand. "Forgive me, Oah," he said, "but I cannot allow you to continue in this vein. I am only one member of a whole team and each was equally important to the success of the mission. As for my choice of Benu, that was nothing more than an inspired guess, for until we actually get here there was just no way I could have known that we could find a planet suitable and acceptable. Many have been the times I have lain awake during our journey trying to assess the odds against us, and believe me they proved to be astronomical. I do not want to depress your high spirits but I must remind you that we still have some very difficult maneuvers to perform before we are safely down on the surface of that planet. We have a very large amount of energy which must be dissipated before we can come to rest, and our ship is not in the best of shape. So let us concentrate our energies and attention on the tasks which lie immediately ahead. There will be plenty of time for celebration and merriment later. Remember that it is always much more difficult to return to normal conditions than it is to get away from them."

Abello thought that he had said quite enough short of depressing the crew, so he sat down somewhat abruptly, startling his audience.

Arabus leaned across to him and hissed; "Now I am certain that you are nothing but a complete fool. You had them all eating out of your hand a few moments ago and you could have insisted on ding exactly as you wanted from now on, including keeping Eloni all to yourself. Instead, you bleat that you are as ordinary as they are and you have thrown away your golden opportunity. It would have been a very different matter if I had had the leadership."

Abello sighed gently to himself and said, "Arabus, Arabus, will you ever learn anything about yourself and the others? Don't you realize that if you present yourself to them as someone greater than you really are, then sooner or later a situation or someone will come along who you cannot best and where will you be then? If ever you become leader of the group then I can see that your decisions, which are only based on emotion rather than reason, will lead to big trouble for them and you and you will be destroyed in one way or another."

"Nonsense," boasted Arabus, "I will have others to carry out my orders and they had better beware that they will not fail in their tasks."

"In other words you will rely on others to correct the messes you will get them into. I wonder how much happiness and indeed probably lives will have to be sacrificed to the vanity of your inflated ego. It is a pity that you have such an exaggerated opinion of yourself and your capabilities. Were you otherwise you would be a very valuable second in command."

Arabus' face turned a deep purple with his effort to maintain his temper which, to Abello's surprise, he succeeded in doing. Arabus turned away muttering to himself and Abello had an unpleasant feeling that the while of his destiny had taken another lurch around to the final reckoning. He wondered if Arabus would attack him on the ship, but calmer and careful thinking indicated this as an unlikely possibility. Rather the attack would be delayed until sometime after the landing, probably sometime after when their life on the planet had been properly organized. With this thought Abello dismissed the subject from his mind, except that he found himself thinking about Eloni and how much he longed for her embrace and the sweet comforts of her body. He had noticed before that these thoughts were extra vivid after a period of high tension over Arabus.

Some ten rest periods later, Omas, the flight engineer, came to Abello with his report. "We are now some ten time the distance between the planet and its satellite from the planet's surface and we are traveling much too fast at this time. If the engines were at their maximum power we would have no difficulty in braking down to a close orbital speed in a matter of a few hours. But for safety's sake I think we ought to start braking gently very soon in order to achieve a low orbit from where we will be able to survey the whole surface in the space of two rest periods. This will enable us to select the best possible place for our landing. Once down, we may not be in a state to fly again, certainly not outside the atmosphere. Remember, too, that soon after we pass inside the orbit of the large satellite the gravitational attraction of the planet will increase our speed enormously once again. We have to get the angle of our entry into the denser atmosphere and our speed just right otherwise we will all be burnt to cinders. Such a fate would be a very cruel joke after such a journey."

"Good idea Omas," replied Abello. "Please make the necessary computations right away. In the meantime, I will give instructions to turn the ship into the right altitude so that our engines fire exactly along our line of flight." Abello then gave orders for everyone to be strapped onto their flight couches, after which the tangential jets slowly rotated the great vessel to the required position. A few hours later, Omas gave the details of his extended calculations.

"We have something of a problem, Abello," he reported. "As we are traveling somewhat faster already than I originally thought, this means we will have to fire the engines at some twenty percent of their power, and as we have only twenty-five percent of the original power available to us that means a thrust of eight percent availability. That is higher than I wanted to use at this stage but we have no choice if we are to land successfully."

"Do you think the engines will stand the effort, Omas?" asked Abello anxiously.

"I regret that I can give you no assurance as to that," Omas said, "but on the other hand neither can I say that they won't."

"Well, as to that," interrupted Arabus, "there is only one way that we can find out and that is to try it."

"You are right in that," agreed Omas, and receiving a nod of agreement from Abello proceeded with the computer sequence for the startup of the nuclear engines. Presently a very slight vibration was felt throughout the ship but this was immediately forgotten as the ship started to decelerate giving the impression of the return of gravity. It was not very long before a number of the crew began to complain of dizziness and headache. Indeed two of the women actually vomited, so Oah and his assistant had to get busy with tranquilizers and anti-motion sickness injections. After this disturbance had sorted itself out the impression grew stronger in several minds that the ship was vibrating much more than it should. Indeed during most of the flight nobody had been aware of any movement at all.

Hour by hour the vibration grew worse until Omas came to Abello and said in a very serious voice, "We will have to cut down on the rate of deceleration before the drive chambers and pumps literally shake themselves to pieces. If we continue like this with the rate of increase of the vibration the ship will destroy itself in another eight hours. We have to slow the engines and the sooner the better, otherwise we perish."

"How much will you recommend that the power be but?" asked Abello.

"Down to ten percent of original power in the first instance and see what improvement we get," was the reply.

"Do that immediately," ordered Abello.

Omas returned to his console and soon the force of the apparent gravity lessened and the vibration died right away. The crew remained perfectly still for many a long minute hoping against hope that the vibration would not return, but there was no sign of it even after a whole hour so faces started to relax and hearts returned to their normal pulse rate. Abello called Omas and Arabus to the observation dome for a conference on their new status.

"Right, Omas," he said when the three of them were seated. "Give us the bare facts on our present situation."

"Yes, leader, these are as follows," he replied. "The power we are supplying for deceleration is now at ten percent of original and I cannot detect any vibration for the moment at this level so the immediate danger of a break-up of the ship is no longer with us. On the other hand, at this rate of deceleration we will not be able to go into orbit around the planet as our speed will be too high. this means that we will sweep partially around the planet and then out into space into an orbit which will spiral us down eventually into Benu. Of course, we will all be ashes long before that happens, but it is not a pleasant contemplation."

"I will agree to that," grinned Arabus.

"Yes, I understand all that," said Abello, "now give me the options that are open to us."

"I think there are several," replied Omas, "some of which I will need a few hours to work out. First of all, we could deflect our course slightly closer to the planet so that we pass through the upper reaches of the atmosphere and this will have a slight braking effect. Very risky, of course, as the skin of the ship will get very hot and a slight error will mean that it will burn away and us with it. I do not recommend such an action or at least only in a last desperate effort for survival, and that will be your decision alone to take, Abello."

"I realize that," agreed Abello, "and I sincerely hope it is one I will not have to make. What is next?"

"If we keep the deceleration at the present level and continue this even after we have passed by the planet we should be able to put ourselves into an orbit around Benu such that we will come back to a coincident point with this planet at the right speed after the planet has completed another revolution around Benu. I would need an hour of computer time to work out the actual flight details but there is nothing impossible about such an operation – it would mean another lengthy period cooped up in the spacecraft beyond that already planned, and I do not think that such an expedient would be too popular."

"By that last phrase I presume you are implying a quicker thought slightly more risky course?" queried Abello.

"Yes, that is right," agreed Omas, "and the plan is this. We continue decelerating for a short while, coast around the planet and out into space again, but this orbit will take us nearer to Benu. While we are coasting, we will be able to inspect the drive chambers and effect some repairs, at least sufficient for us to be able to make a landing."

"But where?" asked Arabus.

Omas smiled at him. "It so happens that Aqa and I were making a few preliminary speculations before the engineering crisis hit us and it would see that the white planet we saw nearer to Benu than the blue one is conveniently situated for us to reach it quickly. It would seem to be of about the same size as our blue friend and therefore probably has the same gravity. More than that we do not know at the moment but obviously if we can effect a landing then only those repairs we can effect under the pull of gravity can be made. We can then safely return to this planet and land properly. But Aqa and I will need a few hours to work out the mathematics and necessary flight corrections before we can be absolutely sure."

"Hm," said Abello, "if I know anything about the pair of you, you are already pretty sure of your ground, otherwise you would not have voiced such an opinion to me. But got ahead, take whatever time you need on your computations. You are right to check and double check to be absolutely positive. There is too much at stake to be anything other than totally certain."

The next few hours were spent quietly, the ship steadily slowing down and the blue sphere becoming larger and larger until it filled the field of vision to close upon half of the total available to the viewers. Omas and Aqa approached Abello once more. He looked up at this assistant with an expectant smile.

"Yes?" he said. "You have completed your calculations and reached a conclusion for me to act upon?"

"We have," replied Aqa, "and it is this. We should adopt the last course which Omas mentioned to you previously and effect a preliminary landing on the white planet. We regret that we cannot at the moment state anything on the ground conditions we are likely to find on that planet other than that which you have already been told. But the conditions would have to be very hostile for us not to be able to land at all and in our opinion that is extremely unlikely. We are too near to the blue planet at the moment to be able to make observations and it will be about ten or our rest periods after we have passed before the white planet will be conveniently placed away from Benu. This will give us ten days without engine power so that the radiation hazards from the drive chambers will have descended to an acceptable level for us to enter for repairs after then. It may take a further ten rest periods to complete our scientific analysis of the conditions on the surface of the white planet, thus all our operations after the next course correction can be taken at an unhurried pace which should ensure that we do not make any mistakes."

"Yes, I understand," said Abello. He looked across at Arabus. "I do not have any doubts about this, do you?"

Arabus shook his head. "No, it all seems straightforward to me," he replied. "When do we make the course corrections, then?" he asked Omas.

"In one hour exactly," Omas replied after glancing at the timepiece on Abello's console.

"Very good. See that it is carried out. Give Ain the necessary coordinates when you pass his place," was the order.

Closer still to the surface now, the spacecraft now visibly speeding up despite the constant decelerating thrust of the nuclear motors. The illuminated disc of the planet was markedly gibbous with the surface details plainly visible even to the naked eye. Vast chains of mountains were clearly seen as pinkish grey areas in the slanting sunlight with glistening white patches of frozen water on the highest ones. Some of such areas seemed to be almost as large as the whole surface of Capernica but there were still equally vast areas of blue-green vegetation. What the voyagers saw more than offset the general disappointment at not being able to end the long journey there and then, naturally, there had been consternation when Abello announced that the journey had to be continued for an as yet unknown period of time.

This despite assurances from Abello that the extension would not be of a great duration.

By now the shining portion of the planet was but a semicircle and the brilliance of it still hurt the eyes of the travelers after so long spent under soft lights. It was at this time that Abello spent a few moments in the observation dome with Eloni and he was able to hold her close to him for a few precious minutes, the warm sweet perfume of her body and hair filling his mind with a deep sense of his love for her and his loins with an equally intense desire for her. But he could do no more than remember past delights for there were others in the dome with them. Thus in a tight embrace they both gazed in wonder and with a deep sense of awe at the beautiful world swinging past them. In their hearts they were reaching out to this strange place already instinctively recognizing it as home. Capernica already belonged to the past, immutable but dead.

The future, their future lay before them, and Eloni remarked, "We should not forget the past, our own and those of our ancestors, for the past is but the stepping stones which lead to the future, ours and the generation yet to come. So courage, my love, brace yourself for the tasks which lie ahead. Always remember that until the moment each of us dies, the challenge to be of service to our fellow beings is before us and the fulfilment of that service is the whole purpose of living. Thus we should aim to leave life a better thing than we found on taking it up." She paused and with a wry smile finished with the remark, "But I doubt if Arabus would see things in that light." Abello smiled at the thought of Arabus expressing such a philosophy and nodded warmly.

Smaller and smaller grew the illuminated area until it was but the most delicate of thin lines around half the globe. At the poles it was noticed that there was a faint extension of this thin line to more than half the circumference which Aqa said was due to the light of Benu being bent around by the dense atmosphere. Suddenly as the light faded in the equatorial region a brilliant green flash was seen followed by a beautiful pink color merging to orange within the atmosphere. Due to the rapid motion of the spacecraft this too faded within but a few minutes to be followed by an inky blackness. This, too, in its turn altered and lessened to a silvery grew color as the light from the satellite which was behind the spacecraft illuminated the topes of large banks of white cloud. A short while later and the sequence of color changes and effects appeared in reverse order, starting at the equator on the opposite side of the planet. The craft then swung out from behind the planet into the full light and warmth of Benu. After the next rest period Abello gave the order to shut down the engines. Full silence returned to the ship and once more there was no sense of motion, speed or gravity. The blue planet shrank slowly in size, much more slowly than it had increased as they had approached, and this brought it home to all the crew that they had lost a great deal of energy during the maneuver and despite the extra passage of time required to effect the necessary repairs, the chances of ultimate success had been very greatly improved.

The next fifteen days were the longest and most tedious the crew had to endure over the entire journey. At least that was the general opinion oat the time. Other periods had been bad, but there was always something new going on, something new being reported by Aqa, the astronomer. But this time there was only the waiting to be done, waiting for some stupid needles on equally stupid dials to slowly go back until they indicated that it was safe for the engineers to descent into the energizing chambers and propulsion tubes for a sufficiently long time so that meaningful work could be done towards the repairs. Black despair seemed to descend on to all the crew with the exception of the engineers who were busy collecting all their tools together, speculating on the damage which they might find and drawing up the contingency plans to deal with it. They were the lucky ones. The rest sand down into their own gloomy thoughts and hardly spoke to one another. Conversation dwindled to a series of grunts which somehow conveyed meaning.

In the end even the engineers lost their enthusiasm and began to move about very quietly and speaking on whispers. But bad things like good things have a habit of coming to an end and one day the needles all spoke their message of safety, the engineers fell to with a will and the spirits of the entire ship rose rapidly. Here was action at last. Omas carefully removed the radiation proof hatch in one corner of the cabin area and with great difficulty forced his body through the narrow aperture. Many were the catcalls at this sight and much advice given concerning the advantages of a slimming diet, all of which Omas took with a broad grin on his face and a final good natured shake of his fist before he finally disappeared from view. The rest of the engineers waited in the cabin while Omas made his inspection and formed his ideas of the priorities which the repairs should require. One of the engineers lay on his stomach with his head through the open hatch so that Omas could be watched and help rendered quickly should it be needed. And what a sight greeted Omas.

Gas entry pipes at all angles but the right ones, where they had been partially melted under the intense heat and radiation and the forced into unnatural shapes and sizes by the very large gravitational forces experienced during the long interstellar acceleration and deceleration periods: the conductors which should have carried the colossal electric charges to the center of the plasma melted back to the very walls of the chambers. The

46

continued discharge of energy had then scoured the walls of the chamber like enormous claw marks. Internal supporting beams had been partially melted and hung in loops, some with one end disconnected from the walls so that they hung free and further distorted the surface of the chamber by their very weight hanging from one side. This was a most disturbing feature as the highest efficiency of the engine could only be obtained with the symmetry of the chamber walls made to a very high degree of accuracy. The other seven chambers built around the axis of the craft were in a similar condition and from two of the chambers came the faint but unmistakable hiss of escaping air through the series of valves which led to the propulsion tubes and thence to the vacuum of space itself.

Omas was not long in make up his mind as to the priorities. He returned to the cabin. "Well?" asked Abello anxiously.

"The damage is very severe, far worse in fact than I had expected to find. We had not been able to allow properly for the effects of the high temperature and enormous pressures involved in the run up to and from full velocity during our hurried tests back on Capernica. Hence my surprise at what I saw. However, the damage can be repaired in the drive chambers, and this is not the immediate task. First, we will need to take down the temporary air locks to the bottom of the chambers numbers two and seven in order to open and repair the valves." He caught sight of Arabus looking at him with one eyebrow raised in an obvious question. "Yes, on those two chambers we will need to work in space suits under full vacuum, as we have to open those valves and we cannot afford to waste our precious air which would otherwise escape out to space. I am not looking forward to that as two men will be required for the work and they will have to work under the most awkward and cramped conditions. Still, the task has to be carried out. After that job is done we will be able to dispense with the air locks and space suits and the entire force of engineers will be able to work easily. The sheer volume of the job is pretty daunting but with a sufficient number of volunteers to hold and fetch for us and act as unskilled assistance generally then I estimate we can finish this part of the work in about twenty-five rest periods. We have that amount of time Aqa?" he enquired.

"Oh, yes," was the replay, "in actual fact you could take about forty-five rest periods of you want."

"That is very good news," said Omas, turning back towards Abello. "It could well be that we shall meet with some snag once we start to work which is not apparent just now. The extra time will be very useful. I still propose that we work as fast as we possibly can, that is continuous working until the job is finished. I suggest that I be allowed to divide my engineers into two or three groups in order to cover the supervision of each complete rest period.

The unskilled work as long as they choose and it does not particularly matter if an individual covers a complete period. Have I your permission to organize along these lines, Abello?"

"Most certainly you have," Abello responded. "Give whatever orders you think fit with my full authority. Indeed, please involve me as well in this work – I am sure I will do tolerably well as an unskilled worker."

Omas, Aqa and those around laughed out loud at the relief of tension which Abello's lighthearted response had produced although Arabus was seen not to join in. but the others took no notice of him and his scowl grew darker still at this further insult.

In point of fact the work was completed in twenty-three rest periods so wholeheartedly did all crew members join in, and it was noted that even Arabus forgot to look glum and scowl at everybody under the stimulation of actually having something practical to do. Abello thought that Arabus might have diverted his black tempers on to the bars of metal which were being hammered and bent with such enthusiasm.

When the repairs were finished Omas requested that one air lock be put back into one of the drive chambers. After it was sealed off, Omas entered the chamber so made and donned his space suit. After double checking that it was air tight on him, he signaled to his assistant who started up the small portable vacuum pump. Omas watched patiently as the pressure dial steadily fell and when it read a steady state of vacuum he carefully opened the vent valve. The remaining air hissed out through the open valve into the vacuum of space, surprisingly slowly, Omas thought.

He then carefully lowered his miniaturized camera on a stout rod through the aperture and proceeded to take a series of pictures of the walls of the tube working methodically around the diameter and down its length. When this was finished, he withdrew his special camera and applying his eye to the narrow aperture found that he could dimly see a small area of the plug nozzle itself. His worst fears were then confirmed for he could see a gaping hole on the wall of the nozzle just where the beam of ionized particles emerged from the tube and impinged on the nozzle where distribution and hence the thrust was equalized, and finally entered space as a complete ring. The other seven tubes distributed their beams similarly. Omas closed the valve, admitted air to pressure and re-entered the cabin. All eyes were upon him as he glided towards Abello to make his report.

"I guess it is pretty bad down there," said Arabus in a fit of deep depression.

"Well, you must appreciate that I have had the opportunity of looking through one of the valve systems and there are eight in all," was the response, "and what I have seen is somewhat depressing although it could have been very much worse. It is my opinion that adequate repairs to the metal surface can be effected but they will have to be carried out under conditions of gravity."

"Why should that be?" asked Abello.

"The reason is that the rest of the plug nozzle was so made and this means that the microcrystalline boundaries all flow in a certain direction and in order to key in new metal its boundaries must flow similarly. If we form the new material under weightless conditions then those boundaries will have randomized crystal growths and there will not be sufficient bond strength between the old and new metal to survive the conditions it will have to endure," explained Omas. "If we run the engines at a low thrust from now on, sufficiently low that is just to get into a low orbit around the white planet, we can then get down to the surface with a further minimum expenditure of energy. This way we will minimize the strain on the already damaged parts as well as the fuel loss. This will give us the maximum opportunity for the final trip. I further suggest that before we fire the motors for more deceleration we look through the other valves to see if the damage is the same all the way around the plug nozzle."

"Good idea," agree Abello. "Please see that that is done forthwith."

After issuing the necessary instructions to his assistants and seeing them started on their task, Omas returned to Abello. "Now that we have repaired the ionization chambers, I can now tell you that it is nothing short of miraculous that the ship has held together after the punishment it has received. It is my opinion that or faith in our ship and the ultimate success of our journey must have assumed a physical identity and held us all in one piece. There is no doubt at all in my mind that had we tried to go straight down on to the surface of the blue planet the s hip would have cracked open like an egg shell with the extreme temperatures and buffeting after entering the dense atmosphere. We have been incredibly lucky once again – it makes you wonder if our ultimate success was predetermined when the universe began." Omas started to move away when a sudden thought struck him and he returned to Abello's side. "By the way," he said, "you are bound to ask sooner or later so I will tell you now. From what I saw I guess it will take a whole rest period to effect the repairs to the plug nozzle, assuming that there are holes in the surface opposite all the valve nozzles. If all eight do not need repair the time will not be affected as most of it is actually waiting for the new metal to harden and stabilize itself. Plan on about twenty minutes outside for each hole to be repaired. Oh", he continued, "there's another thought. Has Aqa finished his astronomical observations yet on the likely conditions we can expect on the surface?"

There was silence for a few minutes and then Abello sighed. "Yes, we have had Aqa's report and none of it is any good. As a matter of fact we have been having long discussions on the situation while you have been on the repair job. No point of beating around the bush, that planet is hostile, so bad in fact that at the moment we do not see how you can survive on the surface long enough to do what you have to do. On the other hand, the deterioration which we might experience with the plug nozzle while we wait for the blue planet to encircle Benu and come back to our orbit means that we may have to take a lot of risks. There seems to be only one place where we can come down and that is on an extremely high plateau just near the planet's north pole. Even there, the atmosphere will be about sixty times more dense than on Capernica, the temperature will be about three times that of boiling water. It would seem that there is a lot of sulfuric acid in the atmosphere and we are worried about the corrosive effects on the skin and exposed engine parts."

"No need to worry on the last point, at least unduly," replied Omas after a pause during which time he had experienced difficulties in getting his eyebrows back to their normal position and unpursed his lips from the long whistle he had given. "All exposed surfaces were specially treated to resist all known corrosive agents before we left and I am sure that sulfuric acid would have been considered. In any case, our stay will be limited to one rest period, always provided that the damage is all similar to that which I have seen. But that temperature and pressure bother me – I will give the matter some further thought while I supervise the rest of the inspection of the plug."

"Right," replied Abello, "we will have a further meeting in the observation dome when you are ready."

Omas departed on his task, but it was more than two rest periods before he was ready for further talk. The task of erecting, using and dismantling the air lock in seven different positions in the confined space was a wearying one and Omas was somewhat jaded in spirit by the time he finally joined Abello and Aqa in the observation dome. On the left hand side of the space ship the brilliant disc of the white planet was clearly visible to the naked eye while back over the line of flight the blue planet with its white satellite had also shrunk to a barely discernible sphere. Omas gazed longingly at the blue object for quite a few minutes before volunteering the information that his thinking had not made any progress on the problem of survival on the white planet.

"How large an area do we have on which to affect our landing?" he enquired of Aqa.

"No problems there, it is very large," was the reassuring response.

"Good," he nodded, "and how smooth a surface do you think it will be?"

"That is much more difficult to answer," said Aqa. "I have been surveying the plateau with our high resolution radar and all I can say from this distance is that there are no hills more than one hundred feet high and no holes of similar dimensions. Naturally, I realize that if we hit an obstacle of that size traveling at any speed at all, then the ship and we will perish. We will probably have to stay in a low polar orbit for three or four rest periods while I make a close study of the area by radar. I should be able to get sufficient resolution to plot objects no larger than five feet and risks of those dimensions are acceptable. It is a pity that we will not be able to see the ground from orbit but I suspect that the clouds are much too dense for that. Indeed you may well need artificial light for your work for I think there will be very little light from Benu penetrating to the surface. Probably the light and sky will be of a deep coppery hue, anyway."

"Not exactly a paradise," grunted Abello.

The three looked at one another somewhat gloomily for some little time. "There must be something that can be done," mused Aqa. "Of course there is still the option of waiting for the blue planet to complete its revolution of Benu, but we will be taking a tremendous risk with a descent to either planet's surface, so as far as that is concerned we might just as well take the nearest planet for the venture. But surely no one will be able to withstand both the temperature and pressure for say thirty minutes, to be on the safe side, in an ordinary space suit. By the way, Omas, how many holes have to be repaired on the plug nozzle?"

"Only two below tubes three and four – which certainly explains why the thrust was so irregular when we needed maximum power," was the reply.

"But that will mean about one hour outside the craft under the extreme conditions," mused Aqa, "so how are we going to design a suit to give the operator a chance of survival and get the repairs done?"

Arabus' head appeared above the open hatchway in the floor of the observation dome. "If you will pardon the intrusion and interruption to your deliberations," he said with heavy sarcasm, "I think I have found the answer to that last problem posed by Aqa."

"If you think that, then come up here and join the conference at once," ordered Abello.

Aqa felt his blood pressure rising as he watched the smug expression on Arabus' face as he entered the observation dome and he was about to burst out into an angry tirade when he sensed that Abello was looking at him with a warning frown. So he remained silent and merely clenched his fists behind his back in order to dispel the tension that was in his mind.

"Well," said Abello brusquely. "If you have anything to contribute let us hear it right away."

"Very well," replied Arabus, with a transparently false meekness.

51

"You will remember that when we built and stocked the spacecraft back on Capernica we tried to provide all the tools and equipment for the sort of work we knew so well and that we were not in a position to provide for situations beyond our experience."

"Yes, yes," said Aqa impatiently, "so what?"

Arabus grinned at him and deliberately arranged his body into a more comfortable position before answering, which infuriated Aqa even more.

"One of the situations we met with on Capernica involved the repair of the water tanks."

"How does that help?" queried Abello.

"Curb your impatience for a few moments longer," taunted Arabus, "and I will tell you. There was one outstanding characteristic of the water tanks and that was that they were very tall, over thirty times the height of ourselves, in fact. This means that the contained water was equally deep and the pressure at the bottom consequently large. How did we repair the tanks from the inside?"

Abello looked at Arabus blankly for a few seconds and then suddenly clapped his hands to his forehead. "Of course, of course," he shouted, "the rigid diving suits. I had quite forgotten about those. Arabus, there are times when your thinking is quite brilliant and I do not know what I would do without you on those occasions. On the other hand, it is well to remember that there are times when I do not know what to do with you."

Aqa noted with intense satisfaction that the leer of triumph on Arabus' face faded instantly with this ally from Abello, to be replaced by the more familiar black scowl, but before he had a chance of adding his contribution Abello had disappeared down the hatchway head fist with the characteristic swimming motion they all adopted under the conditions of weightlessness. Orders were being shouted down in the main cabin and there seemed to be a great deal of instant activity.

Arabus followed Abello down in a more sedate manner but Aqa remained where he was for a long time, deep in his own thoughts and forebodings. Presently he stirred himself and applied his eye to the telescope. Carefully swinging the instrument around to Galactic coordinates which he alone had calculated and then committed to memory. There was no written record nor was it in the computer memory bank, of the two yellow points of light which slowly swung into his field of view. They were quite close together but Aqa realized that that was because one of the stars was somewhat behind the other and that by the time that he, Aqa, finished his life, one of the stars would have swung right behind the other and out again to a maximum separation. Aqa gazed for a long time at the twin suns called Temuna which meant the Faithful Companions. After all, he had been looking at them from the day of his birth and his mind's eye could clearly picture the bright yellow surfaces with the occasional black spots which marred their perfection. He signed and wondered where in relation to what he saw Capernica was actually situated. He could have spent many hours at the computer to determine exactly where the planet was but he decided that it would be a waste of time as his old home would have been far too tine to be able to see from this distance. Anyway, Abello, who was a lot wiser than he, had said that no one was to look back or even think back. They would not, nor could not, ever return to Capernica and while they must draw strength and wisdom from the lessons of the past, it was the problems of the future that they had to face.

With this in mind he turned the telescope to the brilliant cloud tops which were rapidly spinning past his view, a mere three hundred miles below him.

Viewed as a while they appeared peaceful enough but a closer inspection showed them to be in violent motion. Aqa was apprehensive of the buffeting they could expect on the way down to the surface for the accursed repairs, and suddenly the planet assumed a menacing aspect of such intensity that Aqa gave an involuntary shudder. He quickly looked away and directed his instrument back to the small disc of the blue planet which he could still just see with his naked eye. Under high magnification, the blue slightly flattened disc seemed to float under his gaze so that the whirls of white cloud joined together to form dancing patterns. There were no flashing lights from the water surface this time which Aqa knew was due to the fact that the angles between the planet and Benu on the one hand and the planet and himself on the other were not right. To his imagination, however, it seemed that the planet was sad that they had gone by and not landed. The emotion was very strong and the planet seemed to be saying that here was home where they would all be safe.

Aqa felt himself drawn towards the image very strongly. He shook his head. "This is ridiculous," he thought, "I am a scientist and only believe in what I can see and measure. I guess it is a great longing within me to have done with this journey and the restrictions of this confined space that makes me feel such an affinity for that place. It is impossible for it to have an influence on me."

Yet despite his cold scientific reasoning, Aqa felt a great comfort in having looked at the planet and so for the moment he accepted his emotion as an omen of the future, a future which was bright with the promise of a successful conclusion to their journey. Greatly inspired in this way he, too, descended into the cabin beneath to find Omas, Arabus and Abello engaged in an earnest examination and discussion of the rigid diving suits which had been brought out of store and assembled.

Omas had been surprised to find that the suits were so very much taller and larger than the body that was supposed to be inside them. There were two such suits standing on their own weighted feet. He carefully examined the segmented joints at the shoulders, elbows, wrists and knees.

He stood up again, "I think that Fortune has smiled on us to a small extent in as much as these suits will be able to stand a pressure of maybe twenty atmospheres on the inside," he said, "and this will limit the strain on the suit imposed by the application of the much greater pressure which will be applied to the outside once the repairer steps outside the spacecraft. It will mean a pressure difference of forty atmospheres and although that does not sound much better than sixty it may mean the difference between destruction and survival. It we can get an ordinary space suit at two to three atmospheres pressure on to the repairer and all into the rigid suit, then I think there is a good chance that we can affect the repairs successfully. There are some other points to be borne in mind. One is that the repairer will need to carry his own air supply but this will only need to last for one hour with a one hundred safety margin so only one of the small cylinders will need to be carried. The other criterion is that he will also have to be plugged into the refrigeration system of the ship as a small unit strapped to his back will not have the capacity to keep him cool enough for the hour of exposure which we are allowing for the repairs."

"Hm," mused Abello, "these restrictions mean that we need a person with the smallest body to be the repairer. I was going to call for a volunteer but it would snow seem that such an option is no longer available to us."

Oah went to his console without being asked and soon returned with the information that Uth seemed to have the smallest frame but that even he was not all that small.

"Oh, dear," said Abello, "we seem to be in a period of lurching from one crisis to another. Uth, will you come and stand beside one of these suits?"

Uth did this and it was obvious to all that there were going to be problems, grave problems.

"If we can get you and your equipment into one of these," said Abello, waving his hand towards one of the diving suits, "would you be willing to undertake the work outside? You must bear in mind that the conditions out there will be extremely hazardous and that you may not survive."

"Yes," nodded Uth, "I fully understand that, Abello. I also know that if we are to survive, someone has to make the attempt and it might as well be me as anyone else. After all, I do not have any specialized skill or knowledge and in that sense I am expendable. Not that I particularly want to die, of course, but I will be buoyed up by the knowledge that I will have the opportunity of making a vital contribution to the success of this expedition.

In any case, I will not be going to a certain death, will I?"

"By no means," said Oah, "you will have a very good chance of surviving the ordeal. But it will strain your constitution to its very limits, although it is not a question of your physical strength."

"I accept those arguments," said Uth, "and I accept your instructions, Abello."

"Thank you very much for almost volunteering," smiled Abello in reply. "You will be honored for this by us all for all time. Of this I am sure."

There were murmurs of approval for this statement from the entire crew. Nobody felt that the situation called for noise.

"That's settled, then. Everybody must now give their time and energies to the adaptation of the suits. I suggest that one of the suits be used as a mockup so that we can carry out tests on the equipment at least under conditions of full pressure. Let us go to it," Abello ordered.

But before words could be translated into deeds, a female voice was heard from the other end of the cabin. "Abello, did I hear that no great physical strength was required to effect the repairs to the plug nozzle?"

"You heard correctly," Abello answered, "but who is it that makes the inquiry?"

A small figure was seen to come forward to eventually stand somewhat shyly in front of Abello.

"Oh, it is you Arilyn," said Abello. "But why do you ask?"

"Before I answer that, may I ask Omas to tell us all in detail exactly what the repairer will have to do from the moment of going outside?" was the response.

"Omas, please oblige us all with the details," said Abello.

"Very well. I will give you all a briefing as to what will be required," replied Omas. "Listen carefully everyone, for you may spot things which I overlook. First of all the flexible space suit will be donned and the internal pressure of this built up to whatever it will stand. The life support systems will be connected and then the other rigid suit assembled around that person. As soon as this operation is completed then the repairer will enter the main air lock where a number of cans in a large container will have already been placed. This container will be connected to a pulley system so that we can lower the whole load to the ground from inside the cabin here. This will minimize the amount of work that the operator will have to perform and hence the amount of work the refrigeration system will have to do. Once inside the air lock, whoever is inside the suit will have to connect himself to the air pressure vent which is just inside the outer door. He will turn on the small tap you see on the right hip of the suit and from inside the cabin we will control the rate of increase of pressure inside the main suit until it is at its maximum. This will take about two hours. We will then give the signal to pen the outer door which can be done without venting the air out of the lock as the pressure outside is much greater than inside. Backward then down the short ladder to the ground and under the body of the ship to the plug nozzle. A small length of light metal ladder will have to be carried as well in order to climb up to the holes to be repaired. All clear so far?" Omas asked Arilyn.

"Yes," she said, "I think it will be the next part that I want to hear in particular."

"Right. Climb the ladder taking one can at a time, and when opposite the hole remove the lid by pulling on the flap and scoop out the plastic contents using this special tool." Omas held up a small curved metal trowel. "It will take between two and three cans to fill each of the two holes but we will send down ten cans in all to cover any accidents which might happen. When the hole is filled place these two bare wires at each end of the hole and press into the surface gently. Finally, smooth over the shape the surface of the repaired hole with this larger curved trowel which will give the required curvature to the wall of the nozzle. Nothing more is to be done by the operator except to repair the second hole similarly. Abandon any partially used cans, but unopened ones are to be brought back into the air lock, together with the ladder. Any questions?"

"No, I don't think so," Arilyn replied. "Those cans look quite small. Are they very heavy?"

"No," said Omas, "here catch one," and he gently threw a can in her direction. Arilyn weighed this thoughtfully in one hand and then returned it to Omas.

"And what then?" she asked.

"Nothing more will be required of the repairer," enjoined Omas. "We will reduce the pressure in the air lock to that of the atmosphere here, open the inner door and bring the operator and all the equipment inside. When that is done we will pass a large current through the wires in the plastic material which will transform it into metal of a similar hardness and composition to that of the nozzle itself and then we have to wait for a whole rest period for the new metal to reach a stable state. It is that long stay on the ground that worries me, Abello."

"Can the ageing process be speeded up by putting more initiator into the plastic material?" asked Arabus.

"Yes, that could be done," replied Omas, "but the time that would be available to apply the plastic to the hole would be so cut back that I do not think a reliable repair could be effected, and this job has to be done properly the first time. The whole job has to balance one risky operation against another. There is one more thing, the operator must not touch the tap on the hip which will release the pressure inside the rigid suit, on any account, particularly after re-entering the cabin. There will be a large volume of gas dissolved in the blood due to the pressures involved and it will be fatal to release this gas suddenly in the bloodstream. At best it will cause agonizing pains and at worst death by gas embolism. So whoever goes, be warned."

These remarks were digested in silence for a few minutes when suddenly Aqa said, "We will have to fit up a two-way system to vent the air lock. At the moment we can only vent back into the cabin so that we conserve our air supplies. But on reentry the air lock will be full of carbon dioxide and sulfuric acid and we do not want that vented in here – we would cough ourselves to death."

"Good point," observed Abello. He turned to Arilyn with a friendly smile.

"Have all your questions been answered by Omas?" he asked.

"Yes, I think so, and may I say I think you are also being very stupid about this," was the reply.

A shocked silence followed, broken eventually by a dark rumbling of anger from Arabus. The storm finally broke.

"And what do you mean by that remark, woman?" he shouted, waving his arms.

Aqa thought he would have hit here if the two had been alone.

"Allow me to show you," Arilyn replied with a bright smile at Arabus, which only infuriated him the more. She moved quietly to the side of Uth who was still standing beside the rigid suit. Her head barely reached his shoulder and the rest of her dimensions and weight were only about half of Uth. There was complete silence for a long time as the male members of the crew gazed at such an undeniable argument. There was a lot of nervous coughing and embarrassed movements of the crew as they digested this. The silence went on and on until at last Arilyn laughed gently and said, "I think I have made my point."

Abello shifted in his seat, obviously very embarrassed, cleared his throat hesitantly and said, "Yes, indeed yes. I must apologize for the stony silence with which your proposal was received. Believe me, none of us meant any disrespect to you."

"I know, Abello, it is just that you males had never considered that a female might be able to do many of the jobs which you believe to be sacrosanct to yourselves. You should remember in future that we are not just machines for reproduction and instruments for your comfort and pleasure."

"The point is fully taken, Arilyn, there is no need to keep on about it." Abello frowned and Arilyn, cleverly reading the signs, decided that enough had indeed been said and so she maintained a discreet silence. Abello turned to Oah.

"Tell me," he said, "ignoring for the moment the actual personalities of Uth and Arilyn, is the female body and mind capable of carrying out these tasks under the conditions on the surface of the white planet?'

"If any of the male egos here are expecting me to say no to that question," replied Oah with satisfaction, "then he is doomed to disappointment. Arilyn is perfectly capable of the effort. In fact we ought to all understand that the female anatomy and constitution is a great deal tougher than the male in very many aspects. In fact it is only in terms of sheer muscular output that the male is vastly superior. Yes, indeed, Arilyn need no longer stand next to Uth to emphasize all the other advantages. To answer your question exactly as you put it, Abello, Arilyn is the one who should carry out the repairs."

"What do you think of this proposal?" asked Abello, directly addressing Uth. Uth scratched his head reflectively.

"As long as I do not have to make the decision that Arilyn should carry out the work, then I would say that I am in no position to argue with the doctor's statement. I certainly will not let my pride stand in the way of the repairs being carried out as quickly and efficiently as possible. One suggestion I would like to make is that I undergo simultaneously with Arilyn any training that Omas will be giving. I will then be able to back her up without delay should any emergency arise."

"That is a very good suggestion," agreed Omas.

"So be it," said Abello, tactfully closing the matter. "Let us get on with the necessary preparations."

"I will spend an hour or so at my console drawing up a plan of work and a timetable," said Omas. "I want everything to be thoroughly tested and ready for instant action before we start the decent to the surface. Everything must proceed smoothly and at maximum speed once we come to rest, that is until the waiting period for the new metal to become stabilized."

There were mutters of agreement on all sides. While the engineers gathered around Omas' console to consolidate the plans, the rest of the crew lay down on their couches. Abello was included in these. He felt drained of energy as the result of the strains of the last few rest periods. Now that others were taking care of the next requirements and his advice was not needed he could relax and it was not many minutes before he drifted into a deep dreamless sleep. He did not know that Eloni came quietly to his couch while he lay there. She was worried about his health and peace of mind, but as she stood there watching him the lines of tension on his face gradually smoothed out and the slow regular breathing of complete relaxation established itself. She smiled inwardly at this sign and after gently stroking his cheek returned to her own couch to sleep also. She completely ignored Arabus although she could feel his staring eyes burning into her back.

Omas and his engineers took many more hours to draw up their plans than they had originally expected and when they had finished they looked around them to find that entire crew motionless and sound asleep. Not another word was said but after Omas had given a silent but prodigious yawn, with one accord they too lay on their couches and were soon fast asleep also. It was indeed many hours before anyone stirred after which the cabin slowly came to life again. All agreed that the small amount of time which had been lost by the extra amount of sleeping was well worth it, as everybody felt considerably refreshed thereby.

"Right, Omas," said Abello, "let us all hear the details of your requirements and y our timetable."

"The first task will be to pressurize each of the protective suits to the amounts we discussed before. There are small pressure determining instruments on each, as routine equipment, so there will be no problem in finding if there are any leaks," he replied. "After that we......"

"Wait a minute," said Arabus. "That sort of testing is all very well and should be done. But that is not the main test, surely. It is not whether the suit will let pressure out but whether it will let it in, at least as far as the rigid suit is concerned."

"Good point," Aqa grunted somewhat reluctantly.

"You are right, Arabus," said Omas, "that will have to be done but it should not delay the overall program as these tests will take place concurrently with the training of Arilyn in the actual handling of the plastic material. As we have well over two hundred of the canisters Arilyn will be able to run through the while procedure many times before the real thing. She has to be able to do each filling and shaping operation in will under the twenty minutes which I can allow her per repair. In the meantime, one of the engineers will fabricate a model of what there is to see outside and what has to be filled and both Arilyn and Uth will be able to practice with this. At the same time another group of engineers will be making a two-way venting system from the air lock in order to exhaust the noxious atmosphere of the white planet once the job has been completed and the door finally closed. Finally we estimate that the training and engineering program will consume a further ten rest periods and that Aqa and Ain, our navigation officer, can work out the firing details to land on the surface on the first opportunity after the eleventh rest period."

"That seems to be a reasonable though very full program," observed Abello, "but tell me, will Arilyn not be too tired after that? She will need all her wits and strength to do this work."

"You worry too much, leader," grinned Oah. "Have I not said that the female is a pretty tough creature? Anyway, there is nothing to worry about on that score as Omas has assured me that Arilyn will have a whole rest period to herself before the work. I am going to administer a mild sedative which will keep her quiet and relaxed for a whole twenty-four hours. The only thing that will tire her then will be putting on the actual space suits and getting out of the vehicle."

"Oh, very well," acknowledged Abello. "I guess I can safely leave such matters in your capable hands."

Sometime after the second rest period the model of the hole was ready and firmly bolted to the wall of the cabin. There was a gap in front of the hole of about two feet and then a stout board was screwed into the floor and secured at the top by means of a small girder, which made a small chord with the circumference of the cabin. Omas called Arilyn and Uth to him.

"You slide in first, Arilyn," he said. "I will be next and Uth, you slide in after me. You see why I have had to make such an elaborate structure? Down on the planet's surface there will be plenty of gravity to hold your feet firmly and enable you to push the plastic bond firmly into the hole. Up here you are weightless and you would find it impossible to use any strength as you would just fly off in the opposite direct. I am in the middle so that I can demonstrate to you both at once the technique you will have to employ to do the job. So watch me very closely."

He took one of the small cans and shoed them both the small tag which projected slightly from the side right towards the top. Taking the tab between his thumb and forefinger, he twisted it slightly and then gave a sharp pull. The tag came away easily followed by a small sliver of metal which ran around the entire circumference. He lifted the lid and showed them the thick pinkish material in the bottom part of the can. Taking the small trowel, he inserted the pointed end into the plastic material and with a circular motion withdrew the implement which had a fist sized amount of plastic clinging mainly to the underside edge. This he quickly scraped on to the bottom edge of the hole. He repeated this several times, thereby emptying the can. Again with the underside of the trowel he smoothed the plastic into the hole with an upwards motion. A second can was emptied similarly and half a third, by which time the hole was completely sealed. Taking a large trowel he placed it sharp edge down on the model wall an inch or so below the hole.

"You will notice that this trowel fits the contours of the wall exactly," he said. Two heads bent to make the examination. "Yes." Taking hold of the blade with both hands in positions which divided it into approximately three equal portions he moved it upwards slowly but firmly. A small quantity of plastic material was scraped away by this process and an almost perfectly contoured surface was left.

"How long did I take?" queried Omas.

Uth looked at his timepiece. "About twelve minutes."

"Not bad for a first time effort," he said, "but the times I achieve are not important. It's what Arilyn and Uth can do that counts. Your turn now, Arilyn. You stand in the middle so that you are opposite the work. Uth will keep a note of the time you take, but do not worry about how long you take the first time. Concentrate rather on getting a proper final surface."

Needless to say, Arilyn's first effort was something of a disaster. First of all, she had difficulty in getting the tab free from the can and several minutes were lost in Omas showing her the knack of achieving this. Her second can was opened without difficulty. She also took too long in getting the plastic into the hole. She would insist on taking such small quantities of plastic on the end of the trowel.

"Do not be so afraid of it," shouted Omas. "Slap the stuff into place – it does not matter if you spill some. And twist the trowel more as you bring it out of the can."

Her second and third cans were much quicker. Some further difficulty was experienced in pressing the large blade sufficiently closely to the wall and pushing it upwards at the same time. Arilyn was a little flushed at the end of the exercise but all the males watching encouraged her by their assurances that twenty-two minutes was no disgrace for a first effort. Indeed, Arilyn's spirits bucked up considerably when Uth too made a bit of a hash with his first attempt which took eighteen minutes. Her second effort was sixteen and a half minutes against Uth's fourteen, and she very nearly caught up with Uth at the third attempt, Arilyn recording fourteen minutes against thirteen.

"That's enough for now," said Omas, "and I can honestly say that you have both performed very much better than I believed possible. We will have a one fill practice tow rest periods before descent and a three fill practice one rest period before." Omas left to inspect the rest of the work.

Some rest periods passed. Aqa approached Omas. "Last time we spoke together you said that we should make calculation to make the first possible landing during the eleventh rest period. But will you not need some time to get them kitted up and pressurized? Surely several hours will be required?"

"You are quite right, Aqa," was the grateful replay. "Let me see. It will take at least two hours to get them suited and three hours to be pressurized. Better make it the orbit after the complete of six hours after the time that Arilyn and Uth are awakened."

"Very good," replied Aqa, "I will now make the necessary calculations."

On the way back to his own console Aqa reported his news to Abello and Arabus who both nodded their assent. Although Arilyn made several mistakes with her next fill trial and took eighteen minutes she was not downcast, for the next day both she and Uth produced three identical times for the three attempts, all twelve and a half minutes. Arilyn was congratulated by the entire crew, particularly by the other women. Oah led her gently to her couch and made her lie down. He noted her bright eyes and slightly flushed cheeks, the rapid shallow breathing.

"You must not get so excited," he said quietly. "I am now going to give you a mild sedative which will give you a profound dreamless sleep for a whole rest period. When you wake up you will feel infinitely refreshed and very calm. In case I do not get another opportunity of speaking with you, I will say that the thoughts of all of us will be out there with you, willing you to carry out your tasks successfully and, most important of all, returning to us safe and sound." Oah gave her a small tablet to swallow, after which he squeezed her hand gently and then moved quietly away. Arilyn's eyelids were seen to flutter a little, after which they clamped firmly shut and she lay motionless. Only a slight movement of her chest showed that she was still breathing and alive.

While Arilyn slept the rest of the engineers were kept very busy putting the finishing touches to the preparations for the repairs and also completing the building of a decompression chamber in which she would have to spend a very long time while she was slowly brought back to normal conditions. Indeed Omas thought that it was quite likely that they would arrive back in the vicinity of the blue planet before she would be free, if not after an actual landing there.

The hours passed and then Arilyn returned to consciousness. She sat up smiling and chatting to her neighbors on their couches, to whom it seemed that she had entirely forgotten about the ordeal which now lay immediately in front of her. She seemed entirely lacking in nervousness. Probably Oah gave her some very long-acting tranquilizer with her sedative, which was indeed the case. After a meal she and Uth went to where the suits were ready to be fitted on.

Addressing Uth directly, Abello said, "We have decided that you should both be kitted up and pressurized at the same time, and you are to remain in the vicinity of the air lock so that you can pass quickly through. This is in case Arilyn gets into any sort of difficulty with the job or her equipment. You may have to mount a rescue operation on her or the job or both. At the same time Ube, who is Oah's chief assistant, is now going to enter the decompression chamber and he will be up to pressure by the time the job is finished. Inside the chamber are all the conveniences you require for a protracted stay, plus all the necessary medical equipment which Ube is qualified to us in an emergency. As you can see from here, the chamber has plenty of windows which will enable you to see all that is going on out here. There is also a two-way speech system so that full voice contact will be maintained. Thus, you will still be able to take an active part in all that is happening and we hope that this will at least minimize the tedium of the long time you will have to spend in there. Good luck to you both."

As Omas had previously forecast, it took several hours to get Arilyn and Uth into their suits, pressurized and fitted with their life support systems and then into the rigid diving suits. Once these in their turn had also been brought up to the required pressure they were guided down to two special couches near the door into the air lock where each was taken firmly by several males and lowered into a special trapping system. All the time the special electrodes which had been taped to various parts of their bodies were transmitting various physiological data which was both recorded and displayed visually on the screen on Oah's console. Here he was able to keep a very close watch on the body functions and would be able to anticipate the onset of any medical crises. As soon as they were both secure Abello ordered the rest of the crew to their couches where they were to similarly strap themselves down. He checked with each individual that this was done, after which he called up Ain on the two-way speech system and enquired how long it would be before the descent to the surface would begin.

Ain replied, "The spacecraft does not have to be turned around as we arrived here with the engine firing in the deceleration position. I have programmed the computer for automatic firing which will take place in exactly twenty-three minutes time. The motor power will be substantial at first but will gradually ease off over a period of about one hour, by which time our speed will have slowed down to such a point that we can safely lower the rotor mechanisms and come to our land under aerodynamic flight. We will be at a vertical height of about twenty-five miles from touchdown when this happens and sine seventy-five miles to the south. Our path from that point to our landing will be in the nature of a gentle curve. The landing will be about seventy-two minutes from the first firing so that everyone will be able to judge our progress merely by watching the timepieces. Eight minutes before the main motors fire there will be a small adjustment of our altitude to our descent and this will be done by short bursts on the tangential jets as previously. You will be aware of this change by small forces suddenly acting on your bodies in a number of directions although the effects will be very slight. I must warn everybody that we may experience a considerable degree of buffeting once we get to the denser parts of the atmosphere which will be due to the violent winds which blow down there and which are responsible for a great deal of turbulence. The computer will be taking rapid corrections to our flight when this occurs but we may find large air pockets through which we will suddenly drop to be followed by excess pressures which will seem to reverse our descent violently. As we have experienced before, after such a long period of weightlessness the re-establishment of gravity can cause a considerable degree of discomfort."

"Thank you Ain," said Abello. "I wonder if you all realize that in about two hours' time our ship will come to rest on solid ground and that will be the first time in something like fifty-seven of our years. Of course, to us it is only just about two and a quarter years, and that is long enough by any count."

Nothing more was said by any of the crew and once again the only sound to be heard for the next eleven minutes was the faint hum of the small motors controlling the support systems. Then a slight rocking motion startled the crew, particularly Matester who uttered some small cries thereby revealing the tense feelings which they were experiencing. Seven and a half minutes later a more intense whine was heard as the pumps on the main engine started to raise the pressures in the various tanks and then exactly on time, thirty seconds later, the nuclear engine roared into power and the bodies of the crew were forced deep into the cushioning of the couches as the gravitational forces built up due to the deceleration. In fact, it felt as though they had started from rest and were now accelerating in to opposite direction. The forces steadily built up and the child, the women and the two of the less robust males started to make small grunting cries because of the pains in their bodies. However, the pressures eased off somewhat before the oxygen starvation in their brains caused them to become unconscious.

The scene shown on the video screen had altered from blackness with only a thin sliver of white cloud at the very bottom of the screen to being totally filled by white formless brilliance. Because the nose of the craft was not pointing straight down they were able to see a long way forward and as they got closer to the cloud cover they were able to see the top in violent motion with great spouts of cloud being cast up to great heights only to sink slowly back again. And then suddenly the screen darkened and the craft entered the atmosphere. And then the screen became a dull red in color which Ain said was due in part to the high temperature of the outside skin of the craft due to the friction of the then atmosphere rushing past. For a while the descent was reasonably pleasant but then the buffeting began and it was so violent that before long most of the crew would have welcomed death as an alternative. It was as Ain had forecast, and the sudden drops were the feature that caused most of the discomfort. But the distress and terror reached a maximum when suddenly the most violent banging and screeching of metal upon metal sounded throughout the cabin, followed by a steady rocking motion of the ship. Omas called out to calm those of the crew who were becoming somewhat hysterical.

"Do not be alarmed, it is only the adjustment of the rotor mechanisms which is causing all that noise. Remember that they have not been moved for a very long time and the exposure to the vacuum and radiation of space has caused even the special lubricants of the bearings to dry out."

Much calm was restored by this announcement and it was only a few moments later when the blades started to rotate and as they bit into the dense atmosphere, Abello ordered the thrust from the nuclear drive to be cut off. Within a further minute or so the violent motion of the craft largely disappeared and the slower rate of descent was very much more comfortable to the entire crew.

Ain called out, "Five more minutes to touchdown. I can see that plateau ahead of us on the radar screen. It would seem to have a small slope at right angles to the line of our approach. Do not be alarmed when the craft floor does not stand horizontal. There should be no danger of slipping as the surface appears quite rough." Later, "Three hundred yards from touchdown and one minute to go. Everybody brace themselves. Ten seconds, five, four, three, here we go."

There was some shock throughout the craft when the extended feet touched the surface followed by a sliding motion for what seemed a long way. Then there was a heart-stopping lurch away from the slope and then nothing. Silence for a few seconds during which no one even dared to breathe for fear of upsetting the balance, then a burst of cheering which sounded more like hoarse croaking as pent-up emotions were released. The miracle had happened. They had brought their shop to a standstill after so many years of motion. And not one person had been in any way injured in the carrying out of the task.

Omas was the first out of his couch shouting at his assistants. "What is the matter with you all, lying there blubbering like infants? On your feet, there's work to be done and we have to work fast." He tried to heave himself forward to where Arilyn and Uth were strapped in the rigid suits, and fell flat on his face. He had forgotten that gravity had returned. He picked himself up, grinning rather sheepishly. The straps were soon undone and the necessary radio links activated.

"Right, Arilyn," said Omas, "into the air lock with you, and good luck. I will operate the pump and door controls from inside the cabin." He looked back into the cabin and shouted at Abello, "Is the portable television camera strapped to Arilyn working properly?"

"Yes," called Abello in reply.

"I will talk to you again in a few minutes," said Omas as he secured the bolts on the main door. Oah was watching very carefully the various dials which were recording heart beat rate, blood pressure, muscular output, etc. of Arilyn's body. He noted that her pulse rate and breathing rate were rising very rapidly. He called up to Omas. "Omas, I am a little concerned about her early reactions now that the reality is finally upon her. I am going to override all other microphones and have a work with here. You know that only I can break in this way?"

"Go ahead, Oah, but please do not be too long, as time is of the essence," conceded Omas.

A soft voice sounded in Arilyn's ear. "This is Oah and as you know no one else can hear what I say to you. Please do not get agitated at this time. This will cloud your judgment and detract from the absolute concentration you will need over the next hour. Remember that as a female the whole purpose of evolution is worked out through you and the children you produce. At this very moment that evolution in this part of the Galaxy has been brought to a fine focus. You have an enormous responsibility to bear on your small shoulders. Remember this, pause for a few seconds every once in a while, take slow deep breaths and your agitation will decrease. You have to assert the supremacy of your concentration in your own mind. Once you have done this the rest of your body functions will take secondary positions and you will come through this successfully."

"Thank you, Oah, for your comforting words," enjoined Arilyn. "I will try to remember all you say. Please talk to me when you can."

Oah waved a hand at Omas by way of a signal. Omas was now speaking to Arilyn, giving his instructions in an emotionless, scientific manner. "The air lock is now pressurized and I am now going to open the outer door. Oh, Ain tells me that we are very close to the edge of a very deep, sheer sided precipice and that there is a hurricane force upsurge of gases. Keep as close to the underside of the spacecraft as you can and do not go anywhere near the edge. You will be in grave danger of being blown away if you do. Understand?"

"Understood," replied Arilyn.

The door slid slowly to one side and Arilyn gave an involuntary gasp of horror at the spectacle in front of her. Omas spoke sharply. "Come on now, lower the basket of cans. You are not out there to admire the view. That's better." A slight pause. "Now turn with your back to the ladder down and feel with your foot for the first rung. Steady. That's it. Now for the second. As you go down keep a firm grip on the upper rung with your hands. Good. Good. No, don't look down under any circumstances. That's better. Look straight ahead all the time. I will tell you when you reach the last rung. Then the next step will put your feet on the ground. Good. Only seven more rungs to go. Now five. Now three. That's the last rung. Excellent. You are now the first one of us to step on firm ground since Capernica. Don't both to look around you yet."

But Arilyn had found it impossible not to look forward as she descended below the underside of the spacecraft and what she saw did not exactly encourage her. The ground was covered with sharp sided grey to dark brown rocks lying at all angles to one another in the greatest profusion. Around all swirled wisps of white mist swirling in all directions. She was surprised that the deep copper color of the upper atmosphere had given way to an almost white hue and that the amount of light was much higher than expected. She turned away from the ladder and bent down to pick up the steps and the container with the fluidized metal cans. In doing so she saw how desperately near to the edge of the precipice one of the legs of the spacecraft had slid and she reported this to Omas. She could not see very far over the edge of the chasm but she was aware of an equally steep sided opposite wall from which a constant cascade of rocs fell. She could not hear any sound due to her enclosure within the spacesuits.

She carefully placed the steps against the first cowling and jumped several times on the first step to make sure that the footing was secure. She quickly ascended and repaired the gaping hole with the firm sweeping strokes she had practiced so diligently. The first three repairs were affected without any complications but the fourth was full of difficulties as the new metal would not bond to the old at the top most part of the hole. So several valuable minutes were lost and Arilyn became conscious of increasing heat within her suit and of the external pressure. She placed the steps for the last repair and then leant wearily against them, fighting for breath and trying to will back strength into her arms and legs. For just a few moments Arilyn remained absolutely motionless and the whole of the crew watching on the video screens remained still, scarcely able even to breathe. The gentle caressing voice of Oah sounded in Arilyn's ear.

"Courage, my little one," he said. "Think back for a moment on all that you have achieved. There is but a little more to do and I know that you can do it. Remember what is at stake. Your kind will be honored by all the generations to come once you have completed your task. Another five minutes and all will be completed." Arilyn smiled gratefully to herself within her helmet and then bestirred herself into action. Time for her seemed to stand still. Her movements got slower and slower, and Oah and Omas began to exchange worried glances. At a signal from Abello, Ain told Uth to stand by for immediate action and started the pressure pumps to equalize the air lock.

At last Arilyn finished her work and slid down the steps rather than walked. She staggered towards the air lock. "Now, Uth," shouted Omas. The door of the air lock slip open and Arilyn fell into the doorway and Uth's arms. The door closed immediately and the vacuum pumps started up rapidly reducing the pressure from the outside atmosphere. The inner door slid open and both entered the main cabin. Quickly they passed into the decompression chamber where Arilyn sank into a merciful oblivion. Uth divested her of the cumbersome diving suit and then the inner flexible space suit. He laid her gently upon the couch and then took off his own inner suit. Then Uth too lay down, and they both slept for many hours, the one from the fatigue of her exertions and the other from the release of nervous tension that the job was done and relief for the fact that he had not been called upon to venture outside the craft.

For the rest of the crew there were quiet moments of silent gratitude and much wrinkling of noses and coughing as the acrid fumes of the planet's atmosphere spread through the cabin. Gradually the air pumps and purifiers took control of the situation and the air became sweet once more. The gentle buzz of conversation died away and eyes begun to turn to Abello in anticipation of his assessment of the situation. Abello consulted with his chief officers for some time, examining very closely the appearance of the repairs through the video cameras. At last he spoke to the entire crew.

"It would seem that the repairs which Arilyn has carried out have been successful, at least as far as we can determine at this time. But," he continued, "We have now to wait for a full day to pass for the new metal to stabilize and form a perfect join with the old. Only then will we be able to take off from this frightening place in complete safety. So, once again, there is nothing to do but wait. I suggest that we all rest now and sleep as much as possible for we may need our maximum alertness at the time of leaving." There was a general shuffling about as they made themselves comfortable on the couches and before very long the only sound to be heard, apart from the low hum of the life support systems, was that of gentle breathing. Just before Abello settled down to rest he programmed the main computer for the start-up sequence of operations for the take-off to such an extent that all that would be required when the right time arrived was to depress a switch.

Soon, too, Abello drifted into a dreamless sleep which lasted for many hours. Then dream patterns began to flit into his mind and he imagined himself back on Capernica doing the everyday things which were the basis of his life. He stirred easily with the contentment of home. Then gradually things were becoming distorted and he imagined himself becoming listless. Suddenly the imagery changed and he saw himself inside one of the great water towers. His body felt hot and uncomfortable while the water looked cool and very inviting. Although he knew it to be wrong, for this was drinking water, he took off his cloak and plunged into the water. He immediately felt the wave of coolness rush over him but the water too was suddenly too hot for comfort. He quickly came to the surface and as he did so he heard a voice cry out to him from the side of the tank. Abello gave a great start and hurriedly hauled himself out of the water overwhelmed at the enormity of his stupidity.

He slowly became aware of reality, the small light bulb over his head gradually taking shape as his eyes struggled to focus. As he did so he became aware that part of his dream was true. He was hot. In fact, he was wet through with perspiration, the moisture running down his neck, his chest and thighs. His chest was heaving with the effort to draw breath and the air itself was hot and humid. He fought back the black clouds of unconsciousness from his mind and with a supreme effort he sat up. All around him were the crew members glistening with sweat and croaking with the effort to draw breath. "What could possibly have gone wrong now?"

He glanced at the temperature indicator which showed a rise of forty degrees and was not dangerously close to the limit at which life was possible. A glance at the couch of Matester showed that she would not last very much longer under these conditions. A quick survey by the computer showed that the power supply was dropping rapidly and obviously the refrigeration processes were not operating as efficiently as they should have been.

"Must not let the power level drop too low," he thought, "Otherwise there will not be sufficient for the take-off." The pressure of events and the need for positive action helped to clear his mind so that he was able to think more logically.

"What's next?" he mused. "Look at the time." Some twenty hours and nineteen minutes had passed since he fell asleep. "That is still quite a significant time short of the twenty-four hours we have to wait for the metal repairs to stabilize. Can we survive till then?"

More codes were quickly fed into the computer which almost immediately gave a maximum figure of thirty-five minutes. Without a moment's further thought Abello pressed the switch which started the automatic firing sequence. His next thought was to look at the poor unfortunates trapped in the decompression chamber – three supine glistening bodies showed on the video screen. They were all breathing deeply but did not seem particularly distressed. Maybe the temperature had not risen quite so high in there. Finally Abello switched to the outside cameras and inspected carefully each of the repairs in turn. As far as he could see there was no change in the appearance of the metal so he had no means of judging whether the repairs would hold once the nuclear motors started. Anyway, it was too late to worry about that. After all he had no real choice. It was either be boiled in one's own body fluids on that inhospitable planet, instant death by decompression should the fabric of the ship rupture in space, or fry in the upper atmosphere of the blue planet if they should make it that far.

Abello smiled grimly to himself while bustling around the couches as fast as he could to strap his colleagues in before liftoff. He tried to rouse each one at the same time but not very successfully. Only Omas seemed to be eventually aware of his surroundings and what Abello had done but even he was in no fit state to comment or criticize. With five male crew members to be strapped in Abello was aware of the shriek of protesting metal as the power came on to the rotor blades which provided for the aerodynamic flight. Slowly the great rotors began to turn and the ship vibrated with a pattern of ascending and then descending severity. With regret that three males remained unstrapped, Abello reached his own couch as the harshness of the vibration suddenly vanished, to be replaced by a whining note which gradually rose in scale and intensity. They were away from the surface and ascending slowly through the dense atmosphere of the planet. The note rose beyond the limit of hearing, to be followed with a pattern of other low notes rising to high ones and disappearing in their turn. After even only a few minutes Abello noted with satisfaction that the rate of the rise of the internal temperature was falling. The temperature peaked and then started a slow decline.

After nearly an hour of vertical climbing they had risen very high into the upper atmosphere of the planet where the air was thin and the spinning rotor blades no longer bit hungrily into the atmosphere. The ship hung on the blades for several minutes and then the nuclear motors started up with a great roar which faded rapidly as the speed built up beyond that of sound. The rotors ceased their functioning and were drawn back into the engine housing so as to remove as much friction as possible to the atmosphere. The ship rose steadily and majestically above the clouds into the brilliant light of Benu and soon even the last vestiges of atmosphere were left far behind. The crew returned to activity and comprehension fairly fast once the temperature and humidity had returned to more acceptable levels. Only Omas expressed doubts on the events, being nervous as to the state of the bond between the old and new metal after a resting contact time significantly less than had been recommended. The ship was now moving faster than the escape velocity and the nuclear motors automatically shut themselves down.

Abello called to Aqa, the astronomer, and together they ascended into the observation dome. They looked back to where the enormous disc of the white planet showed with its swirling masses of white clouds. A few moments silent observation showed that they were traveling away from the planet at a small angle outwards to the orbit of the planet around Benu.

"That is good," grunted Aqa. "Now to locate the position of the blue planet." He consulted some notes which he had written down before the enforced descent and nodded to himself. Abello looked at him questioningly.

"At the moment we cannot see the blue planet because it is behind us and the mass of the white planet hides it from us. I suggest we continue with our present course for another twenty-four hours or so, by which time we will have drawn far enough away and to one side to be able to see the blue planet, at least telescopically. An hour of observation will then give me all the information I need to design a new course of interception."

"I understand," said Abello, "at least partially. At the moment we are traveling away from both the planets so is it your proposal to use our much greater speed to encircle Benu on and outwardly spiraling and so catch up to the blue planet? That will take a long time."

"No, I don't think that is what I shall be proposing," replied Aqa. "I think it will be quicker if we apply a low power drive at a slight angle to our present trajectory and so swing slowly in a wide arc outwards towards the orbit of the blue planet without losing any of our present velocity. When we get near to our planet we shall turn inwards towards its far side and allow gravity to slow us down to minimize the power we shall need to expend to get to orbital velocity. This is because at the approach we will be approaching from opposite directions and our velocities will be additative so we will have to lose large amounts of energy in quite a short time. But I will need to take actual optical measurements before I can work out the final details of our new orbit."

"Very well," agreed Abello, "let us now see what Omas thinks of the state of repair of the plug nozzle now that the metal has had a chance to cool off after our ascent from the surface." This inspection showed nothing more obvious than a minor amount of pitting of the new metal surface.

"I do not think we are faced with anything serious with the cowling," remarked Omas, "but it is obvious that the surface is not as good as it was when new. This means that we must use the engines with minimum power for the minimum of time of firing. This means that operations will take longer but this is unavoidable."

"That is a small price to pay for safe landing," remarked Aqa.

"True," agreed Abello, "but after all, this time nobody can view an extension of our flight time with equanimity. So we must not draw the attention of the rest of the crew to his unnecessarily." And so it was agreed.

After the new course had been set the routine of the cabin settled down to the monotony they all knew so well. After one hundred rest periods had passed Ain said that the occupants of the decompression chamber were now returned to normal conditions and they could now return to the main cabin and take up their normal routines. When Arilyn herself emerged from the chamber she was swept off her feet and carried shoulder high around the cabin many times to loud cheers. Everybody embraced her and caressed her hair and by the time she came to a halt in front of Arabus and Abello she was flushed and breathless with excitement and pleasure. Abello made a short speech expressing the thanks and gratitude of the entire crew for what she had accomplished for them. He felt very inadequate in trying to express his emotion in cold words and he quickly stopped and embraced her likewise. Arabus notes with scorn the tears in Abello's eyes, but the onlookers observed that he trembled as he swept Arilyn up into his powerful arms, rendering her breathless for a short time. Arabus was surprised to find that Arilyn was so small and slight but he appreciated the softness and warmth of her well-shaped breasts through the thin shift that all the females wore. He made some mental notes for the future but they were rather half-hearted, as his tastes were for the larger variety of companion – she probably already belonged to one of the younger crew members, anyway. The meal that they shared that night before retiring was taken in an atmosphere of high excitement totally free from any cares for the present or doubts for the future and it was a long time before the entire crew could settle into sleep.

Rest period then followed rest period without a great deal of attention being paid by anyone as to the actual number. Aqa suddenly announced that the procedure to put them in orbit would be put into operation after seven more rest periods. There was a momentary silence and then everyone was talking at once. Several of the crew members nearest to the entrance rushed up into the observation hatch and there sure enough was the blue planet with its own white satellite, both clearly showing considerable discs although neither completely illuminated. The blue planet was about half illuminated while the satellite showed a thin sliver of white facing towards the bright part of the planet. Golden Benu was somewhat about the line joining satellite to planet but much closer to the satellite. The white swirls of cloud above the deep blue background were clearly visible although the solid ground they knew to be present from the previous encounter was not well outlined. Probably too far away for the moment, commented Aqa, who was now engaged in a fever of observation and measurement, checking and double checking with the computer. Abello let Aqa work undisturbed as he realized that on him depended the final success of the expedition – he would near the results of the computations as soon as they had been finalized. During the time between the second and third rest periods after Aqa's original announcement the work was finished and Abello and his officers gathered to hear the conclusions.

"Do any of you believe in luck or even a written destiny?" he asked

72

after all had settled down. "Because if you have not believed before this you should start from now on. A most incredible piece of luck has happened. You will all remember the relative positions of the satellite and the blue planet and ourselves when we started the observations two rest periods ago? We are coming in behind them both at a gentle angle and as we sweep behind each one in turn we will be able to use the gravitational attractions as brakes. If the satellite were in a position of half an orbit later we would not be able to use both."

"I do not see your reason for such enthusiasm," grumbled Arabus. "The braking effect will account for only a small proportion of the energy we have to lose."

"Agreed," said Aqa, "but my enthusiasm is for the saving we will have considering the low state of the power supply and for the poor state of the surface of the plug nozzle. We are utterly dependent on those two things for our final descent to the surface. Remember, too, we need to keep some power alive in our atomic source to supply us with the necessities of life after we have landed. But to more urgent practical matters. In sixteen hours and fifty-three minutes from now," Aqa made a downwards chopping motion with his hand, "we must start up the nuclear drive on low power so that we gradually slow down, and before then we must turn the spacecraft around so that the drive is directly against our line of flight."

Abello nodded his agreement and gave the necessary instructions for Omas to implement. In fact, Omas decided to turn the ship around straight away and he applied the tangential jets but with the minimum force so as to conserve fuel. In fact, the motion produced was so slow that the crew were not really aware of any movement and the whole operation took up most of the waiting time to the startup of the retro thrust. This, too, was only on low power and so the discomfort produced by the deceleration was minimal. Only two of the females and Matester experienced a slight nausea with the return of gravity.

First the white cratered surface of the satellite disappeared into an inky blackness as the ship swept around to the unlit side to be followed after about twenty minutes by a narrow line of white light on the far horizon which rapidly broadened as they came out of the shadow. Presently, the nearly complete disc of the blue planet rose above the surface of the satellite with dramatic suddenness and mounted steadily into the sky above the surface. Then the view detached itself from the two bodies and they saw themselves as freely moving in space. The ship was now in a course which would spiral it down to the blue planet after several orbits and at the completion of the first orbit they again passed close to the surface of the satellite but this time between it and its planet. Four more orbits were completed and the voyagers now found themselves moving just above the outer fringes of the planet's atmosphere at a constant speed and virtually constant height.

And yet once again the crew settled down to the boredom of waiting, not that Aqa and Abello had any time to be bored for it now fell upon them to examine every inch of the planet's surface to determine the position of the best possible landing site. Under high magnification it was easy to see where the vegetation was most abundant, where the vegetation ceased in the high mountains and at the edges of vast deserts. Rivers and lakes were also clearly visible as well as the sharply marked coastline. By studying the radiation from the ground by means of infrared photography and records gathered at other electromagnetic wavelengths the two steadily built up a picture of the surface conditions. When their work was completed Abello called the entire crew to attention so that all could hear the details of their chances of survival and make any comments if they were relevant. But Aqa and Abello had done their work very well indeed and there were no hard decisions which had to be made, and Abello felt some relief at this.

Summarizing the recommendations Abello said, "We need to land in an area which has in reasonable proximity plenty of timber and at the same time open ground which we can prepare two or even three crops of food a year in order to build up our reserves as rapidly as possible, just in case we run into problems later on. We will need a well-watered area but not swampy because that will probably be disease ridden. We will also need to be near sources of a variety of metals which we can mine and then fabricate tools. The timber will be needed as a source of fuel for our furnaces. For the metals we will need an area reasonably close to old volcanic activity. Unfortunately no site is perfect but the best choice would seem to be in the region around here." Abello stabbed a finger at one of the aerial photographs which Aqa had taken during this survey. "The area is towards the east of the land mass that is shaped vaguely like a hammer. It is in the equatorial zone but the land seems to be at some altitude above sea level. You will notice that there are lakes to the north, east, south and southwest within reasonable striking distance with further very much larger areas of fresh water to the northwest, southwest and south. There is a long ridge of very high mountains further to the east followed by a coastal plain. You will also observe that there is evidence of a fault line of considerable length running north and south to the west of this area.?

"A question here," interrupted Arabus. "Did you consider this land mass to the west which seems in considerable isolation from these clustered continents. If there are any inhabitants down there they might prove hostile to us and it is likely that the local frictions would have produced the greatest degree of technical advance and hence would constitute the greatest threat to our survival. We will be very vulnerable for the first few months after our landing before we establish defenses suitable to any threat."

"A good point," agreed Abello, "but our thinking is opposite. We can see no evidence of any urban type settlements in as far as no organized patterns of light have been discovered during the passage of darkness. Any forms of organized life would seem to be very primitive therefore, and unlikely to pose any serious threat to us. After all, we do have some fairly sophisticated weapons in the form of laser torches. We feel that if the inhabitants have reached the stage of their development that thy work metals, then we should find the mine workings without too much difficulty. This could save us a great deal of time and effort and we might be able to persuade the locals to dig the ores for us. As for the land mass you mention, it is strange how it consists of two large areas, one to the north and the other to the south of the equator yet joined by the narrow spit of land. That spit is quite mountainous with active volcanoes and from these pictures the land looks very unstable. In the southern part there seems to be but one major inland water which is reasonably equatorial, but look how high in the mountains that is. Vegetation is not all that prolific and the temperatures probably too cold for our seeds to flourish properly particularly at night. There is an area of fresh water of considerable size in the northern land mass in this large multilake systems, but it is winter in this hemisphere and you can see how far south of there the land is frozen and there is a great deal of snow on the surface. Again this is too cold for our plants. We must remember that for a while we will have to depend on our own foods as it would be dangerous to start eating the local foods. These will have to be exhaustively tested to make sure that they are not only not poisonous to us but also that continued ingestion will not have long term harmful effects. But apart from these longer and larger considerations are there any questions about or comments upon this choice?"

"Yes," said Omia. "I have a question. Do we have a second choice of site, should the first prove impossible for any reason which we cannot foresee at this moment?"

Abello smiled a little wearily. "I wish you had not asked that," he said, "although your question is a very good one. I am afraid the answer has to be no. there is no second choice. We will not be absolutely certain about any site until we have virtually landed. By that time our ship will be unable to get back into orbit, nor will there be sufficient reserves of power for a protracted aerodynamic flight. There will be some leeway in that we will be able to keep flying for say thirty minutes at very low altitude which means we can look at quite a number of sites within a small radius in great detail. But a decision will have to be made within that time. My guess is that no site will be perfect and therefore I shall probably decide to go into the first one that looks reasonable." There being no further comments or questions Abello closed the meeting.

Aqa had previously advised Abello that several orbits would have to be completed before the descent could begin. This was so that the approach path would be the most advantageous to the terrain and to minimize the amount of power required for the aerodynamic flight. Thus there was time in plenty to make sure that everything in the ship was securely battened down and those that were subject to motion sickness under gravity could take the necessary remedial steps. It was expected, from the experience of the white planet, that the descent would be turbulent particularly the later atmospheric flight. Well before the time to fire the motor retroactively arrived the work was done and the crew safely strapped on to their couches. The last hour of orbital flight was spent watching the video pictures of the planet beneath them on the large screen at the far end of the main cabin. Five minutes before Abello switched off the main screen and wished all the crew good luck both as individuals and collectively. He confirmed that this was the end of the flight for the shop would stand no more, as the supply of nuclear fuel was all but exhausted. So there was no choice for them to take, no other option open to them but to accept that the blue planet had to offer even if that meant their ultimate destruction. They could not go anywhere else.

A few moments of silence and increasing emotional tension, and then the well-known whine of motors was heard, to be followed a few minutes later by a muffled roaring and each body was increasingly pressed down into the gently yielding cushion of the space couch. After a few moments the pressure eased though still remaining slightly positive. Gravity began to make itself felt then steadily increased giving the ship a top and bottom once more. Then the pressure increased very rapidly and bodies were pressed lower and lower and each felt themselves growing heavier and heavier. Some drifted into unconsciousness which was a great benefit. The pain for the others lasted for several more minutes and then eased off fairly rapidly. Vibrations were now felt throughout the ship accompanied by swaying motions of an irregular nature which indicated that the ship was now descending through the middle parts of the atmosphere. The nuclear motors shut off automatically and the rotor blades were heard to extend themselves. The protestations of metal on metal were not as severe this time as they had been on the white planet when the rotors started to revolve, and so they came to maximum revolutions very rapidly. The flight now felt quite spongy with sudden drops as the ship went into lower density air to be followed by sharp apparent stops as higher density air was reached. However, all were very pleased to note that the turbulence was nowhere near as severe as it had been on the white planet. Abello switched on the large video screen once more and allowed the ship to descend to about ten thousand feet above the ground by reducing the speed of the rotor blades. A brilliant scene met their eyes and for the more sensitive of the travelers was of overwhelming beauty. The sip was coming in on a course running roughly from north of west to south of east. Immediately below stretched mile after mile of dense green rain forest stretching away to the north where a thin line of bright blue showed on the horizon which was the southern shore of the northern lake. The other two lakes were too far away to the southwards to be seen from this low altitude. In front of them and but slightly to the north rose the wooded slopes of a mountain, only the very top of which was bare rock. Behind that and dead ahead could be seen the bare peak of an even higher mountain, while again more to the north and towering over both was a very high summit which glowed with a pinkish white color which was the reflection of Benu shining through some low cloud and mist near to the horizon on to the snow around the summit. Benu itself was away to the southwest and low in the sky. Indeed Aqa estimated that it would be dark within the hour and this thought gave extra urgency to all the pairs of eyes searching the screen for a clearing in which they could set down. After several minutes they could see on the southeastern horizon a long ridge which was fee from large trees. As they approached nearer this ridge became the vast outer ring of a huge volcano many, many miles in circumference. Arabus pointed to this and said to all and sundry, "Lucky for us that that is extinct." To the north of the crater wall the land levelled out to a series of grassy plains, some of which were only a few hundred yards in extent. Omas now brought the craft down to only a few hundred feet above the treetops and the crew were able to see strange moving creatures grazing on the grass in these places. As the roar of the rotors bore down on these creatures they lifted their heads and started to run in all directions in sheer panic, eventually disappearing under the cover of the trees.

Abello caught sight of a flash of light within some trees which wound their way around several open spaces some way away. "Aim over there, Omas," he ordered, "I think there is a small river in the trees and we will need to be near a supply of fresh water."

At that moment, the screen went nearly black as a furious rain squall hit the craft together with violent winds which spun the craft around several times. So violent was the buffeting of the wind that two of the rotor blades snapped off suddenly and the craft lurched one-sidedly as the blades no longer gave sufficient lift to keep the ship on balance. The craft dropped sharply downwards and spun sideways. By this time Omas had lowered the landing wheels which were in multiples at the bottom of each rotor housing and one of these slipped the topes of the trees at the edge of a small clearing.

This gave a further increase to the spinning motion just before the craft hit the ground with a violent thud which made everybody's teeth rattle in their jaws and set up not a little panic. As luck would have it Abello had not given any instructions for the crew to take off their safety belts and so there were no actual injuries. The ship careened sideways, one engine digging itself deeper into the soft ground as it went, causing it to lean over at an ever increasing angle until all motion was arrested by an outcrop of rock. There was another violent shock and all the lights were extinguished, adding to the general confusion and panic. Then a few of the emergency bulbs lit up to reveal a chaotic scene. Order was quickly restored and the work of assessing the damage commenced.

Most of the instruments of navigation had been destroyed and Abello realized that they did not know their position relative to the river or the lakes within an area of one hundred square miles. A lot of instrumentation concerned with the analysis of their environment was also out of action but whether permanently or temporarily it was impossible to determine for the moment. The atmosphere pumps still seemed to be in working order. There should be no trouble over temperature control as the observations from orbit had indicated an acceptable level.

After a short while Abello said, "That was hardly the landfall we hoped to make, but at least we are down and everybody is safe. Aqa tells me that it is dark outside so we will not attempt to leave the ship until tomorrow. Then new adventures will befall us the like of which we cannot even begin to guess. But let us give thanks, for our journey is over."

CHAPTER IV

For quite some time those simple words "For our journey is over" hung in the air of the cabin, their true significance just waiting to be born. Then with one great shout the whole cabin erupted with relief and joy which far outdid in length and intensity any other moments of relief from tension that all had shared. But calm and understanding did at length reestablish itself and then Abello told the crew what the next steps would be leading to their exit from the spacecraft the next morning.

"As I said earlier, it is now dark outside and it would be unsafe for us to open the main door, for we do not know what dangers might lurk in wait for us outside. In the meantime, Oah is running some final checks on the nature of the atmosphere, at least as far as he is able in view of the damage that was caused on the landing. They will be complete in another hour or so. Unfortunately, the outside video cameras are not functioning so we cannot have a look around us either. So I suggest that we settle down and get as much rest as we can before we face the excitements of tomorrow."

"Before we do that," interrupted Omas, "Is it possible that the microphone which is on the outer skin is still functioning? If so it might be interesting and maybe not a little instructive to hear the night sounds of our new home."

"Yes, the power demand for both of these is virtually negligible," answered Omas. At this moment Eloni came from her couch and stood at Abello's side and her hand slid into his and his fingers entwined with hers. Omas operated the necessary switches on his console, waited a few moments to check that the circuits were completed and then slowly turned up the volume. The crew were still and absolutely silent as the strange sounds filled the cabin. There were high pitched whistling notes very close which were immediately answered similarly from some distance away. Silence, and then the notes close by once more to be similarly answered. There were also chattering noises which seemed to come from up in the trees nearby, followed by scampering. The gentle soughing of the wind formed a background to this fascinating cacophony. Suddenly, close to the ship there was heard very coarse breathing and sniffing sounds. Although they could not hear the footsteps of whatever it was upon the ground a faint swishing sound was just heard from time to time.

"A large animal walking around the ship sniffing the intruders in his world," whispered Abello into Eloni's ear, taking the advantage of the situation to give her a brushing kiss on her neck.

"Why are you whispering?" Eloni said with a little chuckle, "it cannot hear us talk."

Abello forced to admit that it was the emotion of this moment and his unwillingness to break the spell which had made him whisper, but only Eloni heard his confession. A few moments later there was a sudden roar in the microphone which made everyone jump with sudden panic. A moment's silence, then a scream full of fear and pain which died with a choking sound. For a few seconds the whole of the new nature was still and silent. Then the musical notes and chatterings started again just as though nothing had disturbed the rhythm.

"Seems as though it is also a cruel world," commented Eloni, adding beneath her breath, "which will probably suit Arabus' ideals of life and living."

The crew listened for some time longer until it was suggested that any more sounds would disturb their sleep with possible bad dreams of the unknown.

Oak spoke. "There is one thing we could enjoy that would be more useful and beneficial to us than listening to the noises from outside. I have now completed my final tests on the atmosphere outside and I find it is absolutely harmless although it is a lot more humid than we are used to. I propose to link up one of the air pumps to the outside and draw in some fresh air. We might get quite a surprise when we find out just how stale and fetid our air had become. Shall I do this?" he inquired, looking at Abello.

"Very definitely," was the response.

It took but a few moments for Omas to make the necessary connections and a few more moments for the new air to make its presence felt. And Oah was right about the contrast. Apart from the freshness, what Oah had not prepared everyone to expect was the smell of the air. This had a background odor of moist soil, green vegetation and the heady perfume of a rich ménage of tropical blooms.

"That is absolutely wonderful," said Eloni filling her lungs with the sweetness, the terror of the animals of a few minutes previously having faded from her mind in an instant. "It must also be a very beautiful world," she added, wrapping her arms around Abello and squeezing him tightly.

Little Arilyn came and stood by Abello and Eloni. Both of them smiled at her. "There is one more thing which we can do this night to get a little appreciation of our new home. Would you be very upset, Eloni, if I asked a very big personal favor of Abello?"

"Of course I would not mind," was the reply. "You have the right to ask whatever you will. How can we deny you considering the debt we all owe to you."

"I hope you will feel just as calm when you have heard my request," laughed Arilyn, "but this is what I would like, Abello, will you come alone with me into the observation dome and look with me at our new home?"

Despite a sudden nervousness which caused him to pause momentarily before he replied, a fact which Arabus noticed with a slight grin, Abello willingly agreed and together they went up into the lighted dome. There was a faint whirring sound as Abello removed the protective screen from the dome and then the crew members saw the light turned off – this was greeted with loud whistles and catcalls but Arilyn and Abello ignored this, for they were lost in a wonderland of their own.

It took a few minutes for their eyes to adjust themselves to the difference in the level of the light inside the craft to that outside. In front of them at an elevation of about thirty degrees was the face, the brilliantly silver face of the satellite which was illuminated between full face and half face, the phase being that after full. The light was sufficiently bright to bathe the scene around them in a soft silver glow, not bright enough to show the actual green of the vegetation around, yet showing each leaf as a separate dark object. The topes of the trees could be seen quite distinctly moving to and fro in the gentle breeze. They could not hear this through the transparent shield, the microphone had previously been switched off. The craters and dark areas on the face of the satellite could also be distinguished quite readily. They gazed in complete silence, forgetting time. "It is so wonderful," breathed Arilyn, "and so different from Capernica. How can we ever be unhappy in such a place?"

Abello did not respond other than a slight shake of the head. Arilyn stood very close to Abello and slightly to one side. He put one arm around her waist and drew her gently to him so that her right shoulder pressed into his chest. He held her close with great affection and felt refreshed by the contact.

"You are still very young Arilyn," he said softly, "but I hope that because of that none of us will ever forget and be profoundly grateful for what you did for us. It is thanks to you that you and I can gaze out on the breath-taking scene this night."

"Thank you Abello," she replied, "but my part was but a tiny fraction of the effort which you put in to bring us all safely to this time and place."

"Let us just agree," Abello smiled, "that we played our part fully in the enterprise." They continued to gaze out into the night scene, absolutely motionless and each one deeply sunk into his own private world. Eloni's head appeared in the hatchway.

81

"You two are very quiet up here," she said. "What are you doing?"

"You must come up here and look with us," replied Arilyn beckoning with her hand.

Eloni came up and stood on the other side of Abello and slipped her hand in his to be followed up the steps by Aqa who went to the other side of Arilyn. The four companions spent a long time in silence and quietly pointing out to one another the strange happenings outside the craft which caught their eyes from time to time. A few more crew members drifted in and out but Arabus did not climb the steps, preferring to save his first glimpse of his new home to that magic moment when the outer door would glide silently open the next morning.

None of them slept very soundly that night and their restlessness was echoed by Arabus' daughter, who became fretful and whining. Most of them were alternating between excitement at finally stepping on to their new land and apprehension as to what lay in front of them. They had spent the previous day eagerly looking out of the windows and taking turns to clamber up into the observation dome to look at the wall of green low scrub vegetation. They had marveled at the complexity of life and were entranced with the various groups of animals which skittered across the clearing. They had heard through the microphones cries and howls as the animals foraged through the night. Abello sat at the back with Eloni, taking turns to rock the baby, and conscious of the sweet nearness of them. He thought about the ultimate success of the flight and he wondered how they would all fare in their new life. If he had been given second sight then he would never have stepped off the ship.

The dawn came swiftly and unexpectedly as though the darkness had cracked and let out the light. With it came a rival in the noise from the birds and tribes of tree climbing animals. Abello stood up.

"My friends, the time is upon us. All reports are favorable and I will now open the door, and we all shall set foot on our new land. A work of caution. You will be weak from lack of exercise, so do not exert yourselves too much and do not leave the clearing. None of us know what dangers are out there."

"Just open the door," interrupted Arabus, and the cry was taken up. Abello moved to the large metal door and started synchronizing the many locks and bolts. When all were set he nodded to Omas who was at the computer control and who pressed a button. For a moment noting happened, but then slowly the door swung out and sunlight came rippling in, illuminating the faces of the people and etching Abello's outline against the door. Suddenly there was a concerted movement as everyone rushed to the door, Abello stood to one side as Arabus, who headed the crowd, swept by.

With a swift bound he was down the steps and onto the ground. Turning he helped Anice down and then the others followed. Abello stretched his hand for Eloni.

"Come, my one true love, and we will enter our new life together." He carried her down the steps and almost dropped her at the bottom.

"Careful, Abello," she laughed.

"I did not realize how weak I was," he answered. They stood with arms around each other, feeling the sun warming their bodies. The others were standing, sitting or lying on the ground. Some had already instinctively sought the shadows of the ship to enjoy the comparatively cooler air. As he looked around Abello could see that they were in an almost circular clearing surrounded by trees except for the space where the ship had landed. From where he stood the mass of trees and various plants looked solid as a wall. There must be ways through it. Some of them were already walking towards it and Abello and Eloni followed them. As they got closer they could see small openings and they saw great swathes of plants and enormous, brightly colored flowers which climbed around many of the trees. It was cooler here and they rested on the thick grass which grew abundantly at the edge. The remainder of the day passed in the same casual fashion with a little exercise followed by rest. It was humid, more so than they had ever known, and one by one they all sought shade. Their thirst was fierce. As the day drew to a close Abello ordered them all back to the ship.

"I do not want to go. I would rather sleep out here," said Arabus, and several others echoed him.

"There may be dangers here as I told you, and I think until we are sure we are secure we must stay in the ship at night. In time we will build some other shelter but at least for the immediate future you will be safe on the ship."

Arabus hesitated and then with bad grace clambered back into the ship. When on board Oah came to see Abello.

"I have observed that even today the humidity is causing problems. Many of them are already complaining that they do not feel too well and at the rate of liquid consumption we are going to finish our supplies within the week. The food is not a problem as we are all vegetarians and it looks as though we will find plenty to eat although strict tests will have to be made. I am going to see what can be done with those who are not feeling well and I would like you to tell them all to keep out of the sun, move slowly and try to control their thirsts."

"Thank you, Oah, for informing me," said Abello, and then asking for their attention he told them what the doctor had said. This brought a somewhat discouraging note to the first day and one or two complaints were voiced that maybe this place was not as marvelous as they thought.

"This is just the first day and you must expect problems, and I expect solutions from you as well," snapped Abello. "You are not on Capernica now where everything is handed to you by the robots. It is up to us all now."

For the rest of the night all was quiet and most of them slept deeply. In the morning Abello stayed with Oah in the ship to ask about the conditions of the patients.

"Most of them are better," he affirmed. "You were right to suggest a leisurely pace for a few days. However, we should try to find a source of water." Abello thanked him and joined Eloni outside. He told her about the water.

"What are we going to do?" she queried. "We cannot fail now we have come so far."

"I realize that, my darling, and I plan to ask them all what they would do."

Accordingly, Abello went around to every man and woman and asked them what they thought would be the best solution. He found that some of them took an active interest in being asked and that some of them were quite indifferent. Surprisingly Arabus was concerned. He listened intently as Abello told him of the problem.

"We will have to explore," he said. "We should send a small group out each day and they must mark where they have been."

"That is a good idea," said Abello.

"Just practicing how to be leader," mocked Arabus.

That evening Abello asked for volunteers to look for water. Most of them volunteered and Abello selected Omas, two others and Oah. "He will be able to tell if they should find water if it is suitable," Abello explained. Early next morning they left. The rest of them were quiet during the day as they all hoped for an early success. The four of them came wearily back on the late afternoon without having seen any water. For the next three days a different group went out but all reported failure. By this time they had been forced to stop all but the most elementary washing. Only the baby had a bath and even then the water was saved. Oah suggested that a pit be dug some way from the ship and this would be used as a toilet. They were not to go alone, but have someone else to act as a look out.

On the fifth day about noon the sky darkened dramatically. Instinctively they all returned to the ship. A crack of lightning jagged the air followed by a rumble of thunder and it began to pour with rain.

"Quick, quick, let's catch some of it," call Abello, and they rushed outside with whatever containers they could find. Some of them began to take their clothes off and let the water flow over them. Soon all of them were running around naked, laughing and singing. As quickly as it had begun the rain stopped and the sun returned to beat down with renewed intensity. They all dressed, and their clothes were soon dry. Abello had found that they had collected a fair amount of water and so they were safe for a while. The day continued but as night came there was no sign of the four that had set off to explore that day.

"Let us go and try to find them," said Arabus.

"What do the rest of you think?" asked Abello.

Some were in favor of going but most of them were a little afraid of setting off through the jungle in the approaching darkness.

"I think we should build a fire," a voice said and they all turned. It was Anice who spoke up. "That way if they are lost they will see the light and be able to find their way back."

All were in agreement and started to search for wood. Soon there was a big hole in the middle of the clearing. Abello asked Omas if he knew of a way to start a fire.

"I think the best way is for me to make a taper and try and light it from the microwave oven. When this is done I will light a piece of wood and come out here and set it to the pile of branches."

"So be it."

In actual fact it took several tries before the branch would even stay alight long enough to carry it to the wood but after about five attempts one of the branches finally caught and soon the flames of the fire threw strange and fanciful shadows across the clearing. They ate the evening meal outside as there seemed little point in going on board the ship when four of their comrades were still outside in the jungle. Later on some of them went to the ship to rest but others lay down beside the fire. Abello arranged for at least two of the men to keep watch in shifts. One of them called out, "This used to be what the robots did on Capernica. " But no one paid any attention to this remark. The watching in shifts that night was the first break in the long process of changing an established way of life. All night they waited but no one came. During the following morning there was talk again of a search party, but Abello reiterated that it was better for them to stay all together. After all, he pointed out, take another four or even six and this leaves just fourteen men to look after the women, the supplies and the ship, and if four more leave, well, we may all spend days traipsing around the jungle after each other and no more than fifty years away from each other. Instead he fetched some paper and pencils and passed them around the group.

"I think you should all draw your ideas for the new homes. Yes. We cannot live in the ship forever and we must make a base from which to explore. I want to hear from each of you."

"Always our dear leader getting us to do this and that. We have left Capernica and the rules are different here," said Arabus.

"Until such time as the rules are changed I will remain Leader," retorted Abello. "I was going to ask you if you would like to design the gardens. We have brought seeds with us and the sooner we get started the sooner we shall be enjoying the food we are used to as well as the new tastes we are finding here."

"Look!" a voice shrieked from behind him. He turned. There, hobbling across the clearing, was Aqa supported by Uth and Ua and Efa. They all rushed to help them and carried them to the shade of the ship.

"What has happened?" they chorused.

"First get some water," ordered Oah. Eloni ran to fetch some from the ship. Oah gave them all some to drink and then set about cleaning Aqa's foot and ankle, or rather what was left of it.

Uth began, "It was horrifying. We had made good time and passed several places where the marks showed that some of you had been. We came to a fork and took the left one. The path became practically impassable with roots, undergrowth and bushes all knotted together. It began to get very mush under foot as well. We decided to turn back." Uth paused for some more water. "The daylight hardly filtered through at all and we became confused. We could not find the original path. We were taking a meal break when suddenly the storm was upon us. We were all frightened and huddled under a tree. The noise seemed to envelop us all. It was then that a streak of lightning hit a tree not more than a few yards away from us. All at once there was a terrific crash followed by a roar. We heard something crashing through the jungle towards us. Without a word we each started to climb the tree. Three of us made it safely but as Aqa was just going up on enormous animal came bounding out and seeing him grabbed at his foot. I unleased my laser gun and killed it but not before it had practically torn his foot off. We made him as comfortable as we could. We did not know what to do. After the storm passed and all was quiet we took turns to carry him back along what we thought was the way we came. Finally Efa suggested climbing a tree to see if we could catch a glimpse of the ship before nightfall. He saw the fire and, well, here we are." He sand back exhausted.

"Take them all into the ship and let them rest," ordered Oah.

Abello walked beside Uth. "You did well," he said.

"It was lucky you started the fire," he replied, "or we might all have been lost forever." Most of them seemed to comprehend the gravity of this sobering thought and the little community was very quiet that evening.

Next morning Oah reported that Aqa was better although his foot would never heal properly and he would always have one leg shorter than the other. "He is sleeping now."

From then on the established routine was always to keep the fire going and a double lookout was maintained. More of them had taken to sleeping outside. They got used to the flash storms and as each day passed they grew fitter. Abello was busy checking all the plans for the new compound about a week later when Oah came looking for him. "Aqa is fully awake now and wants to see you."

Abello entered the ship and made his way aft where Aqa was lying propped up on one of the couches. "How are you feeling?"

"Better, thank you, although I do not relish spending the rest of my days hobbling about. But I want to tell you that when we were eating our meal I was conscious of a noise. It was not an animal noise. The others heard it, too, but they have probably forgotten it, but I think it is important. I have never heard anything like it but with the damper ground underneath I wondered if we were close to water. Maybe when one of them was up the tree he could see something. Anyway, ask them." Abello nodded and left. He found Uth sitting in the shade and relayed the information that Aqa had given him.

"I had forgotten," he said. "I don't think I saw anything in the trees, but you had better check with Efa as well."

Abello found Efa sitting rather glumly by the edge of the clearing. He told him what Aqa had said. Efa brightened up. "That's it," he exclaimed. "Something was bothering me and I think that is it. When I looked around I thought I saw something shimmering in the distance. It could be water. We should go immediately and look for it."

"Would you mind going back in there?" asked Abello.

"Well, I think there should be more than four of us. When something unexpected like this happens it makes us seem very vulnerable. If someone else had been hurt I don't think we would have made it back here." He paused. "You know, Abello, I never realized how lucky we were on Capernica. After the accident it seemed as though every insect in the entire area settled on that animal or Aqa's ankle. This new life is going to take some getting used to."

"Yes, I am becoming very aware of this," said Abello. "But now I will go and tell the others. If there is a chance of finding fresh running water not too far away we must find it. We can catch rain water but should there be a lull in the storms we could be back to rationing again. And if we are to make our home here we need a permanent source of water."

For once there was total agreement among the community that an expedition should go as soon as possible. Arabus volunteered immediately and surprisingly so did Anice.

"After all," she pointed out, "there are still four women left to take care of his daughter and any other tasks. I want to see more of my world and I can take care of myself."

After considerable argument it was decided that Arabus, Anice, Efa, Uth and Omas would go. Abello insisted that Omas would be in charge. This brought an angry reaction from Arabus but Abello was adamant.

"I realize that you were the mainspring of rebellion and therefore had some form of leadership on Capernica, but here I want someone more even tempered. None of you know what you are facing in that jungle and you are still inclined to be impatient in the extreme. Omas has proved his judgment on the journey and I feel it is right that he should take the responsibility. And I will remind you that I am still Leader and my decision is final."

Arabus glared at him malevolently but held his tongue and walked away. The remainder of the day was spent in making preparations for the trip. All of them took containers of water and some feed and each was given a laser gun. Efa was to lead the way with Arabus behind, Omas was to be in the middle so that he would be able to take stock of any situation easily enough.

Abello went and told Aqa about the plans and he nodded approvingly, "I am only sorry that I cannot go too. I should suggest to Omas that after they reach the spot where the accident took place, and Efa will recognize it, he should send someone to climb the trees at regular intervals to make sure that they are still on the right track. The path is practically non-existent through this part, indeed if I did not know better I would say that the only reason for it being there is that..."

"Well, what, Aqa?"

"Well, it is almost as though it had been trodden out over the years."

"I expect it was the animals."

"No, it wasn't wide enough."

The two men stared at each other and simultaneously shook their heads. The thought was too much for them to entertain. Abello should remind them on the expedition that the wild animal could still be laying there, and he left to explain this and other last minute details to the exploring group. He passed Eloni coming into the ship. "I am going to get Aqa's supper," she said. Abello nodded and carried on.

Oah called to him. "Can I have a word with you?"

"Yes, what is it?"

"I am concerned about the effects of several days' walk in the jungle and so I would like Ain to go along as well. He can take some medical supplies. I have been experimenting to see what is most effective against the insect bites and other possible hazards. I have found one or two things which might help and I would like Ain to try them out."

"What a good idea," exclaimed Abello. "I had no idea you were even working on these problems."

"I am always experimenting," said Oah quietly. "I will go and tell Ain."

Abello watched him go. He looked at the others sitting or lying on the grass watching the fire flicker and flame. They looked so carefree and relaxed. How soon we adjust, he thought. It is as though we have been here for many months instead of nearly two weeks. Already the effect of the sun could be seen, all were a darker brown and the effects of the journey were wearing off. Most of them were a lot fitter now and given another months, he thought, and if they found water, they would have forgotten about Capernica. He returned to the ship to tell Aqa about Oah's suggestion.

"Shh," whispered Eloni, "he has fallen asleep."

"Let's go and sit in the dome for a while," suggested Abello, "this is the first time we have been alone since we left Capernica." He helped her up the steps. It was dark in the dome but outside a myriad of stars winked and glistened in the firmament.

"To think we passed all those," said Eloni.

"Are you glad you came?" asked Abello.

"Yes, so far all has been perfect, especially now." She smiled wickedly and kissed him hard. The feel of her strong lips on his sent spears of desire to his loins.

"Oh, my love, it has been so long since I had you, and I have missed you so. To see you so near every waking hour and yet just to only hold hands with you. I could hardly bear it." She made no verbal reply but pressed her body against him. He drew her down to the floor of the dome caressing her all the time. Their touching became hard, searching, feeling, and their breath shortened. He stripped off her robe and she did likewise to him. For a moment he stared at her naked body, her breast pale white against the tan of her neck, face and arms and the contrast of her long brown legs against the milky cream of the rest of her body. He could wait no longer but thrust himself inside her and within a few minutes they reached their climax in joyful unison. For a long time they lay there in each other's arms content and warm. At length they fell asleep.

A finger of sunshine crept across the dome and touched their sleeping bodies. They stirred. It widened as it drew more strength until it was like an outstretched hand. It caressed their faces. Eloni opened her eyes. "Abello, wake up my love, it is morning."

Abello sat up with a start. "I had no idea of the time," he exclaimed. "I should be outside checking on the expedition." Quickly he dressed and ran downstairs. He met Arabus at the bottom outside step.

"Abello, I wondered where you were. We are all ready to go. I gather

Ain is coming as well. Not a bad idea. I thought you would have been out here checking."

"I was just coming," replied Abello.

"Well, let's get a move on." Arabus smirked. "Now I see why you are so dilatory this morning."

Abello turned. Eloni was coming down the steps. "Must be nice for the fortunate ones," grunted Arabus. "Well, we'll see about the share and share alike when we get back."

"Oh, Abello, what does that mean?" said Eloni.

"Don't think about it, we will deal with the matter when he comes back. Just as well he is going on the trip. It may give him a change of outlook."

They stood side by side watching the five men and Anice disappear into the cavernous mouth of the jungle, "I wonder if Anice knows how Arabus feels," said Eloni.

"I think they both know how each other feels. But I expect the presence of the four other men and the march itself will cool their ardor. Let us hope they all return safely. Now I want to go over the plans for our new compound with Oah, for health reasons, and I would like you to add your point of view."

They walked over to where Oah was sitting.

"We have come to discuss the planning of the compound with you," Abello said, and soon the three of them were deep in discussion.

A week passed. All of them were busy with planning the new buildings. They felled trees by laser beams and finished the construction manually. Abello was privately concerned at the reckless abandonment with which they used the lasers because these could not be recharged. They used parts of the ship for roofs. They had departed from the Capernica ideal of a round compound but instead built rather an elongated 'L' shape row of houses. Most of the supplies from the ship were now ready to be unloaded and stored. Large pits had been dug in the shade to store many items and the interior of the ship was left for Oah to turn into a combined laboratory and sick bay. Plans were made to square off fields to grow the seed which they had brought with them, and one evening Aqa produced his lyre and the community enjoyed an evening of music.

"We found it, we found it!" It was Arabus crashing joyfully out of the jungle. "We found a river," and the remainder of the party took up the cry. "It is not too far from here, about four days' walk. We stayed to bathe and dry out and bathe again. The river is wide and sluggish, full of weeds and enormous animals in the middle of it. We came to no harm though; they paid no attention to us at all."

"We even went in at night," chorused Anice with a self-conscious smile.

They sat on the ground while the others brought them some refreshment.

Omas took up the tale.

"We marched for a day without seeing or hearing anything. When dusk came we made camp. The insects were terrible, swarming around our faces in crowds so that we could hardly get our food eaten fast enough. The ointment that Oah had given Ain, though, proved a blessing to us as we used it often and were not so severely bitten. We broke camp early next day and walked for about an hour before I sent Efa up the tree. He thought it was the place where he had been attacked but there was no sign of the animal that attached us. It seems incredible that it should disappear so soon. Efa could not see anything this time so we pressed on. The fourth time I sent him up a tree he saw it – water, in the distance about five degrees northwest. Much encouraged by this we carried on. Sometimes there was a path and sometimes there was not. We could hear a roaring sound now, and the ground was damp and muddy. Then we ran into a fine spray of water which half blinded us. We rounded the corner and there was the wall of water stretching across a cavern, thundering and charging its way down a sheer drop. We stood in silent amazement. Indeed it had to be silent as we could not make ourselves heard. Arabus and Anice were laughing and embracing and soon we were all caught up with the spirit of it. We then moved off north as we assumed that the river would quiet down further along and we could find a shorter route back to the camp. We must have walked half a day before we found a quiet stretch complete with a sloping bank. I should think we were all stripped and swimming within a minute of finding the spot."

"All of you?" asked Eloni.

"Yes, all of us," replied Omas. "Well, the rest you know. We have marked the route clearly with crosses in every fourth tree trunk. We have cleared all foliage and creepers, etc. from around those trees so that they stand out. We can explain the quicker route back."

"Well done," said Abello, "we all owe you a debt of thanks. This is great news indeed, and I must go and tell Aqa. After all, it was he who first told me about it."

He disappeared inside the ship. The others sat around listening to all the half-forgotten details as they came back in the telling of the journey. Abello could hear the talk and laughter as he sat by Aqa's bedside. Aqa was much better and beginning to hobble about with the aid of crutches cut from wood. He was delighted with the news but mused as to whether he would ever get to see the river. Abello promised to take him somehow, and went outside.

"Abello, while you were inside talking to Aqa I have decided that we should all to the river tomorrow," said Arabus.

"I see, well I don't think we should all go and leave the camp unattended. I am not sure if your daughter would be up to the journey and we have to think about Aqa."

"Aqa can manage and I'll take my daughter. Anyway, what's the use of staying at the camp? Nothing is ever going to disturb this place."

"Arabus is right, we should all go. Aqa will be here and we have not seen any danger," spoke some of the others.

"No, I cannot agree to you all going. I think we should have a roster and that way we can take turns to go."

"You and your roster. I say we all go, what do you say?"

"Let's go."

"I will stay with Aqa," said Abello.

"And I will stay too."

"No Eloni, you come with us." That was Anice. "Abello will be all right here with Aqa and I want you to come with us."

"Then it is settled. We will all go tomorrow except for Abello and Aqa."

It was a happy crowd who sat down to the evening meal that night. The talk was full of the forthcoming trip to the river. Abello had seen to it that each man would take a container for the water. Later that night Omas drew him to one side.

"Abello, I fear there may be trouble ahead. Arabus was talking about the relationship between you and Eloni and pointing out that now we are on a new planet it was not right that you should continue to have her for yourself. He said we should have a new system of leadership and he added that with only five women and twenty-two men we should learn to all share. And then," and he paused, obviously embarrassed, "Anice offered herself for any of us to…"

"I understand," interrupted Abello, "and I appreciate you telling me of these feelings. I anticipated trouble but not so soon. I thought we all would be so involved with our new planet that all would be peaceful for a while, but I underestimated Arabus. He is so impatient and so ruthless. Anyway, thank you."

He moved away to find Eloni. He told her of Omas' conversation.

"Must you go tomorrow, by love?"

"Well, Anice was so insistent, and I would like to bathe in pure running water," she said.

"Just be watchful, my darling." They embraced, and parted.

Next morning Abello and Aqa watched them all leave. It seemed quiet and empty in the clearing without them all. Abello moved restlessly around. He felt uneasy but could give no reason why. He watched Aqa hop about the ship. He was practically recovered by now. It must be so awkward having to balance on one foot. An idea struck him. Putting some earth in a pile he poured some water on it and patted it down. When he was satisfied that it was all smooth he found Aqa and carried him down and outside. They he made him stand with his good foot on the ground and the remains of the other resting on the mud. Aqa watched him with amusement. "I hope you know what you are doing."

"I am trying an experiment."

"You sound like Oah. He is experimenting all day long. He is always weighing, measuring and grafting bits of this on to pieces of that. He has made quite an intensive study of the insect life already and has started to fill several volumes. Now he is building cages and I think he is planning to catch some of the animals. I also think he wants to start keeping monthly checks on us with regard to general physical conditions, etcetera."

"I see," murmured Abello. He thought about this as he waited for the mud to dry. He then carefully cut out the shape and took it inside the ship. He found some wood and tried carving it in the same shape. It took him many efforts before he achieved his aim. He made small inserts in each side and nailed pieces of rope to them. He thin took it to show Aqa.

"Try it on and tie it up and see what you think." Aqa did so.

"It is marvelous," he cried after a few simple experimental walks. "Thank you."

He spent most of the rest of the day walking around the clearing humming to himself. They shared a quiet meal that evening and fell asleep by the fire. Abello woke several times in the night, restless and uneasy, but after listening he could not hear anything. He contented himself by heaping more logs on the fire. The following day passed very quietly. As Abello was going to urinate that evening he happened to glance to the right and noticed a line of small footprints disappearing into the jungle. How odd, he thought. Those feet look so small. He made a note to check the sizes of the other's feet when they returned. He did not mention it to Aqa. The days passed peaceably enough with the two of them doing a few chores and talking. About three days passed before the rest returned all laughing happily.

"You must go, Abello, it is marvelous," sparkled Eloni.

"Aqa, what have you on your foot?" called Arabus.

"It is marvelous. Abello made if or me."

"Well, I can see he can take my job as a carver over and I will take his."

A nasty silence ensued, broken by Arabus' daughter crying for her food. That night they held the naming ceremony for her, as although she was already past the time that was customary for this they felt that it should be done now that they had settled in their new land. Arabus had chosen the name Matester after her grandfather and mother. Matester cried continually during the ceremony but after having a sip of the fermented drink which

Oah produced she quieted down. Oah modestly explained that this was one of his experiments. The bottle was passed from lips to lips with carefree abandon. Much embracing and feeling of breasts ensued and even Abello was hard put not to carry Eloni off to the jungle and mate with her. At length the excitement dimmed and one by one they fell asleep by the fire.

The community settled down to a regular schedule of building, planting, with each of them taking turns to go in groups to the river. Abello went as often as he could, especially when Eloni was in the group, but it seemed as though Anice or Arabus would be along too and he had no opportunity to be alone with her and make love. Oah made checks on them from time to time and was busily involved in trying to catch one of the monkeys and in carrying out even more experiments. Life acquired a certain rhythm to which their bodies were becoming finally attuned. If anyone had landed there from Capernica they would not have recognized them. They seemed unaware of their increased capacity for hard physical labor. Abello kept them all busy, because he alone feared that when they became idle there would be trouble, but it was precipitated by an entirely unexpected incident several months later.

CHAPTER V

Many months had passed since their landing. The clearing no longer felt like an alien land to them, full of the unknown, but rather now it was a secure base from which they were building their new home. A row of houses filled one side and with their orange roofs, taken from the outer skins of the ship, they added yet another splash of color to the clearing. The ship itself had been stripped clear of anything that could possibly be of use. Oah had virtually taken over the interior and converted it to a combination of a hospital, surgery and laboratory. He had quite a collection of animals inside and seemed deeply involved in mysterious experiments. The remainder of the people had been busily making gardens in front of the houses and clearing away the trees behind them. In these clearings they had sown the seeds they had so carefully brought with them. Even now they could see the results as some of the seeds and taken to their new environment with voluptuous growth, while others had barely pushed their stalks above the ground.

A few parties of explorers used to leave about once a month to extend their knowledge of the new land, but now they had a source of water and the homes built there was not the urgency. There had been sorrow in the community as well. Two of the men had died. Oah had been unable to ascertain the exact cause of death, but they had sickened overnight and died. But they had reason to rejoice as well. Eloni had told Abello that she was pregnant. They had kept the secret to themselves at first but before it became obvious they told the rest. Most of them were delighted and looked forward to the first birth on the new land, but a few of them were upset. Abello was increasingly aware of these undercurrents and took even more care to make no affectionate gestures to Eloni when any of the others were around. He was not surprised, therefore, when Anice came to see him one night.

"Abello," she said, "I have been chosen as spokeswoman for all of us. We cannot continue in this segregated life specifically as you are so fortunate as to have your own woman. The men, and the women, feel it is unfair and that you should make a decision as you are still our Leader at the moment."

"I appreciate your feelings, Anice, and I am fully aware of the problem."

"Then you should do something about it," she retorted.

"But with five women and twenty men what am I to do?" he cried.

"You are the Leader and you must decide, but we will not continue this way any longer, especially now with Eloni pregnant."

"Bring the women here and I will discuss it with them"

She disappeared into the darkness and Abello paced up and down. He wished he had foreseen this problem when he had originally passed judgment on them all on Capernica, but he realized that it was only the fact that Eloni had elected to come along that had hardened his desire to be on the journey. Now he must face the consequences. Anice reappeared leading the four other women, which included Eloni.

"Sit down around me," he commanded. "As you know, Anice has come to me with the problem of basically having five women and twenty men. As you can imagine, the idea of sharing Eloni with anyone else is anathema to me and to her as well. But I am the Leader, and we have all been raised on the concept that we are all equal when we are born. Leaders were chosen in case an occasion arose wherein a final decision was needed. Until my term of office this never arose. However, I decided that you should be banished and I alone decided that I was contravening the rules because of my love for Eloni was too great and that I could not renounce her at the end of my term of office. Therefore I came with you and I must stand by the consequences. I believe the important thing is that you decide among yourselves how you would like to resolve this situation. I feel this is the just way to solve the problem as you have the minority rights."

"Am I to be included in this as well?" questioned Eloni.

Abello took a deep breath, "Yes, you are. It is only right that the decision among you must be a majority and although you are now pregnant once you have delivered our child you must be prepared to join in." She accepted this in silence, her expression carefully marking her emotions.

"Come on, Eloni, come and join us over here while we make our decisions," called Anice.

Abello watched them as they sat in a circle a few yards from him. He could see Anice gesticulating and various degrees of assent and dissent as the discussion ranged back and forth. They were there for about thirty minutes before they called him over.

"We have decided that for the time being we will leave Eloni out of it as you suggested. That leaves each of us with five men each, although I suppose you would rather be excluded." Abello nodded. "Therefore the four of us will take a first choice and thereafter we will draw lots. It will be up to the men to decide if they would like a nightly change, a weekly change or longer. Of course if we become pregnant then any of them can share the joys and responsibilities of becoming a father."

"I see. Well, let us go and tell the men."

They walked over to where the men were waiting in a group. Anice repeated what she had told Abello. There was quite a stir in the crowd.

"I should like to add that if any of the men feel that these arrangements are distasteful he should speak forth and we will try to come to some other organization," said Abello. Silence.

"Well, let's get on with it," said the familiar deep voice of Arabus. "Who are the fortunate ones tonight?"

The women went to their various selections. Abello was surprised to note that Anice passed by Arabus and went instead to Ain. Arabus looked very disgruntled but Anice just smiled and ignored him. The couples disappeared into the huts and the rest of them sat by the fire. Nothing much was said as obviously they were all fully aware of what was going on behind them.

From that night a lot of tension went out of the life of the community. All of them appeared to have adjusted to the rhythm of the new life and very little comment was made about it. Eloni continued to fill out and to Abello became almost impossibly beautiful. Oah took a great deal of interest in her and was often seen taking blood samples and other tests on her. His laboratory was quite extensive now and at all times of the day and night a variety of noises emanated from inside the ship. Abello went to get some of the ointment from him one day to help keep the insects away from Eloni. He found him in the middle of surgery on a monkey. He had one of the tree climbing creatures on a small table in front of him. It lay quite still as Oah made an incision in its body.

"Abello, quiet now." It was Aqa. "He is at one of his experiments again. He found this animal on his walk yesterday. Apparently it had been in some kind of accident and was lying on the ground. Oah picked it up and brought it back here. It had broken one of its legs. He set it but did not seem satisfied. Now he is trying something else."

"But it looks dead to me."

"Yes, but it is not. He gave it some of the fermented drink he has been making and it fell asleep. But let us watch him."

Oah had cleaned out a section below its stomach and was carefully pulling out a small object which looked like a little sack. He carefully put this into a container and then quickly sewed up the little creature. As he went to return it to its cage he caught sight of the two men.

"I did not realize I had an audience."

"What were you doing?" queried Abello.

"I was just taking out its womb," he replied.

"Whatever for?" exclaimed Aqa.

"Well, I am making some tests on various insects and animals that I now have. I am curious as to how their reproductive cycles work in this sort of climate and what, if anything, I can learn from it. As you know, gynecology and its related studies was my particular study on Capernica and this is one of the reasons I wanted to come on the journey. I actually was never part of Arabus' group there. When I heard your sentence I could not resist coming too. I knew there were at least three other competent doctors on Capernica and I suppose I too was ready for the unknown."

"But we may have all perished."

"I realize that, but I still wanted to study all of you on the journey. I am interested in psychology as well and specially in the sort of ratios we have here. To me it is worth it. If I had perished, well, there was no one in particular on Capernica who would have missed me." Abello and Aqa were unable to say anything after this and Oah left to attend to the little creature who was beginning to stir.

Aqa and Abello walked to the door. "I had no idea that Oah was so impersonal," remarked Abello. "He appears the total scientist."

"Well, there is another side to him," replied Aqa, "but I expect you will not find out for a while."

"Abello, can you come back here a minute?" called Oah. Abello walked over to where he was standing. "I would like to ask you a few questions about your diet and exercise, etcetera, since you left Capernica."

There followed about twenty minutes of questions and answers between the two men. "Why do you want to know all these details?" asked Abello.

"Well, you are our Leader and soon to be the first father on this new land. I want to know all about you. After all, it may all be up to me whether you survive or die. I must ensure that we are all healthy both physically and mentally. I am checking all of you in turn. I have not yet discovered why those two men died or why even some of us have no trouble in becoming deeply tanned and adapting to the new life, while others cannot go out into direct sunlight without coming up into blisters. As a matter of fact, I am even curious as to why some of the plants have adapted so well and some not at all. Maybe we are doomed to the same ration. Now if you will excuse me I must attend to the creature, who is now fully awake."

Aiello wandered out into the sunlight. He could wonder at what Oah was doing and felt uneasy as to the exact path of the experiments. Eloni beckoned and called to him that she was going for a swim with Matester and he ran gaily after her, all thoughts of Oah trailing in the backwater of his mind.

A few weeks later Ain came back from swimming one day and complained of pains. Overnight he seemed to shrink into nothing. Huge, suppurating sores appeared over his body and as fast as they were swabbed out, more appeared. Three more were suffering by the end of the next day. The disease spread rapidly and soon only Anice, Efa and Eloni were free. Oah instructed Eloni to stay clear although she wanted to look after Abello. Reluctantly she kept to the other side of the clearing. Oah directed the other two as best he could from his sickbed. Despite all their efforts two more of the men died. The survivors looked haggard and scarred. Even Arabus had lost his customary blustery nature and seemed content to sit by the fire all day. As soon as Oah was well enough to stand he was back in the ship checking and rechecking all his findings. He seemed particularly interested in Efa who was the only man to survive without a trace of disease. The two of them spent many hours in the ship together.

Another month passed and normality returned to the community. As a result of the stringent burning program ordered by Oah, clothes became a major problem. What few each of them had left were now becoming tattered. They had long since given up wearing shoes and their feet had become hardened to long use. Many of them had forgotten how little they had used their bodies for physical exercise. The men had taken to just wearing a garment around their loins but for the women a more formal robe was required. Poor Eloni was reduced to one change of clothes now that her time was close. Arabus was all for them running around naked but the majority did not take him seriously at that time. The problem was solved for them in an entirely unexpected way.

An expected severe rainstorm had come drenching down, sending them all to the shelters. The fire disappeared in a defiant hiss and the only sound in the area was the beating of rain on the roofs. The storm continued well into the night. Eloni was first awake the next morning as she found it difficult to lie in one place for a long time. Gently she caressed the sleeping form of Abello before going to the aperture which served as a lookout for each house. She stifled a scream and rushed to shake Abello awake. Gesticulating at the window she half dragged him over there. In the clearing by where the embers of the fire were was an enormous golden, black striped animal with huge teeth. They stood awed for a moment. Quietly Abello crossed the room and picked up his laser gun. Recrossing he stood again by the window. He took aim and fired. It gave an agonized howl and keeled over. For a moment they stood there but then rushed to the door. By this time the rest of the crowd were streaming out of their huts. Slowly they advanced towards the animal, uncertain as to whether it may spring into life again. Even in death it was a magnificent beast. Oah appeared carrying a knife and proceeded to cut it open. He removed certain parts and returned to the ship.

"It is so good to the touch," said Anice who was running her hand over

99

its body. Aqa began to try to move it away from the fire and several of the others went to help him. Oah returned and began to cut more of the flesh away. Soon only the skin was left.

"We should now rebuild the fire," said Eloni, and soon all were involved in the daily routine once more as the skin of the animal lay drying in the sun.

At dusk Abello and Eloni went for a quiet walk as was their custom. They liked to be alone together at the end of the day and now Eloni was near her time she found it easier to walk than to sit or lie.

"Abello, I must tell you some news I heard from one of the women today."

"What is that, my love?"

"Well," she said, "they have all tired Arabus but none of them are willing to lie down for him anymore. Of course, I do not know exactly what the problem is but they all plan on pleading sickness when his turn is around."

"How long has this gone on for?"

"Quite a while, and Arabus as you can imagine is getting very impatient. The other night he tried to persuade Aqa to let him take his place and even threatened him. He did not succeed, but I fear we are in for some more trouble."

"I had thought that Anice's solution was workable and I did not foresee any more trouble. They walked back to the compound. Later, as she slept, her head cradled in his shoulder after tender, gentle lovemaking, Abello thought about her comments. He could see no solution to Arabus and even if he had had a glimmer of what was going to happen he would not have believe it.

It was Aqa who made the final discovery about the animal skin. He had tripped as he passed by and falling on it found it smooth and flexible. He got up and draped it around himself. "Why don't we wear this?" he asked. The others were dumbfounded.

"What a good idea," said Anice. The women busily cut up the skin and sewing it together made passable clothes for themselves.

"We should kill some more," said Arabus.

"Perhaps we could build a trap for them," said Efa.

After much discussion it was decided that scouting parties would go out and look for signs of animals and Abello did not approve of the use of the laser guns except for extreme emergencies as the source of power was not renewable. They tried several different methods of forming weapons and finally settled upon taking branches and filing one end down to a fine point. Arabus took a fiendish delight in wearing his tied to his shorts, making him look like a furious beast, especially as his hair was long and he had gown a massive beard.

Aqa came to find Abello one afternoon as he was chopping wood.

"Come to the ship," he said. "Eloni's labor has started."

Abello raced ahead of him to the ship. Inside he found Eloni lying on two of the bunks, her face quite serene. She grimaced for a minute and then relaxed. He sat down beside her.

"You will have to leave when the birth is closer but it will be a while yet," said Oah.

Abello held her firmly and whispered endearments to her. She seemed so relaxed and he remembered the stormy birth of Matester and the others. Word had spread throughout the compound and looking through the porthole he could see them all gathered around waiting. The time seemed to dray by. Finally Oah sent him outside as her pains became closer and closer. He paced up and down, up and down. Silence. A thin wail and a bigger one. Oah appeared at the door.

"You have a son," he yelled and a great cheer went up. Abello bounded up the steps and burst inside. Eloni was laying on the bed, the baby in her arms. He went and kissed them both tenderly. "How much I love you, and now our son," he said.

"You must leave now," ordered Oah. "Thy both need rest."

He went outside to receive the congratulations of the others. Even Arabus slapped him on the back. A general celebration followed and the fermented drink that Oah made was passed around. Abello could hardly believe his good fortune.

The days slipped by. Eloni and the baby, who was as yet unnamed, grew strong and well. Matester was fascinated by the baby and would often be found standing by his crib grabbing his little fingers. Abello was busy making his hut suitable for them both and he did not notice that Arabus was often missing from the compound. One particularly hot day he decided to go to the river for a bath. As he walked down the now well-trodden path to the river he heard voices. He thought it was probably some returning bathers but he could see no sign of anyone as he rounded the corner. He could still hear the voices and curious as to what or who it was he turned off the path and tried to see if he could locate them. As he drew nearer he could recognize Arabus' voice but he could not place the other. He concluded that he was probably with one of the other women and returned to the path and put the incident from his mind.

"It is interesting," remarked Oah to Abello one afternoon as he sat beside Eloni's bed. "How long is it since we have had this sharing of the sexes?"

"About four months, I think. Why?"

"Because, although it is early yet to tell, so far none of the women have become pregnant although their menstrual cycles are changing. On

Capernica they used to have two a year during their fertile cycle but some of them have told me that since landing here they have already had two if not three. They are evidently changing biologically in order to increase their chances of fertility but as yet no change in the men. Now I have been experimenting with the creatures I have captured and as yet have only managed to fertilize one or two."

"You should not be doing such things," protested Abello.

"But we have to create life if we are to survive and after all I am not carrying out experiments on the community, just these animals. Arabus thinks it is a good idea."

"Does he indeed. Well, he should have no complaints. His wife had a multiple birth."

"I am well aware of that and I am trying to find out why," said Oah peevishly. He returned to his surgery, adding "You can take her to your hut tomorrow."

Abello smiled at Eloni. "That is good news indeed. I will go and make the final preparations."

By the time Abello came to collect her most of the others were waiting at the steps. Gently he escorted her across to the door and a cheer went up as she appeared holding the baby. Slowly they progressed across the clearing to Abello's hut.

"I thank you all for your good wishes and I would like you to know now before we have the naming ceremony that he will be called Abeno after the two of us.

There were many congratulatory remarks after this, and finally she entered the hut and laid Abeno in his crib. Abello stood watching them both.

"I am so proud. This journey and the decision I made has succeeded beyond my most private hopes and dreams. I would not trade places with anyone right now."

"May I never have to share you with anyone," she replied and they embraced.

The community settled back to normality. They had not experienced any success with capturing any of the animals although Arabus seemed determined to catch one. He was often gone for a day and a night but always returned empty handed. Oah and Efa were also gone, presumably to try and find more specimens for the doctor to work on. The rest of them were involved with the planting and harvesting of crops as one season chased upon the heels of another. Some of them produced some sketching materials and began drawing pictures of their new homes. Others produced instruments and soon the sound of music filled the air in the evenings. As yet none of the women were pregnant and it was about this that Oah spoke to Abello one evening.

"I would like to ask you when you think the conception took place. Was it shortly after we arrived here?"

"Why yes," said Abello.

"I see, and did you repeat the act very often after that?"

"No, and I really do not know why you are so interested."

"Well, I am trying to find out why the two of you were in the right cycle at that moment. Could I have a sample of your sperm?" he asked casually.

Abello was speechless and angrily pushed him away. He told Eloni later that night, and told her to stay away from Oah. "I cannot comprehend what he is up to but I want you and I to have no part of it," he said.

He was so incensed that he found it hard to settle and stormed off towards the river. It was quite dark but he knew the way. Again he could hear voices and again he went to find out who they belonged to. He moved quietly through the undergrowth and soon he could recognize Arabus' voice and he thought he also recognized Oah's. He paused to find the location and then crept on. Finally he could sense that he was close. He inched his way forward and peered through the grass. As his eyes adjusted he was filled with revulsion and nausea. Arabus, Efa and Oah were all lying naked on the ground, kissing and caressing each other. He could not bear to watch. He back along the trail and when he found the river path he was violently sick. He sat down. He was sick again. He could not believe it. He sat there for a while before he realized that they may come out and see him there and instinctively he realized that this was not a wise thing to do so he withdrew into the tall grass. After a while they passed him, clothed now, with arms around each other's shoulders, laughing and joking. Abello felt a choking rage within him but he sat still. What could he do? Who would believe him and how would he stop it? It was hard to believe that only a little while ago he had been so full of happiness and contentment. He thought of Eloni and the great love they had between them. He thought of Abeno and wondered if he would ever grow up to see this sort of thing. Maybe he would turn out like Oah. I would kill him, he thought, and immediately rejected the idea. That would place him on the same level as Arabus. Wearily he made his way back to his hut and told Eloni what he had found out. She was horrified.

"We should leave," she said. "We should not stay and live with people like that. To think he delivered my baby." She began to weep. Abello comforted her as best he could and they fell into an uneasy sleep.

A week passed. Nothing changed outwardly. Eloni and Abello made excuses that Abeno was unwell and remained close to their hut. They could not help but watch them all and several times they felt like bursting out and telling them. Arabus left them alone but they had to tolerate regular visits from Oah who sometimes brought Efa with him. It all seemed so obvious now and they found themselves checking the others for signs of deviation. After a few days they forced themselves to take part in the normal day to day life of the community. Various plans were still being mooted for the capture of another wild animal. Several of them including Uth had become quite expert at tracking them through the jungle and indeed they had surrounded one of the animals, but they still had no effective way of killing them. Now that they were after their skins they had realized that the laser did too much damage. None of them were brave enough to approach one and throw a sharply pointed stick at it. It was Efa, who had spent many hours helping Oah with his operations, who suggested the solution of melting down some of the tranquillizer medicines that had been used on the journey and dipping the sharp end of the sticks into it. After all, he reasoned, if we could fire enough at the same time we could probably put it to sleep. Oah had been using some of the fermented wine to put the small creatures to sleep while he operated on them. But the stronger medicine would be needed for the larger animals. This was voted an excellent idea.

"How soon we adapt to new ideas," said Anice one day as she sat beside Eloni. They were watching the men practicing their skills at throwing the spear as far and as accurately as they could.

"We all seem to have adapted very well," replied Eloni.

"Most of us, anyway. I hardly give a thought to my life before I came here and if that ship was not still here we might have all been born here."

"I never thought I would find such happiness, said Eloni. "And to have a son."

"Are you fully recovered now?"

"Oh, yes. I am now normal," she laughed and blushed.

"Well, don't forget that you are part of the arrangements we made. You should start thinking about someone else besides Abello."

Eloni was horror stricken. She immediately thought of Arabus. Anice reached out and took her hand.

"Don't look so worried, Eloni, it is really not that bad. Think of it as doing something for your new home. After all, you are the only one that has been able to conceive so far."

Eloni grasped her hand and smiled wanly. "Thank you Anice, but you must excuse me."

She ran back to the hut and stood looking at Abeno asleep in his bed. What am I going to do? She thought. She was still standing there holding on to the bed when Abello arrived.

"My love, what is the matter?" he asked, taking her in his arms. She pushed him away. "Oh, Abello, I have been talking to Anice and she reminded me that now I am well again I must be thinking of other men."

"No, I cannot bear it."

"But you are the one who stated that we are all equal and must share and share alike. And you are the great Leader who told the women and the men that I was only exempt until after the birth of my child."

"But I never thought anyone would refer to it. I thought they all realized that you are my love and mine alone."

"I expect that Anice is busy telling all the men now that I am recovered and that even now they are taking wagers as to who would be the fortunate one." She sunk on to the bed clutching at her body. "What am I to do?" she wailed.

Abello sat down beside her. "I cannot share you," he said. He kissed her hard and sudden desire ignited them. Their love making was a consumed passion. "Never, never," cried Abello as they reached their climax. They fell asleep.

Oah came to see him a few days later. "Have you seen Efa?" he queried

"No, we have not. Why?"

"He has disappeared. I have not seen him for two days and I discover now that no one else has."

Abello resisted the temptation to ask him if they had had a lovers' quarrel.

"Perhaps he has gone after some specimens for you."

Oah nodded.

"Is Arabus here?" Abello asked.

"Yes, he is."

"Well, I am sure there is an explanation and we will not worry unduly for a while," said Abello.

Oah stomped off.

Uth came bursting into the clearing. "One of them is coming this way," he yelled. "An enormous animal."

"Quickly, into the huts with the women and Matester. Everyone to the trees and hide," said Abello. Within seconds the clearing was empty. They waited, tense and fearful. A great gray animal came lumbering into the clearing. It paused and looked around and raised its long trunk like a nose in the air. Slowly it looked from side to side. It was obviously uneasy, for it turned and lumbered off down the track where it had emerged from. A sign of relief flowed through the men. None of them had felt very enthusiastic about tackling a monster that size. The incident made them realize that they were far from perfecting a way to catch animals.

There was still no sign of Efa. Most of the community seemed unconcerned about his prolonged absence, only Oah was constantly asking questions of each of them. Abello and Eloni remained aloof from the others, both of them consciously avoiding the doctor. Abello concluded the Efa may have decided to go on his own exploration or had had a quarrel with Arabus and decided to stay away for a few days. One morning as Eloni lay awake she heard a scratching noise. Idly curious she listened more intently. The noise had a definite rhythm to it. She got out of bed and walked over to the window and saw Efa scratching at Arabus' door. She went to call a greeting but thought better of it. She crept over to Abello and woke him. Putting her finger to her lips she pointed to the window. The two of them stood watching. Efa had succeeded in arousing Arabus who was now standing outside the door. Evidently he did not want his sleeping companion aroused. Efa was, by the multitude of gestures, explaining something to him. Arabus looked as though he wasn't convinced. Finally Efa showed him something which he took from the pocket of his shorts. Arabus seemed to concur and disappeared. He reappeared a couple of minutes later and the two of them disappeared along the path towards the swimming pool.

"I am going to follow them. Quickly, give me my laser torch and drinking flask." Eloni quickly found these things and gave them to him. "Take care of yourself and Abeno," he said and was gone.

He could hear the two men chattering away but he could not hear what they were talking about as he dared not get too close. They continued towards the bathing pool but instead of carrying straight on they swerved right and started to make their way upstream. Abello followed cautiously as he did not want to betray his presence to them. They walked for about half a day and Abello was beginning to think that it had all been rather a waste of time when he rounded a corner and almost ran into them. Efa was pointing to the far shore and hand miming to Arabus. Abello watched him and then looked towards where he was pointing. At first he could not see anything and he crept closer to the two of them until he could see their expressions. Fortunately he was hidden behind tall grass. Carefully he parted the strands and looking across the green, glassy expanse of water he saw a woman. Naked. Black, the sun giving her skin a brilliant ebony sheen. She was bathing. Happily splashing about in the water. He looked at Arabus and was horrified to see a look of wanton lust on his face. Efa was tugging at his arm and shaking his head obviously trying to restrain him. Eventually they lay back down again and Abello turned to watch the woman. He discovered that she had been joined by other women and children. They were all splashing about totally involved with enjoying the water and warm sunlight and totally unaware of being watched. Abello wondered what their reaction would be if he should suddenly stand up. He noticed too, that there were no men to be seen and he was curious as to why. The three of them must have spent about two hours lying in the grass watching them. Abello could see that they were busily plotting something by their furtive manner. Once or twice they glanced in his direction but he did not think he had been see.

About noon the women and children suddenly dashed out of the water and disappeared up the bank. Arabus and Efa immediately moved forward to follow them and Abello followed these two. They did not cross the river but swung right and disappeared into the undergrowth. Abello gave them about a five minute start and then walked after them. Fortunately the undergrowth was not too dense and he could follow them fairly easily. He could hear other sounds now as though they were close to animals. He glimpsed the other two stopping, and he immediately halted and dropped down. As he crawled closer he could see that they were on the edge of a clearing. A group of black men were busily digging a large hole in the ground. He watched as it got deeper and deeper and then they started to fill it in with branches. When it was filled up they threw some dirt over it and then they led a small, brown colored animal with horns over to the side of the large hole and tied it up. The men disappeared as swiftly as shadows vanish as the sun rises. The animal stood there for a moment and then back and forth emitting noises.

The time passed and darkness fell. The air vibrated with the noises of the night animals and the noise of the little animal grew more plaintive. More hours passed and still they waited. A screech of terror rent the air followed by the screams of an animal. Abello strained forward but he could see nothing. He heard sounds of things being hurled through the air and then all was quiet. He waited and eventually dropped into a fitful sleep. At the first touch of dawn he was awake. He looked over to where he had last seen the animal. It was gone. The men were busily uncovering the hole, and removing an enormous striped animal from it. It had several spears sticking out of its sides. Carefully they dragged it out and then with a synchronized effort they picked it up and carried it off down the path. Abello stood up, forgetting about the other two.

"Abello, what are you doing here?" said Efa.

"I might have known you would spoil everything," grunted Arabus.

"I was curious to see where you two went, so I followed you," he replied.

"But quickly, don't let us stand here and argue, let us follow the men."

"Did you see the women in the river?" queried Arabus.

"Yes, I did. I had given up all hope of finding other human beings on this planet. I had no idea."

"I did," said Efa. "Aqa had noticed some tracks and I was determined to follow them. I thought at first they were animal tracks but as I came closer to the river they became more pronounced and I was almost sure they were human."

"I will be interested to see how they live. Maybe we will be able to communicate with them and they with us," said Abello.

"For what I have in mind it won't matter," grinned Arabus.

"Oah would be interested in them, too" said Efa.

As they talked they continued to follow the men. They came to a clearing with a row of mud huts. They hid and watched as the men laid down the animal. Women and children came running out of the huts making noises and clapping their hands with glee. Both men and women began cutting up the animal as the children played around it. One of the women took a chunk and spearing it went to a nearby fire and held it over. The rest of the women did the same and soon the smell of roasting flesh filled the air. While they were doing this the men took the skin and stretching it, laid it on the ground putting rocks on it to secure it.

"I am hungry," said Efa.

"It certainly smells good," said Abello.

"I am going to have some," said Arabus, and before the others could restrain him he strode out into the clearing. Complete silence. Abello and Efa followed him. As they advanced towards the fire the others stood up and then backed away. Arabus went to grab a chunk of meat but Abello stopped him. He approached the man who stood in front of the others as though the leader. He smiled and put out his hand. The man grunted but did not move. Abello rubbed his stomach and pointed to them eat. The man still did not move. Abello then took one of the pieces and bit into it. The other two followed suit. The people watched them, still silent. They finished the meat and Abello turned to the man. He bowed. The man was still silent. "We had better leave," he told Arabus and Efa. They left the way they had come, conscious of the silence.

It took them a few hours to walk back to the clearing. Conversation was sporadic. All of them were full of what they had seen and heard. None of them realized that they were followed.

Eloni flung her arms around Abello. "I thought you were gone forever," she sobbed. The others were all apparently glad to see them. That night they sat around the fire and recounted their adventures. Oah expressed great interest in the size, shape and color of the primitives, as they had decided to call them. Much discussion took place as to the best method of approaching them. Surprisingly Arabus, Abello and Efa were all agreed that they were quite mild and unlikely to attack them. It was definitely decided that they should try to establish some sort of contact. They were all very enthusiastic upon hearing the description of the catching, killing and cooking of the animal. Aqa suggested that they should try this the next day.

A new air of enthusiasm pervaded the camp the next day. A party of twelve left to dig a pit and six more went in search of a suitable animal to drive towards it. They had no idea as to how to secure a beast such as the primitive had. Abello, Efa and Oah were busily discussing the primitives. They had gone into the ship as Oah wanted them to try and sketch a picture of them. He was most enthusiastic and pressed Abello for a date to go and see them. Abello suggested they wait for a few days and then go.

"We should not take too many of us," he said, "as we may frighten them. We will make a roster."

"Always the leader," said Oah.

"I see you are having some success with your experiments," said Abello, indicating a couple of rather pregnant-looking tree climbing animals.

"Yes, yes, I am delighted to say that I have succeeded in fertilizing them. Of course only you have succeeded on the advanced level. It is extraordinary. I think that now Eloni should spend about three weeks with another male, say Efa, and see if he can make her pregnant."

"Shut up," said Abello. "I will not have that kind of talk about any woman. She is mine and mine alone."

"But you make the others share, and I know for a fact that Anice would like to just have Aqa alone but she goes on sharing. And what about Arabus? All the other women are boycotting him."

Abello strode out of the ship. He was livid. He stormed over to his hut.

"Abello, whatever is the matter?" cried Eloni. He told her, reluctantly, about the conversation with Oah. She began to week. He cradled her in his arms.

"Don't fret, my darling, I will find a solution," and he whispered endearments as his hands fondled her breasts. Soon her weeping ceased and she began to caress his private parts. Soon he could feel the hardness in his loins and the moistness between her legs, and he entered her. No sooner had they climaxed when Abeno woke up and started crying. He lay contentedly on the bed, watching her feed him. I will never share here, he thought. Never.

"I think it would be a good idea if you and Abeno came with us to see the primitives," he said.

"I think we should take Arabus as well," she said.

It was his turn to query.

"Because it will keep him out of trouble and occupy him. I have a feeling he is going to cause trouble and I think that Oah's helping him. Not because Oah is a trouble maker but because of his scientific bent."

"I see. I will talk it over with the others tonight and we will make plans to go the day after tomorrow."

In the evening when they were all gathered around the fire Abello explained the idea to them. Most of them accepted it with equanimity. The twelve who had gone to dig the pit wanted him to go and inspect it the next day which he agreed to. The six who had gone in search of animals reported several promising sets of tracks in the vicinity. Arabus was rather surprised to be included in the party and soon he and Oah and Efa were huddled in conversation. Next day Abello followed the others to the pit. It certainly looked large enough and they all worked hard during the day to fill it with branches. Uth suggested that they should try to tie some rope around it so that when the animal fell into it they could tighten this around its neck to make an easier job of holding it down. Efa and Uth left to fetch the rope from the ship. They came rushing back to say that they had seen some prints and that they thought an animal was coming this way. Quickly they all hid and waited. Nothing. Screams. Harsh, piercing screams. They all rushed towards the sound. They saw Uth being dragged by an animal. It was a re-enactment of Aqa's encounter all over again. This time they had no lasers with them and desperately as they tried by hurling branches, rocks or whatever else they could find, they could not get the animal to relinquish its hold. The screaming stopped and the animal let go of Uth. In silence they trooped home. All of them numb with shock. One minute so vitally alive and the next, practically dead. As soon as they reached the clearing the others crowded around. Abello left them to find out from the others and went wearily to his hut. It was a quiet community that night. All of them realized that little by little they were being eroded away.

Two days later six of them left to find the primitives again. Among them were the doctor, his assistant, Abello, Eloni and Abeno and Arabus. They made fairly steady progress the first day and camped close to the position where Arabus had seen them dig the pit. Next morning they hurried on and in a short while they rounded the corner and came upon the primitives. They were standing across the central path looking almost as though they had expected them. Arabus went first with Oah hurrying after him. Eloni, carrying Abeno, was at the rear. At the sight of these two a murmur of interest ran through the primitives. They crowded around her and pointed at the baby. Eloni took it all very well and presently sat down on the ground and laid Abeno in front of her. The primitives formed a circle around her. Abello could see that Oah was filling his notebook with jottings. He also noticed that he was counting the number of children who dodged in and out of the crowd unconcernedly. He walked over to him.

"I wish I had some way of communicating with them," he said impatiently. "There are so many questions I would like to ask them."

"Such as?"

"How many children each woman has had. Are any of them barren? Do they share or are they monogamous. Also I would be interested to know if their breeding cycles are as comparatively far apart as our women's. I have noticed that two of our women are starting to menstruate more regularly."

During this time the primitives had started passing sticks of meat around. It looked and smelt rather fetid and most of them declined. The primitives looked puzzled at this and produced some long grass-like shoots which they lit and then started to suck on them. One of them passed his on to Arabus who took a long puff. After a moment his eyes watered and he began to cough and sneeze. The others laughed and the primitives joined in. With the tension broken all of them squatted on the grass and tried to smoke. Abello noticed that the women were still passing Abeno around, touching him and playing with him. Abello picked up one of their babies and began rocking it. One of the women came and sat beside him. She seemed quite at ease. Arabus came over and stood staring at her. Abello pushed him away. He found that even after two of the initial puffs his vision had become somewhat blurred and he seemed to lose control of his movements. Presently they all fell asleep.

Eloni was first to wake. Suddenly conscious of the cries of Abeno, she started to feed him and she noticed that several of the primitive women were doing the same with their babies. They smiled at each other, a wordless communication bond forged between them. Soon after the men woke up and Abello indicated it was time to leave. He went and shook hands with Oah, who was most surprised and then offered his hand to one of the primitive men. Shyly he proffered it and Abello grasped it firmly. As soon as he let go the man disappeared behind one of the huts. The others turned to leave when the man reappeared, leading one of the animals that Abello and the other two had seen him tie up in front of the pit. Grinning widely he took Aiello's hand and placed it on the rope which held and which was tied around the animal's neck. He then seized his other hand and shook it. Abello impulsively took his knife by his waist and handed it to him. The man carefully ran his hand over it. Abello took it and cut a piece of grass. The primitives watched intently. After several repeat performances they crowded around muttering. Abello signaled to the others to lead and with Eloni and Abeno behind him they set off for home.

When they all arrived at the compound they received quite a welcome and they spent the rest of the time discussing what they had experienced. They christened the animal Capernica after their planet. They took turns in guarding it during the night and the next day several of them built a pen for it with a wooden shack for it to be locked up at night time. Oah was apparently very interested in the animal and could often be found examining it. He was standing staring at it a couple of days later when Abello stopped by to give

111

it some water.

"You are looking rather downhearted," he said.

"I am. I certainly am."

"Buy why?"

"Two of my tree climbing animals gave birth last night."

"But that is wonderful news," exclaimed Abello.

"No, no, they all died. The babies were too big and the strain of birth was too much for the mother's hearts. I have failed again."

"Oh come now. You may have success with the others."

"I suppose so. I wanted success so badly so I could move on to larger animals."

"Well, maybe we will get something in the pit."

"Yes," he said, and moved off into the trees. No doubt to find some consolation with Efa, thought Abello. He still felt very uneasy about the experiments. He did wish that some of the other men could get the other four women pregnant. He felt a splash of rain on his shoulder and looking up he realized that the sky was black and menacing. He ran to his shelter to find Abeno and Eloni already there. It was a tremendous storm. Quite the most violent they could remember, and lasted for well over an hour. They sat together on the bed hugging Abeno. At last the rain abated and the huge sun reappeared to dominate the surroundings. They and the others emerged into the steamy heat.

"Our great Leader sharing the storm with his woman," mocked Arabus, who stood in front of Abello.

"I naturally took shelter in our hut," he replied.

"But you could have gone anywhere else. We are all to share."

"I chose to go to Eloni. She is my woman and the mother of my son."

"Strange to think that on Capernica you couldn't get her with child but it certainly did not take you long down here."

"And what are you implying?"

"Well, it does seem strange. Anyway I think you should share her."

"Never."

"No? But I say yes. You are the Leader and you made the rules. We are all to share. She is able now and Oah has passed her fit. You should share her."

"No. No, I will not."

"Well, I am going to have that lovely white body of hers," and he stepped forward. Abello moved to bar his way.

"You are going to stop me?" he sneered and charged at Abello. He knocked him down. Abello scrambled to his feet and wrenched his hand off Eloni.

"Let her go," he yelled.

"No, I want her and I will have her now." The others had drawn back.

Arabus charged at him again but this time Abello was ready for him and stepped aside. Arabus spun around and punched his arm at him. Abello returned the blow and soon the two men were fighting hard. Neither would give in and now the onlookers were beginning to divide into two groups. Those for Arabus and those against. Meanwhile Eloni had taken refuge in the hut with Abeno. The two men fought on, then Arabus tripped and sprawled on the ground. Abello stood over him.

"Leave her alone," he yelled.

"I will. I will."

Abello stepped away and turned around. Silence.

"Look out." It was Eloni screaming as she came out of the hut. Arabus had picked up a branch and was poised to crash it down on Abello's head. He swerved and it missed him by inches. Again and again Arabus tried to smash his skull in but Abello managed to keep ahead of his movements. In desperation dropped the branch and drew out his knife. He moved threateningly towards Abello.

"Look out love," yelled Eloni. Slowly Abello backed away from Arabus. All eyes were upon them.

"Look out." It was Anice who ran to grasp Matester who had toddled over to see what was happening. Arabus brushed her aside. Abello backed up some more. He could hear Eloni sobbing. He glanced at her, as he did so he tripped and fell. Arabus jumped forward and plunged the knife into his chest.

"Ah." A wrenching scream from Eloni as she rushed forward to throw herself on Abello. But it was too late. He was dead. She sobbed, cradling his head in her arms.

"You can leave him alone now. It is time for the living." It was Arabus. "Get up and come here," he commanded.

She paid no attention to him. He strode over and roughly dragged her away.

"You are going to be mine now and I will have you now," he said.

"No, no. You cannot. Please, I implore you. Let me be alone." Turn⸒ she looked at the others. "Please, please let me be alone."

"I think you should let her be." It was Anice.

"No, woman. Be quiet. I am going to have her now." With a sh⸒ knocked Eloni unconscious, dragged her to the ground and raped he⸒ unconcerned by the onlookers. The others were incredulous, and t⸒ or two of them began grabbing at the women. Soon a general ⸒ going on. There were men and women together, with Oah produ⸒

of his fermented drink. Eloni lay unconscious on the ground for a while. When she regained her senses she managed to crawl across the ground into the hut where she passed out on the bed with Abeno beside her.

CHAPTER VI

The dawn crept slowly over the community. Many months had passed since the death of Abello. Eloni stirred restlessly on her bed, her sleep disturbed my memories of him. Her hands strayed over her swollen body and she turned sideways as though to ease the burden of her unborn baby. After Abello's death she had taken Abeno and gone into the jungle to hide and to try and cleanse from her mind and body the awful remembrance of Arabus pressing upon her, his fetid breath filling her mouth, his body bearing into her. One of the primitives had found her and she had spent at least a month with them in their village. She returned to the compound without explaining where she had been, but in fact no one now seemed particularly interested. Most of them had abandoned any semblance of effort at creating a new life and seemed bent on passing their days in an orgy of drinking and copulating. Indeed, they had become so sloppy about eating and drinking and also urinating wherever the need took them that they became prey to fevers and several more died. Oah had finally taken charge of them, chivvying them into cleaning up the area. His experiments were now in full swing. Arabus also was given to days of wild abandonment with women and men, after which he would disappear into the jungle for a while. Eloni had noticed his presence at the primitives' compound when she was there and had tried to explain to them what had happened. Whether they could comprehend or not she was unable to ascertain. She flinched whenever Arabus came close to her but all he would do was to sneer and pass by. Aqa was the one who spent the most time with her. He would play with Abeno and see if there was anything she wanted. He seemed disturbed at the rapid change of events but because of his lameness he seemed reluctant to challenge any of them.

Eloni heard a knock at her door. Wearily she arose and went to open it. Oah was there.

"I came to check that you were all right," he said peremptorily.

"Yes, I am."

"I want you to come over the clinic this afternoon as I want to do some more tests on you."

"More tests? But I have had enough."

"I need more."

"Very well," she said, and slammed the door. Soon afterwards she heard

Anice who arrived, bringing Matester to play with Abeno. She let her in.

"Eloni. Is everything all right? I saw Oah leaving."

Eloni nodded.

"I know you must be feeling awful, but I still envy you. Yes. I have had sex with all of the men here and am still unable to conceive, and you, after having sex with just Abello and Arabus, are pregnant again."

"One."

"But I saw, I mean, Arabus did."

"It is Abello's child, I am sure of it," she replied. "I will not carry any other man's child."

"Does Arabus know?"

"No."

"I would not tell him. He is in strange moods these days and has only laid off you because Oah has warned him not to touch you."

"I don't care. What have I to lose?"

"Oh, Anice, what am I going to do? Is there no finality to my suffering? I came to this new life because I could not bear to relinquish Abello and I lost him anyway. I should have stayed behind."

Anice put her arm around her.

"Oh my pains. My pains have started," moaned Eloni.

"But it is too soon," exclaimed Anice. "Quickly like still and I will fetch Oah. She rushed outside and ran across the clearing. Soon she returned with Oah, who examined her and turning to Anice said, "I think it is a false start but she must remain still for a while. Will you stay here and look after her and the children?"

Anice nodded, and he left. Anice sat by the bed and watched as the children played. Their reverie was broken by the sound of strident singing. Anice went to the enclave. Across the clearing came Arabus, leading one of the primitive women by means of a rope strung around her neck in much the same fashion as they led the goat around. He was obviously drunk, and was alternatively singing and fondling her. The woman looked terrified, and twisted and turned as though trying desperately to escape her bondage.

"I have got myself a woman," sang Arabus. "She is all mine. Nobody else is to have her. I will be like Abello, our late Leader, and keep her here on my own, as he did."

"You must let her go." It was Efa. "You cannot just take her and keep here."

"Are you going to stop me? I will kill you too," said Arabus quite cheerfully, but he stopped and put his hand on his knife. Efa back away.

"Arabus, what have you done? Bring her here." This was Oah.

"I have my own woman now."

Oah advanced towards them.

"What do you want?" queried Arabus.

"I wish to examine her," said Oah. "This is the first opportunity I have had, bring her to the ship."

Anice ran outside. "Arabus let her go."

"Jealous, are you, my darling?" mocked Arabus. "Well she is min."

Anice followed them into the ship. The woman was now passive, at the end of the rope. Oah indicated the table and Arabus lifted her up and laid her on it. "What are you going to do?"

"I am going to operate on her, of course," said Oah testily. "I have been waiting a long time now to have one of these in here and I am not going to waste my chance now."

"But she is my woman."

"I know, but I am not planning to have intercourse with her. You should know that, Arabus."

"Well, I am, so what are you going to do?"

"I am going to do an ovarian transplant."

"Not now, surely?"

"Yes, I am," said Oah, who was busily getting his equipment ready.

"But I have brought her here to have sex with her," protested Arabus.

"Go ahead," said Oah. "It will be some time before I am completely ready."

"All right." Arabus leapt onto the table.

"No, no, Arabus, please no," said Anice.

"Shut up woman. You have had your turn."

She ran for ward and tried to pull him off, but he hit her in the face with his foot and knocked her out.

"Now my black beauty, you had better be ready for me." He ran his hands over her breasts and then thrust it between her legs. The woman lay still, her eyes wide and staring. "Get on with it, then," said Oah.

"Right," said Arabus, and shedding his animal shorts he proceeded to force himself on her. Oah watched dispassionately as his animal-like grunts finally gave way to a satisfied sigh. Slowly Arabus pulled himself away and climbing off the table, dressed. The woman lay there with blood dripping from between her legs.

"Hm, she must have been a virgin," said Oah as he set about mopping up operations.

Oah walked over to Anice who was still unconscious on the ground. Gently he turned her head from side to side. Why, he wondered, to himself, could I not take advantage of her? Carefully he undressed her and stared at her smooth, creamy body. He ran his hands over her body gently and stroking her breasts watched her nipples harden. Suddenly he arose and ran over to the door, which he bolted. Stripping off his clothes he lowered himself onto Anice. But it was a failure again. He tried repeatedly, but he was a total failure, as Arabus was a total success. Anice moaned restlessly and Oah sprang up. Hurriedly he dressed, and then fetched some medicine which he administered to her. He also gave the same thing to the primitive girl, who had long since passed out. He then set about and cleaned her up before making a neat incision over her uterus. Speedily and economically he carried out the same sort of operation that Abello had watched when he was alive. Finally he sewed her up and gave a grunt of satisfaction. He lifted her off the table and carried her t one of the beds. As he went to clean up his gaze fell on Anice. Well, why not, he thought. He carried her to the table and performed the operation on her, but doubling the quantity. After he had cleaned up he held a cloth under Anice's nose, and after a few minutes her eyes opened.

"Oah, what happened?" She grabbed his arms.

"You are quite all right now," he said. "Arabus knocked you unconscious and you cut yourself on the edge of the table as you fell. This is why you have a small scar on your abdomen."

"And the girl. How is she?"

"She will be all right in a few days' time. She is sleeping now."

Anice went to get off the table but fell back at the wave of pain that enveloped her.

"Come and lie down in one of these beds," suggested Oah. "You will feel better in an hour or so." She acquiesced.

There was a knock at the door.

"Coming." Oah crossed the floor and opened it. It was Efa.

"Have you got the primitive girl in here?" he asked breathlessly.

"Yes, yes, I have. What is the matter?"

"I have been over to the village this afternoon. I saw Arabus take her. He knocked down two of the men. One of them did not get up. I think they are very angry and I saw a whole group of them coming this way."

"I see. Thank you for letting me know, Efa. I cannot let her go now. Come and help me hide her in the dome."

Together the two men carried the still unconscious girl up the stairs. "You had better go and see what is happening," ordered Oah, and Efa trotted outside.

In his rush to tell Oah he had not mentioned his findings to the rest of the community, and most of them were still lolling about unconcernedly, drinking or sleeping, and he saw Eloni playing with Abeno and Matester. Arabus he noticed was flat on his back, snoring soundly. Why should I tell them, thought Efa, suddenly. We are all individuals and we can make our own decision. I will go and find Aqa, he thought. He always seems to know what to do.

Eloni looked up as a shadow crossed her vision. She gave a gasp. The primitive man touched her, and then pointed. A group of his men had surrounded the sleeping form of Arabus. Upon a signal from the man they began to prod him roughly. Arabus woke up with a snort of anger. He tried to get up, but one of the men slammed a spear into the ground beside him and several of the others followed suit. The man took hold of Eloni and led her to Arabus. He pointed at her and then at Arabus, and grunted.

"Oah, Oah has her," Arabus cried but he did not understand. "Tell him, Eloni, she is in the ship."

Eloni touched the man and pointed at the ship. She repeated the action several times. Finally the man nodded and pushed her in the direction. Stumbling clumsily she went to the ship. "Oah, they have come for the woman," she called.

"She is not here, come and see."

Eloni went inside and looked around. "Anice, what is the matter?" she said. Oah laid a restraining arm on her. "Nothing is the matter. She had a slight accident, but I have taken care of her and she is resting. She will be all right tomorrow."

Eloni went outside again. She saw that Matester had run over to her father and was squatting beside him crying. Eloni went over the group and looking at the man she shook her head. The man looked puzzled and grunted to the others. They stood together uncertainly for a few minutes. All eyes were upon them. Suddenly one of them bent down and picked up Matester who began to cry even more loudly. Arabus leapt to his feet, but one of the taller men knocked him to the ground. The man gave a low hiss, and turning they ran into the trees. Arabus stood up slowly. "They have taken my daughter. After them. We must go after them," he bellowed.

"But where is the girl?" yelled Eloni.

"I told you, Oah has her."

"But I went into the ship and I could not see her there."

"You are a stupid woman. He has her. I had sex with her on the operating table, and I should know. Besides Oah and Anice were there, too."

A gasp ran through the others at this, but Arabus ignored it. He chased across to the ship and bounded up the steps. "Oah, Oah, where are you?"

"Here I am."

"Where is the girl? They have taken Matester and I want her back. Give them back the girl."

"Because you have had your enjoyment of her?"

"Yes, yes."

"No, I will not. I have not finished with her."

"But you don't enjoy women."

"Never mind she is part of my experiments, and I need to keep her for a few days."

"And Anice, is she one of your experiments as well?"

Oah looked uncomfortable. "N, she is not," he said defiantly.

"Give me the girl."

"No."

"Are you going to kill him too?" It was Efa.

"No, I am not."

"They will not harm her, I am sure," said Eloni, who had joined the others at the bottom of the steps. "They are kind people and will only keep her until you return the girl."

"Listen to Abello's sainted woman, will you. I will have my daughter back," he reiterated.

"What are we going to do?" said Efa.

Everyone puzzled over this. "I am going after her," said Arabus, who appeared at the doorway carrying a pair of laser guns.

"No, don't go after them like that. They have not harmed us in any way," said Aqa.

Arabus ignored him and charged down the steps. "No, don't harm them," cried Eloni. Suddenly Uth stuck his foot out and Arabus went flying. Before most of them could react Aqa jumped on his back and held him to the ground.

"You are not going," he said.

Arabus writhed underneath him. Aqa hit him hard on the back of the neck and Arabus fell forward unconscious.

"Aqa, Aqa, you have hit someone," said Efa.

"I had to," he replied. "I could not let him go. Now quickly let's make sure he does not get away."

"What shall we do with him?" Efa queried.

"Put him in the goat shed and keep a guard over him for the night," suggested Oah. The others agreed and then manhandled him over to the shed and shoved him inside. Two of them volunteered to guard him and the rest left.

Next morning Arabus was unrepentant and they decided to keep him inside all day. Anice came over to see Eloni, and told her of the events she had witnessed in the ship. "I wish I knew what had happened to me after I was knocked out. I am still in considerable pain," she added.

"And you, have you had anymore pains, Eloni/" She shook her head.

"What are we going to do now?" Anice said. "I am certain that Arabus means to kill those men to get Matester back and I am equally certain that Oah will let the girl go in time."

"Maybe I should go to them and stay with them until Oah is ready to release the girl. I am sure I would be safe with them and you could tell Arabus what I have done. I would not do it for him, but I am glad to be away from this community."

Anice nodded. "I will tell Oah, and then I will come with you to the primitives."

"No, I will be all right."

"But in your condition and with Abeno to think of as well you should not travel even that comparatively short journey along."

"I will be all right," she said impatiently.

"Well, I am going to lie down," said Anice, and left.

Eloni rose slowly and taking Abeno in her arms, left her home. As she walked by the goat house she called out to Arabus. "I don't know if you can hear me or not, but I will tell you that I am going over to see the primitive men and I will stay with them until Oah returns the girl. I am indifferent to you but I care for Matester and this is why I go." She paused, but heard nothing. She walked stiffly on.

Halfway towards the primitives' village one of them appeared silently beside her, grunted and took Abeno from her. The silent trio walked on. Meanwhile Anice had gone to see Oah and to tell him what Eloni had done.

"She should not have gone," he said harshly. "She is a high minded fool, just as Abello was. I am sure Matester will come to no harm and Eloni is risking her live and her unborn child's, going over there."

"Well, you should not have kept the girl," retorted Anice sharply. "Just what have you don't to her and me? I am sufficiently aware of my own body to realize that this scar is nothing accidental."

"But you were knocked out by Arabus and you fell."

"And finish up with a neat scar on my abdomen. And I have checked on the primitive, she has a similar one. Oh yes, I am quite resourceful."

"I know that. You had better sit down before I tell you."

"Just tell me," she stamped her foot impatiently.

"As you know, I have been concerned at the inability of all except Eloni to become fertile, and so I have been carrying out experiments on the various animals that I have been able to capture. I have had some success. In fact, the tree climbing animals all became pregnant but unfortunately they all gave birth to malformed young and most of them died in the effort of birth or shortly afterwards. I have long been interested in the primitives' reproduction cycle and when Arabus brought one over here I seized my chance."

"You mean you operated on her."

"Only after Arabus had taken his fill of her, so I will not be sure if it is his or mine. I did think that only Abello was the fortunate one."

"And me, what about my scar? Did Arabus have me as well?"

"No, no, I."

"You finally succeeded," she laughed. "I don't believe it."

"Stop it, woman."

"But you. You have never even expressed interest in any of us."

"Well, I have now, and you may be pregnant because of it."

"You make me pregnant? Never." She started to laugh and broke it off abruptly and stepped back from him, her eyes widening in horror. "You experimented on me, didn't you? And I am to have a malformed horror. You didn't, tell me you didn't."

"I did, and you will have a normal child, I am sure."

"And that wretch up in the control room. She is to undergo the same horror?" Oah nodded.

"I despise you," she said, "and I will never have one of your experiments. I will die first," and she stalked out. She stormed through the clearing and without being fully aware she followed the path to the primitives. Again halfway there two of them appeared beside here, and escorted her to the village. She found Eloni with Abeno and Matester in a hut at the far end of the clearing, and bursting in she related her conversation with Oah. Eloni was horrified.

"We must find a way to get rid of it," she said. "You stay here with me until we have solved this problem. You will be quite safe here."

Several days passed and then the primitive girl arrived. The whole village clustered around her, poking and prodding at her. They were obviously fascinated by the scar and each in turn ran its fingers over it. After this she was brought along and thrust into the hut with Eloni and Anice and left alone. Anice indicated her scar and the girl looked at it curiously. She compared it with hers, but try as they could the two women could not explain anything to her. Finally she crawled into a corner and lay down. The next morning Eloni noticed that her face was swollen and that she had difficulty breathing. By the afternoon she was much worse, and in spite of the women's efforts to keep her cool by constantly bathing her she was burning hot. Anice went to find one of the primitive men and returned with two of them. She made them touch her body and then hers to indicate the difference in temperatures. The men ran out of the hut and back into another one further away. There was hardly any change in her condition overnight, and the next day Matester started to complain of the same symptoms. Later that day a primitive arrived, and grabbing Eloni propelled her down to another hut. Inside she found several more men in varying stages of the same symptoms.

Running back she told Anice, "Go and fetch Oah," she said, "and go quickly. We may all be doomed."

Anice left without another word. Eloni rounded up several of the primitive women, together with some water pots. She took them down to the river and had them fill up the pots. When they returned to the village she showed them how to bathe the men. Once they had grasped the essentials of this operation she left them and went to check on Matester and the girl. Both appeared better, and Eloni lay down on the floor and went to sleep.

While she was asleep Oah arrived with Anice. He went from hut to hut checking the occupants and making notes. He found Eloni asleep with Abeno curled in her arms. He gave a cursory examination to Matester, and then calling for Anice to hold the instrument bag, he knelt down to examine the girl. He spent about fifteen minutes checking her, and wearily stood up.

"I am afraid that she has carried a disease back from the compound and transmitted it to these people."

"But we are all healthy enough," said Anice.

"Yes, but we must have built-in resistance to certain diseases. These people have never been exposed to our way of life and their bloodstreams are unable to cope with the germs which pass unnoticed in our midst."

"But we cannot let them die," she cried.

"I am fully aware of that fact," said Oah stiffly. "I am mainly concerned that the disease seems to have spread among the men at first. Most of the women here are healthy enough at the moment."

"And what should we do?"

"We must separate them."

"Separate them? But how?"

"We must try to explain to them that this is the wisest course. Then we will take the women back to the compound until the disease has spent itself. I will leave you and Eloni here, although Eloni in her condition cannot do much. The primitives, however, appear to trust her, and her presence may have a calming effect on them. I know that you are very capable and you can look after the men. I will send some of our men over to help you. Now let us go and find the one who is supposed to be the leader and tell him of our decision."

Anice followed him down the path to the hut in the middle. Inside she recognized the man who had come asking for the primitive girl Arabus had stolen. She indicated this to Oah. She noticed another man lying, moaning, in the corner and she went to attend to him. Oah, meanwhile, in a series of miming gestures was trying to indicate to the man what his intentions were. The man seemed completely unable to comprehend and eventually slumped down on the ground.

"I have done my best, Anice. I will leave now and take the women with me. I do not anticipate any trouble, and as soon as I reach the compound I will send some help. Do not tire yourself," and he pointed at the scar.

"If it will help me to get rid of your monster, I will," retorted Anice, and Oah then went from hut to hut, pushing and prodding the women until he had all of them lined up in the middle. One or two of them resisted his efforts, but when he produced a surgical knife and threatened them they acquiesced. He made no attempt to explain his actions but shoved them down the track towards the compound like a flock of recalcitrant chickens.

Night was falling by the time he reached the compound where he was greeted by many ribald remarks and obscene gestures. He ignored all of them and shepherded the women inside the ship and indicated to them to sit on the floor. He then stepped outside and locked the door. He turned to face the group who had crowded around the steps. "I have brought the women here because of a disease which has spread through the primitive village. At the moment the men seem more susceptible to it than the women and so I have brought them here to keep them isolated. I have had to leave Eloni there, and also Anice who is taking care of the men."

"I expect she likes that," chimed Efa, and much laughter followed this remark.

Oah ignored this and continued, "I would like some volunteers to go over and help her and to bring me reports of the disease's course."

Nobody seemed very eager to go. The men wanted to stay and see what was going to happen to the women. Several of them had caught their breath in anticipation of sampling the younger beauties. None of them had ever see fifteen naked black women, their breasts proudly jutting forth, pass by so close. Oah asked again for volunteers, and finally they drew lots and Aqa and Omas lost. Reluctantly they left.

"What are you going to do with the women now?" called Efa.

"I am going to check them over thoroughly and after I have taken all their statistics," amid laughter he continued, "weight, age and so on and examined them I will let them sleep. Tomorrow I will let all of you take a turn with one of them." A shout went up at this. "I plan on keeping them here until I can ascertain if any of them are pregnant or not."

"But that will be at least two months. The primitive men will want them back before then."

"I have ways of keeping them too sick to care," retorted Oah and turning, unlocked the door and disappeared inside the ship.

"What about Arabus?" queried one of the men. "We ought to tell him what is going on."

They all walked over the goat hut.

"Arabus, we want to talk to you," called Efa.

A grunt was heard. Efa walked up to the door and peered inside. Arabus was lolling on the ground. Briefly he told him what had transpired since his imprisonment two days ago.

"Oah, eh? He is an odd sort of fellow. Why can't we have the women tonight/" he said, and getting up he strode purposefully across the compound and banged on the ship's door.

"Who is it?"

"It is Arabus."

"What do you want?"

"I want my women tonight," he yelled.

"No. You cannot."

"Don't tell me no, open this door."

"No, no. I have much to do. Wait until morning."

The argument raged on for a few minutes, but Oah was adamant.

"Well, I am not going without tonight," stated Arabus, and marching back to the hut he pulled the goat out and began to mount it. The others looked on, horrified, and one or two turned away. None of them dared to stop him. The animal bleated frantically but Arabus was determined to have his way, and eventually the two of them collapsed on the ground. The night eventually passed. For some of them it was too long, and at the first hint of daybreak they were banging on the ship's door.

"Coming, coming," said the querulous voice of Oah, and he unlocked it. One by one the women trooped out. Their ages ranged from a young girl whose breasts had hardly formed to an old woman whose breasts hung pendulously in front of her. The men converged upon them and led them until they formed a circle around the fire. They pushed them to the ground, and while the women watched they stripped, the sun's first rays etching the contrast between the fair skins and dark. As the women realized what was about to happen they all rolled over on their stomachs and knelt. The men turned them over, but each time the women would roll back.

"Interesting, interesting," said Oah, who was watching the proceedings. He stood up. "Men they are obviously deeply primitive, and having only seen other animals copulate they do not realize that there is any other way to have intercourse. You will have to do it their way to start with."

The men grunted, and soon the clearing echoed only to sounds of grunting and labored breathing. Soon even this was gone. Seeing that they were all finished Oah rounded up the women and took them back to the ship. The remainder of the day he spent studying and evaluating them. The other men slept and attended to a minimal amount of basic chores. Three of them went off into the jungle to see if they could find any meant. They still experienced difficulties in trapping any game although they had tried many ways including making lassos and tying strands of branches across an opening which, when snapped, dug into the animal. But they only seem to attract small animals, which after being skinned out did not provide much meat. For a while they had been using the laser guns indiscriminately firing at anything that moved, but as these were running low they abandoned them as well. Generally they had reverted to being vegetarians again, living off the luxuriant plant life that grew in abundance around them. Several of them had taken to smoking the plant which the primitives first gave them, and were even trying to cultivate it in a small patch behind the huts. Oah had taken some samples of it and was trying to analyze it.

Omas came bounding through the clearing and rushed up the steps of the craft. He pounded against the door, rattling it hard. "Oah, Oah. Hurry, hurry."

"What is it now?" said Oah crossly as he opened the door.

"It is Eloni. She is in labor. We need help as she is very weak and the baby will not be born."

"Coming, coming," Oah replied, and he disappeared inside the ship to re-emerge with a bag in his hand. As they passed through the compound Oah called Arabus. "I am going to deliver another of your children."

"Hm. I hope it is a boy this time," replied Arabus. "It had better be all right, or I will tear you apart." Oah smiled and followed Omas out of the clearing.

When they arrived at the clearing there was hardly any sign of life. A few children were standing around listlessly, and a couple of primitive men were asleep in the sun. Omas indicated the hut where Eloni was living and Oah hurried inside. He found Abeno sitting on the floor screaming, and Matester cowering in the corner. Anice was helping Eloni, who was on the floor in a pool of water, while Aqa was bathing her forehead. "Take the children out of there," order Oah.

Aqa scooped up Abeno and Anice took Matester by the arms, and they left. Outside he said to Anice. "Take her back to her father, she needs to be with him. They are very alike."

Anice looked questioningly at Aqa but he did not elaborate. "I will take care of Abeno here and help Eloni."

He stumped off down the pathway to find an empty hut, the few children that were outside gathering around him and trailing along behind.

Meanwhile Oah was struggling to deliver Eloni's child. Her body was weakened by several hours of labor, and Oah could not get a firm enough grip on the baby to drag him out. Finally, in desperation he cut her open and pulled the baby out. Quickly he dewed Eloni up and then gave her a sedative. The baby was a puny little thing. He only gave feeble cries now and again and then was still. Oah injected him with some medicine and for the rest of the day he stayed with them. At one time Eloni woke up and turned restless searching for the child. Oah gave him to her, but after she looked at him she pushed them both away and sank into sleep. Later the baby died without even a whimper. Oah carried him outside and looked for Aqa. When he found him he showed him the infant. Oah explained what happened. Aqa shook his head sadly. "You must burn him now before she is really fully conscious and it will ease her pain. I will help you after I have made sure that Abeno is all right. I have one of the children watching over him."

He was gone a few minutes before catching up with Oah, who had put the infant down and was started to carry branches into the center of the clearing. It did not take the two of them long, and Ain a short time they had a fire going. With a last look they flung the body onto the flames. They heard a gasp behind them, and turning caught sight of two of the primitives fleeing down the pathway.

"How odd," remarked Oah, "I cannot imagine doing anything else with a body, can you?"

"No," admitted Aqa, "although I do not think that this is the way they do it."

"Interesting, interesting. I must check on it, but now I will go and check on the rest of the primitives. Since we have this fire burning now we might as well drag out the other bodies and burn them. Can you help?"

"As much as I am able with this leg."

"How is Abello's special shoe?"

"It is wearing now, but I find I have to rest after I have been on it for half an hour."

"I must have a look at it sometime when we get back to the compound," said Oah as he walked into the first hut. It took them a lot longer to drag the bodies to the fire than originally anticipated. Halfway through Aqa had to leave to attend to Abeno, who had woken up. By the time Oah had finished night enveloped the clearing. After he had settled Abeno again, Aqa had wearily lain down on the floor beside Eloni and fallen asleep. Oah looked in at them to check Eloni before he too found a hut that was empty and fell into an exhausted sleep.

The community was awakened by the sound of something crashing

127

through the jungle towards the clearing. Oah emerged from his hut, blinking in the harsh daylight, to find Aqa was already standing stretching in the sunlight.

"What can it be?" called Oah.

"Probably an animal attracted by the smell of burning flesh," replied Aqa.

"But they would have come last night, surely?"

"I suppose. By the way Eloni is awake. I told her what had happened to the baby. She seemed quite indifferent to his death and is now looking after Abeno."

Oah nodded. "I had better come and see her. I will get my things," he said, and disappeared into the hut. As Aqa turned to go back inside he caught sight of a movement at the end of the clearing. He put his hand over his eyes so he could get a better view. He sucked in his breath and darted inside.

"Eloni, Arabus is coming. I just caught sight of him. He has Efa and Uth with him. You had better hide, for I am sure he will get very violent after he finds out about the baby."

Eloni smiled. "No, Aqa, I will stay. If I am to die, then I cannot stop it from happening. But I feel that Abello did not bring us safely here from Capernica for us all to perish. No. Just help me up so at least I may look him straight in the eye."

Carefully Aqa helped her up and watched as she straightened her clothing and ran her fingers through her hair in an effort to straighten it.

"At least let me take Abeno somewhere in case his anger will be directed at him."

"You are right. Take him and hide in the jungle somewhere close to the lake and I will come for you when it is safe."

Aqa hoisted the sleeping child on to his shoulder and limping as fast as he could he slid through the doorway and hurried to the back of the huts. For a moment he paused but no shouts followed him. He breathed out and slowly wended his way to the lake while Abeno remained asleep.

"Eloni, Eloni, where are you?" sang Arabus as he led the other two down the central path. "Eloni, my darling, this is your successful lover here. Have I another daughter or a son this time? Come on out, I am going to find you." The three of them sauntered along and as they came closer to the line of huts Arabus went over to one and strode inside. "Nothing in there," he grunted, crossed over. "Come on, come Efa, Uth. Hurry up and find them. I cannot wait to see my children born of the beautiful Eloni. I am so fortunate."

"Here I am, Arabus."

He spun around and saw Eloni standing in the middle of the street.

"My love, let me congratulate you," he grinned and advanced upon her.

"Congratulate me for what?" she replied coolly.

"For the child, of course. Tell me, is it a boy or a girl?"

"It was a boy."

"Perfect, perfect. You hear that, Efa? A boy. To be like me. I hope we have many more, and you two had better get one of those black savages pregnant or he will be reduced to the goat, too, when he grows up."

"Eloni said it was a boy," pointed out Efa.

"Was? Was? Well woman, what do you mean?"

"It was a boy because it has died."

"Died? Died? Come on woman, tell me the truth. It cannot have died. You had Abello's baby and he is perfectly healthy."

"And your children are accursed," she retorted. Arabus' face went crimson and his eyes became stone hard.

"Lies, woman, lies. Where is my son?"

"He is dead."

"Show me the body. I want to see his body. The baby of the beautiful Eloni and Arabus." He advanced towards her again and Eloni turned her head to try to avoid the awful smell of his body.

"He has been burnt," she spat at him. "Burnt, you understand. Gone and forgotten as far as I am concerned. You forced yourself on to me and impregnated me with your seed. I hoped at first it was Abello's, and I still have no way of telling, bit it was a hard, long pregnancy. No sleep, too much movement. Kicks. A little savage, after his father. Twice he tried to come into this world before his time and he should have done. The sooner the better as far as I was concerned. I was well rid of the bastard."

"You. You set yourself up as a superwoman. Who would not be part of the new community. I am Abello's. I will not share him, etc., etc. You are no better than the rest of us. Worse in fact, since you hide your feelings behind the whitewash you dish out. Come here, you slut. You are going to have my next child and the one after that and after that." He knocked her down.

"Arabus, Arabus, stop. She is just out of childbirth. Think of Rester. You virtually killed her. You want Eloni to die too? She will never have your children then," Oah pleaded.

Arabus stepped back from where he had straddled Eloni, leering down at her. "Well, it is the good doctor who let my son die. I told you I would kill you if anything happened to my child. Are you ready?"

"But I did all I could, I swear to you," said Oah as he backed away from Arabus.

"You didn't do enough, did you then? I want my son. I think, you killed him deliberately."

"No, no. I did all I could to save him."

"I want to see his body."

"But Eloni told you I burnt it."

"Very convenient. No, come on, step forward and be a man." He jeered as Oah continued to back towards the hut where he had slept. "Oh, I forgot the great doctor is no man. He cannot rise to the occasion, as we would say. He has to content himself with experiments and watching others, don't you Oah?"

"Stop, Arabus, you have gone far enough." This was Efa.

Uth nodded in agreement.

"Gone soft on me, have you?" said Arabus as he turned to face them. "Well, run and hide if you have no stomach for this. But I am going to kill him."

Oah re-emerged from the hut. "Come on then. Stop talking and get on with it. Or are you just a blowhard?"

Arabus charged forward, fists clenched. As he neared Oah the doctor stepped forward and jabbed a needle into him. He watched as Arabus, caught off guard, charged around in a circle holding his left buttocks. Each time he came at him Oah sidestepped. Gradually the pace slackened until Arabus crumpled in a heap.

Oah looked down at him, and then at Efa and Uth. "Get him out of here unless you want him to die of the disease. Leave us alone."

"Aren't you coming back to the compound?" queried Efa.

"In time. In good time," replied Oah.

"But what about the primitive women?"

"They will be all right for a day or so."

Uth opened his mouth to say something but thought the better of it. Oah walked over to Eloni and gathering her in his arms carried her to a hut and laid her on the floor. She smiled sweetly up at him, and he stroked her brow. "I will give you some medicine to sleep, and do not worry, I will stay with you."

She nodded gently and watched him as he prepared the injection.

"What about Abeno, where is he?" he asked as he administered the drug.

"He is all right. He is in good hands," and she drifted off to sleep.

Oah sat there stroking her arm, marveling at her shapely body. She looks so serene even though she has been through so much. She has known joy and despair in both the conception and birth of her two children, and especially the joy of true loving sexual intercourse. How fortunate she is, and why cannot I achieve the same thing? As Arabus taunted me this afternoon, I am useless as a man, I fulfill a role as a doctor and that is all.

What would it be like to have a body like Arabus? I would have stayed on Capernica where my celibacy passed unnoticed. He continued these musings until he too fell asleep.

In the meantime Efa, and Uth had grown tired of dragging Arabus through the jungle and had left him by the path. "He will find his way back, no doubt," said Efa, and Uth nodded his agreement. The two of them made their way back to the compound. This was a scene of absolute chaos. The men had grown tired of waiting for Oah to return and had finally succeeded in breaking down the door to the ship. They had herded the women out and were all busily engaged practicing every form of sexual deviation on them they could think of. One or two of them, having palled of this, had returned to the shop and snooped through all Oah's medicines and notes. Most of them they did not understand, but they administered several of the different medicines to the primitive women. Now most of them lay sound asleep on the grass while Anice moved about trying to take care of the women. Seeing the two men return she called to them to come and help but they ignored her and choosing two of the younger women dragged them into the huts. Anice finally shrugged her shoulders in disgust and left to look after Matester. She found her sitting contentedly on the floor pulling the legs of a spider she had found. Anice paid no attention to her but flopped on the bed angrily.

"Where is father?" said Matester.

"How should I know?" replied Anice crossly.

"I want to see him," she wailed.

"Oh, shut up. He has gone to see your new brother or sister."

"I want a brother. I want a brother. I want…"

"Shut up, will you." Anice swung her legs over the side of the bed and stood up. How peculiar, she thought. Neither Uth nor Efa mentioned the baby. She strode out of the hut, Matester running behind her. She found Uth lying in the sun. "Is it a boy or a girl?" she asked.

"Boy or girl, what are you talking about?"

"Eloni's baby."

"It is dead," he said flatly, and went on to recount the events of the afternoon.

"And she said it was Arabus who fathered it? She told me she knew it was Abello's. Good for her. It is time Arabus received a few shocks from the women. Where is he?" Efa told her where he had left him.

"I had better go and check on him. Matester wants to see her father, anyway."

"I should wait until morning now. Darkness will be here soon."

"No, I will be all right. I know the path," she said and the two of them walked off.

It took Anice a lot longer than she had anticipated to reach the spot where Efa had explained to her he thought they had left Arabus. Her delay was solely due to Matester, who sat down frequently and would not move. It took most of Anice's patience to persuade the child to keep moving. When at last she found Arabus, still sprawled in the grass beside the path, she gave him a hefty prod with her foot. Unfortunately Matester copied her, and Arabus woke up to find his daughter kicking at him.

"Stop it, you little bitch," he swore and slapped her hard.

Matester, taken aback by this unexpected wrath, retaliated by spitting at him and then promptly sat down and started bawling.

"Can't you stop her?" he queried angrily.

"Why should I?" Anice retorted. "You should care for her yourself. Especially now she is all you have got."

"Who told you?"

"We all know now. You haven't had the success you thought you would. You had better wait and hope one of the primitive women bears your child – or perhaps you are waiting for the goat."

Surprisingly Arabus did not rise to this but rolled over on to his stomach and said lazily, "That's right Anice, always ready to charge after others, but I don't see you with a swollen stomach. After all the different chances you have had these past few months I am a little surprised that you are still barren. It certainly cannot be for the lack of trying."

"Well, maybe I am."

"Are you?" he said as he stood up and grabbed her arm. "Are you sure?"

"Let go," she said angrily twisting away. "What if I am? It is hardly likely to be yours."

"Well, who then?"

"You will be the last to know. Let me go." Arabus shook her angrily and was about to strike her when Matester grabbed one of his legs.

With a snort he let Anice go and bent down to pick up Matester. "What is it, child?"

"I am hungry."

"You had better go back with her said Anice. "Although it is dark I am going on to see Eloni and the primitives." She vanished into the dark and Arabus stumped off towards camp with Matester slung around his shoulders.

When Anice arrived at the primitive village she found Eloni, Abeno, and Aqa asleep in one of the huts. The whole area was quiet and still, even the noises of the night animals seeming muted and far away. Anice peered in all of the huts in turn out of curiosity and found all the men and the children asleep. Finally she too crawled inside between Aqa and Abeno and fell asleep.

Meanwhile Arabus had arrived back at the compound to find an argument raging. Oah had rounded up the women and shepherded them back into the ship. Although the door had been battered down he had placed a row of cages across the doorway, each containing an animal or an insect. These he informed them all carried deadly bites, and he could electronically open the cages as soon as he heard someone coming. Most of the men were skeptical about this, but none of them felt eager to put the theory to a practical test. Arabus found that he was forced to attend to Matester before joining in the argument. It took him somewhat longer than he had anticipated to attend to her needs, and by this time the men had given up and gone away. Arabus went over to the ship and called Oah who eventually came to the doorway.

"What are you doing in there?" he called.

"Just making the usual tests and collecting data."

"But why? You must have plenty already. You should be over with the men looking after them."

"They will be all right. I have seen to that."

"Why are you so sure?"

"Because I am a doctor and I can take care of these problems quite easily."

"And is my baby really dead?"

"I am afraid so."

"Then I want one of these women for my own. I want to have another child."

"You have had your turn."

"But so have the rest. I want to know that it is mine."

"Well, they may all be pregnant already."

"But surely we could not make our women pregnant, so why should these be now?"

Oah withdrew into the ship and Arabus yelled after him.

"I don't know,' came the reply.

Arabus walked away. As he drew near his hut he remembered that Anice had told him that she too thought she was pregnant. He shook his head. Oah? No, it can't be. I must talk to Uth and Efa tomorrow and we must try and find out what is going on. We men must have free rein here without the doctor using us as experiments. He resolved to have a meeting the next morning. Basically he felt uneasy at the thought of Oah working on his own initiative. Without realizing it he was facing a problem of leadership which the death of Abello had left unresolved. He fell asleep somewhat uneasily.

When he tried to interest the others next morning he met with a wall of indifference. This was Oah's doing, albeit unwittingly. He had let the women out and the men were too busy making choices. After a few abortive attempts to get their attention Arabus gave up and seizing one of the women dragged her along to the hut. However, he remembered that Matester was in there and so he went on into the jungle with the woman. Later in the afternoon Oah rounded the women up and put them back inside the ship. After setting out his cages of animals and supplementing this with other deterrents he left for the primitives' camp. In addition to checking on the remaining men he wanted to send Aqa back so that he could keep a careful check on the women. He was till puzzled as to why they were all so passive. He was also anxious to find the first signs that his experiments were successful and in this regard he wanted to keep a check on Anice. Thus the pattern was set for the next few weeks, with Oah dividing his time between the two camps. Aqa now spent most of the time with the women and he was joined by Anice, who took a keen interest in the experiments. She had taken Matester over to rejoin Eloni and Abeno, who seemed quite happy to stay with the primitives. No one seemed to care that it was taking so long to cure the primitive men of their illness although Eloni observed all the visits and treatments that Oah made. Towards the end of the sixth week when Oah came to check on the mean and also to see how Eloni was progressing he remarked that the men seemed to be better. "Another two weeks and I shall be able to return to the women," he said.

"But why has it taken so long?"

"Well, with creatures like this they have no built in resistance to any diseases brought from another source. Therefore they are very susceptible to any germs, and of course it take quite a while to effect a suitable cure."

"And how are the women?"

"They are fine. Anice has been helping Aqa to look after them."

"An Anice, is she all right?"

"Yes, yes, why not?"

"She told me what you had done to her and I assume that you have done the same to these poor wretches, keeping the men almost comatose until you can reap the fruits of your experiments."

"Well, not exactly," blustered Oah.

"You should not have submitted Anice to it. She does not deserve such treatment. I went through nine months of carrying a man's child I despise, but at least it was fathered by a man. Hers comes from what? Or is it you?"

"No. It is not. I would be the first to tell everyone if I was the father, but I am sure all will be righted in the end. After all, the other women have not complained."

"Probably because they are unable to assimilate what you have done to them. What are the men going to think when all their women, including the unmarried ones, return to them pregnant?"

"Well I am sure that upon seeing them there will be a spasm of intercourse and they will feel it to be the natural outcome."

"And what about the poor girl that Arabus raped?"

"They will make a decision when the child is born."

"If they are capable."

"I am sure they are."

"I wonder. They all know it was Arabus who took her and they will assume it is his even though it may be one of your experiments."

"I am certain everything will be perfect."

"Not like the monkeys," she retorted as she left to find Abeno.

Oah stood there for a while. She may well be right, he thought, and as he mused he went rather uncertainly down the path towards his patients. Most of them had been permitted to recover and the remaining few were genuine sufferers.

He noticed that although the men submitted to his examinations without any visible signs of emotion, as soon as he had finished they would scuttle away. Altogether about fifteen of them died, leaving about ten men. Oah reckoned that now the ratio would be about one man for every two women, and of course there were the children who had passed through the epidemic comparatively unscathed. He wondered if the imbalance would have any effect on the primitives and smiled ruefully to himself as he realized it was the reverse of his situation. No doubt it would not take his fellow men long to discovery the fact. He realized, too, that he would have to return the women to the village. With this thought in mind he walked off to find Eloni. To his surprise he could not find her anywhere. Puzzling he searched the huts again but there was no sign of her. Well, I will just have to leave without her, he thought, and strode off down the path. He was surprised to overtake her and Abeno at roughly halfway.

"Eloni, what are you doing?"

"I am going back to the compound."

"Buy why?"

"I did not want to stay with the primitives any longer."

"But you have always been quite content over there."

"But I am afraid of their reaction when the women return, despite your protestations, and I wanted to return Matester to her father. She is becoming too much like him and she needs a father's discipline."

"Where is she now?"

"She ran on down the path and I could not catch up with her as Abeno is too heavy to carry for long spells."

"But all will be well, I am certain of it. Their minds are not advanced enough to conceive of any evil. And although I told you I would return the women in two weeks I am resolved to take them back tomorrow. The men are well enough now and the community must resume its normal life as soon as possible."

"Normal life. I doubt that. How long is it since we have had any normal life. Anyway I am surprised to hear you admit that what you have done is evil."

"I did not say that. For us to survive here we must have children, as I have often said, and if we cannot conceive them naturally then I must help."

"You should have concentrated on us. There must be other ways."

"But this is not Capernica. I did not leave there with any hope for the future at all. However, now that I am confronted with the problem I owe it to us all to find a solution by any means possible."

"But surely you could have left the primitives alone."

"Well, they were there."

"And you wanted to experiment."

"Yes," said Oah firmly, at last admitting the truth. "Why not? I will become the father of many children at last."

Eloni stared at him for a moment.

"Oah, you experimented because you are impotent. But surely you could have tried to solve y our own problems. You may have changed since leaving Capernica and you have your choice of women here. Would you like to take me now?"

"No, no. I cannot. I tried with Anice," he said hesitantly, "and it was not to be."

"Poor, poor Oah."

"Enough of this. We must hurry if we are to reach the compound before night." The two of them, with Oah carrying Abeno, hurried along.

When they arrived Eloni followed Oah to the ship. The others were lying around the fire place. There was no sign of Arabus or Matester. Eloni looked curiously around the ship. Most of the women were sitting rather apathetically and she was surprised to find Anice there as well.

"I have been helping to look after them. After all," she laughed nervously, "we are all in this together."

"Why don't you come and share my home tonight," said Eloni. "I have come to stay a while and would be glad of another woman's company, especially one that I can converse with."

"Yes Anice, do go. I have Aqa here if I need any help, and there is not too much I can do. I will be leaving early in the morning with them to take them back to the village." Anice nodded, and the two women and Abeno left.

Eloni found her home undisturbed and thankfully put Abeno to bed. She and Anice talked for a long time and Eloni asked her about her experience with Oah. She was surprised to learn that she had no knowledge of it.

"I wish this thing inside me was his, then I would not feel so apprehensive. Aqa has been telling me about the other experiments and particularly about his failures with the tree climbing animals and others. Do you realize that although all transplants have been successful inasmuch as the animals became pregnant, all have died giving birth to misshapen offspring. I am so frightened."

She began to week and Eloni consoled her as best she could. She vividly recalled the agony she went through of carrying a child and not being sure of its father. How much worst it must be for Anice with her extrovert character. Presently they went to bed and Eloni lay there thinking about her life. She was quite certain that Abello had not brought them this far to die in vain and have all the rest of them die as well. Surely, she pondered, it would have been better if we had all perished in vain. Slowly she went to sleep.

When Abeno woke them up the following morning they found it was quite late. Looking through the aperture they could see the door of the ship wide open and none of the usual barricades in place, so Oah had obviously set off with the women. The rest of the community was stretching itself into wakefulness and she still could not see any sign of Arabus, for which she was grateful, or Matester. Thinking about Matester she went outside and seeing Uth asked him if he had seen her. He informed her that she had wandered in yesterday and that she and Arabus had disappeared into the jungle fairly soon afterwards. Eloni thanked him.

CHAPTER VII

Oah motioned to Eloni to wipe the primitive female's forehead with the rag soaked in cold water. The girl was bathed in sweat as she strained to deliver her offspring. She and Oah had been in the hot hut all day waiting for the child to be born, and the heat combined with nervous anticipation had made him tense and irritable. He felt certain that the birth could not now be long delayed. For the hundredth time that day he explained to Eloni that because of the difference in size of the two races, the primitives being quite small and narrow in the hips, great difficulty was experienced in the actual birth. He had tried to speed up the process by pushing against the girl's swollen abdomen but he could not use much force as he did not wish to damage either the mother or the child. This one just had to be delivered successfully. He had waited for a long time for this moment of triumph and this would herald the safe arrival of many more babies who would carry on the traditions of Capernica and its way of life. But these efforts were in vain and it was obvious that nature would take its own time. From his external examination and felling inside her he was sure that the child was perfectly normal. For the hundredth time also he wondered if it were Arabus' child or the result of his own experiments. As the girl grunted and sweated, he was aware of Eloni's condemning silence and also of the primitives sitting outside waiting. Eloni attended the girl compassionately as she relived the memories of her own two confinements. She bathed the girl's head and as much of her body as she could conveniently reach without getting in Oah's way and was rewarded with looks of gratitude and the pressure of her fingers. As for Eloni, she wondered if the baby was Arabus' and she knew that Anice was waiting for news back at the camp in a considerable state of nervous tension.

The thought of Abeno crossed her mind and she reflected upon the fact that the children seemed to develop so quickly, for he was both walking and beginning to talk, although the seasons had revolved but once. On the other hand she had observed that the adults seemed to age with equal rapidity and she thought how flecked with grey Arabus' hair and beard had become of late. But she had noticed the same with her own hair. She smiled to herself as she fondly recalled how Abello had loved to see her lying naked on the bed with her long black hair cascading over her young breasts. Oh well, that was all in the past now. Maybe it was just as well as there was no time for personal grooming and she did not have a looking glass with her. She had tried once or twice to see herself in the still water of a pool but usually Matester would catch sight of her and rushing up to the bank would throw in lumps of mud or pebbles. Eloni would experience feelings of annoyance as her image dissolved into a thousand ripples.

Thoughts of Matester caused Eloni to wonder how she was faring with her father. A strange, tense relationship seemed to exist between father and daughter. However, Arabus often took her with him on trips to secret places and Eloni had seen the two of them at the village of the primitives on more than one occasion. While her father was grunting after the females Matester would seize one of the smaller children and proceed to terrorize it. She seemed to enjoy this infliction of her superiority, and Eloni had noticed that Arabus would make no effort to stop her, shrugging off the incidence with a laugh. The primitives would shrink to the ground whenever he came near as though in total awe of him.

Her reverie was interrupted ay an agonized cry from the girl. "It's coming, it's coming," yelled Oah, and for the next fifteen minutes both he and Eloni were very busy bringing the infant into the world. Oah gently washed the screaming child with water and, turning proudly to Eloni, said "It's a girl." Eloni bent to examine the infant carefully and then started back in some horror for the child's skin was pale cream color.

"Take it," he commanded, but Eloni shrank back with distaste and so Oah walked by her and went outside the hut. For a moment he held the child aloft as though in triumph and then lowered it to his waist. "Look, come and look, it's a girl." The primitives crowded around, mixed feelings showing in their eyes.

At that moment Arabus was seen striding along the path towards the settlement. "What have you got there?" he called.

"A girl, a baby girl."

Arabus ran up to have a closer look.

"What a pale skin. Whose is it?" he queried.

"It's yours, of course," replied Oah.

"Mine? Yes."

"Yes, this is the child of the primitive girl you raped in the ship, before my eyes. Here, you take it."

He thrust the squalling infant into Arabus' arms, much to the latter's astonishment. A gasp of horror ran through the crowd of primitives and they fell to the ground. Arabus just stood there, staring first at the child and then at the primitives. Oah watched him take several deep breaths and push out his chest as though praising himself. After a few minutes he turned to Oah and handed the baby back.

"You may take charge of her now," he said, "and I will go and try to think up a suitable name. Remember what happened to my child by Eloni and make sure that there is no recurrence of that event. I expect she will be quite glad to take care of this infant."

Oah decided not to disillusion him of this.

Turning now to the primitives, Arabus announced grandly. "I am the father. Take note. I shall be here more frequently than before."

Eloni, who had been watching and listening from the open doorway guessed that these remarks would probably go right over the primitives' heads. She saw Arabus arrogantly pat one or two of their bowed heads as he swaggered back down the pathway, Matester skipping happily by his side.

"Oah, how could you?" challenged Eloni as the still protesting infant was brought back to the hut.

"Well, it might just as well be his. After all, it could have been." He thrust the child at its mother who took her and put her to her breast quite impassively. Eloni watched as the child started to suckle and then left. She wanted to find Anice to tell her that all would be well now that she had visible proof of the success of Oah's experiments.

While he was at the primitive settlement, Oah made his rounds of all the pregnant females who were at varying stages of their pregnancies. The few men who had remained after the illness followed him apathetically. Looking at them, Oah found himself wishing that they would all fall to the ground in front of him. After all, wasn't it he who had got their women pregnant? Hadn't he cured their men? When it had suited him, of course. What would their lives have been like if we had not landed there? He wanted to yell at them that he, not Arabus, was the great one, the genius. But it was no good. He could not communicate directly with them. He smote his fists together in utter frustration. He would have to think of some other way to demonstrate his superiority to them.

Back at the landing site, Eloni found Anice and told her the news. Anice looked a little unconvinced but Eloni reassured her that all would be well when her time came.

"I will go and see Oah when he comes and ask his opinion," she said distrustfully.

"All right. You do that. I am sure he will confirm all that I have just told you. Look, here comes Arabus. Go and ask him."

"Arabus, wel…."

"Go on. After all he is the father."

The two women walked across the clearing and stood in front of Arabus as he headed towards the ship. He raised his arm in a mock salute.

141

"Hail, my two good looking members of the sex I like best."

"Glad to hear that," murmured Anice, but Eloni just shook her head.

"Well, don't just stand there, say something or move out of my way."

"Is it true, Arabus, that you are the father of another baby?" asked Anice hesitantly.

"Yes. Yes, I have another daughter and this one is healthy," he replied, shooting a blackbrowed look at Eloni who ignored him.

"And are you sure you are the father?"

"Of course I am. After all, you were practically there. Oah witnessed the intercourse and the baby is of our coloring. What more proof do you expect, woman?"

"Nothing," replied Anice.

"Just a minute," sneered Arabus, "now I am beginning to realize. You are pregnant too, and you suspect I might be responsible. Is that it? Giving her breasts a hard squeeze.

Anice stepped back. "No. No, I was just curious."

"No, you were not. Anyway, I am not the father of your child. That is Oah's responsibility."

"Oah? But he cannot. At least he never did with me."

Arabus let out a great bellow of laughter. "Well, well. The great doctor makes fools of us all. Maybe he struck it rich with you when you weren't looking. You will just have to question him, won't you? After all, who else could it be? Uth? Aqa, eh?"

"Stop it," screamed Anice, racing away across the clearing with her hands clamped over her ears.

"Well, whatever got into her? You women." He eyed Eloni. "Would you like to have another child besides your precious Abeno?" he asked speculatively. Eloni stared at him.

"I would rather lie with all the remaining crew and the primitive males before submitting to you again, Arabus," and she stalked away to find Anice. She eventually found her crouched in a dark corner of their sleeping hut.

"Whatever is the matter with you, Anice?"

"I am frightened."

"But surely you have nothing to worry about now that a baby has been born and is quite normal."

"But just look at me," cried Anice. Eloni stared at Anice as she stood up and then turned sideways. She realized that although she was only about six months pregnant she was simply huge.

"It could be that you are going to have a double birth like Rester had on Capernica."

"But Oah? Oh no, Eloni, I cannot believe that. I am sure I am the victim of one of his ghastly experiments," and she flung herself down on to the ground and started to sob. Eloni tried to comfort her as best she could but finding this less than completely successful she left the hut to find Aqa and Abeno. She found them sitting companionably together under the shade of a tree at the edge of the clearing. Eloni related to them all that had happened. They went on to discuss the pattern of events from the time of their departure from Capernica.

"I still cannot believe that we have come all this way for nothing. There must be some purpose behind it all," said Aqa.

"Very difficult to see at times, but I do agree with you," replied Eloni.

Just at that moment Matester burst into the clearing carrying something in her hands. "Look, look what I have found," she shouted.

"What have you got there, child?" called Aqa, and Eloni rose to have a closer look.

Matester held the object out for her inspection. Eloni caught her breath with shock.

"Give it to me," she ordered.

"No."

"What is it? What is going on?" It was Arabus mooching over.

"Look father, look what I have found, and there are plenty more."

She thrust the object at Arabus who took it and dropped it.

"It is a skull," he cried.

"Where did you find it?"

"I am not telling."

"Oh, yes you will. Come here, child," his voice changing to a wheedling whine. Matester stood there uncertainly and while she was making up her mind the remaining members of the compound drifted over to see what was going on.

"I think Oah should see it," – this was Uth who had joined the crowd.

"I agree," said Eloni.

"Be quiet, woman," snapped Arabus.

"I still think Oah should see this," reiterated Uth.

There was a murmur of assent from the others. Arabus strode over to Matester and snatched the skull. Matester immediately gave him a well-aimed kick on the leg. Arabus tossed the skull aside and Uth picked it up. As the others watched the scuffle Uth ran over to the ship.

Oah examined the skull with rising interest. "It is definitely human. Tell me again where you found it."

"I told you, Oah, Matester found it."

"And where did she find it, I wonder?"

"Go and ask her yourself," said Uth rather rudely. Looking at Oah's rather thin figure with his gaunt face and high forehead Uth wondered if he really saw day to day living in the same light as the rest of them.

"Where is Matester now?" he asked Uth sharply.

"Arabus was wrestling with her by the edge of the clearing."

"Well, let us go and see what we can elucidate from the child."

The two of them made their way back to the little crowd and Oah thrust his way to the front. Eloni had hold of Matester who was kicking and biting. Arabus was standing scowling at the two of them.

"Matester, were did you find this?" asked Oah peremptorily.

"I told you I did not have it," screamed Matester at her father.

"All right, all right. Where did you get that?" asked Arabus, pointing to the skull which Uth held.

"Uth brought it to me," answered Oah, "and I demand to know where you found this."

Matester stopped her activities momentarily surprised by the authority in Oah's voice.

"I will show you if you will let me help you with one of the experiments you do."

"No, definitely not."

"I will not show you my secret place, then."

"Come on Arabus, make her tell us where she found it. This could be very important."

"Oah, all you are worried about is the experiments and research. I will not force her to tell you unless you let her help with one of your experiments."

"Very well, I will."

Matester erupted with shouts of joy and it was some time before she calmed down enough for her to lead the way.

"Is it far?" queried Eloni.

"No."

"Well, can we get there and back today?"

Matester looked doubtful.

"Maybe we should go tomorrow morning."

"I want to go now," said Oah.

"Don't be so selfish," retorted Eloni.

"What do the rest of you think?" Oah appealed to them.

"Tomorrow," said Uth, and the others nodded.

"Tomorrow it is," said Eloni. "Matester, you come and spend the night with Abeno and me and then we shall be ready to leave together in the morning."

"Go with Eloni," ordered Arabus as he disappeared into the jungle. The rest of them disperse, Oah striding back to his ship.

They were all ready early next morning. Eloni left Aqa with Abeno as he was uncertain as to how his leg would stand up to a long walk. Matester was unable to give anyone any indication of the distance. She seemed fairly cheerful this morning and ran beside Oah, pestering him with questions. The doctor had difficulty in restraining his temper. They had walked for about an hour following a barely discernible path. Most of them were rather quiet as though they feared what they would see. Matester seemed totally unconcerned laughing and skipping and obviously thoroughly enjoying her unaccustomed role as the star attraction. Presently she dived to the right and disappeared in the undergrowth.

"Matester, come back," called Arabus.

"Not if you want to see the skulls," came the reply.

"Very well," and Arabus went to join here.

"Just a moment," said Uth. "We should take precautions. This is still wild jungle."

"Rubbish," said Oah. "Let's go. We are wasting time."

They stood uncertainly on the path.

"Well, I'm going," said Oah and left.

"We had better follow them," said Uth. "We do not want to lose them."

They all followed his lead as they started to wind their way through the undergrowth. They could hear the others crashing about ahead of them, in particular Oah who was apparently having some difficulty in negotiating the dense foliage. Progress was slow for them but evidently Matester, being so small, had no such difficulty and in the distance they could hear Arabus yelling at her to slow down.

"I wonder how she found this place," remarked Eloni to Uth.

"That child is capable of anything," Uth replied.

They all pressed on for a while when they became aware of the silence. Anxiously the pressed forward. Suddenly they were upon it. A small hollow in the middle of the brush, free of vegetation except for long grass which swayed and rippled in the slow moving air. Scattered among this were skulls. Eloni estimate she could see about twenty of them, and Oah was already on hands and knees examining one of them. Matester was playing games around them and Arabus was kicking one around with his foot. The rest of them sat down on the bank and gazed at this sight.

"Those primitives must cut off their heads and bring them here. Maybe this is a sacred place to them," said Uth with an involuntary shiver.

"No. I think they must bring whole bodies out here as when I was helping Oah when the primitive had their sickness we never could find any bodies."

"I think it is horrible," said Uth.

"Look here," cried Oah, who had moved to the far side of the clearing.

They rushed over to have a look. Oah pointed down at the body of a young girl propped up in the grass. Some fruits lay beside her.

"I think they must have put her here," he said.

Eloni gave a shriek of horror. "Oah, Oah! It is the girl who had the baby!"

"Nonsense, Eloni."

"But it is, it is."

"Let me have a look," he said kneeling down he bent to examine the body.

"Can he not tell by looking at her features?" said Uth.

Eloni shook her head.

"I would have thought so," she replied.

"Eloni, you are right. It is her," said Oah standing up. "And I cannot find a cause of death. How extraordinary! She was perfectly all right when we left here, wasn't she?"

"All right?" Eloni looked at him in horror. The doctor really did not comprehend what he had done.

"The baby. Where is the baby, I wonder? I must go and find her." She said, and ran.

"Well, I am going to gather some of these for further examinations," said Oah.

"Maybe you should not touch them," said Uth.

"Don't be ridiculous," said Oah. "These people are primitive. They have obviously never tried any other way of getting rid of their dead. We must show them about burning. Much more hygienic." He picked up several of the skulls and presently returned to re-examine the girl. He evidently was not satisfied but reluctantly decided to leave. As they all filed back along the path Matester came bounding up.

"Can I help you re-examine one of these skulls, Oah?" she asked.

"Well I will try to find something for you to do," he said, and they continued on their way. No one apparently noticed that Arabus was gone again.

Eloni was running back to the compound as fast as she could. She was actually not worried about the primitive girl's baby as she was about Anice. She mustn't know, she thought. I will have to keep her in the hut and forewarn the others.

Anice had taken advantage of Oah's and others' absence to explore the doctor's laboratory in the ship. Every single item, whether bottles or pickled pieces of tissue, were all neatly labelled. As she read each one Anice was conscious yet again of the violent movements within her and she realized that

146

soon it would be her time. After a thorough check she turned her attention to the drawers beneath the shelves. All the notes that Oah had made were there in chronological order. Anxiously she scanned them, stuffing most of them back into the drawers with an impatient shake of her head. Finally she found the notes pertaining to the experiments and was soon deeply absorbed in reading them.

"Anice! What are you doing?" said Oah, and she gave a guilty start.

"I was looking for details of your experiments, dear doctor, particularly those in reference to the girl who has just had her baby."

"And what did you think you would find?" he asked sarcastically.

"The truth about this creature within me," she replied.

"And did you?"

"No. I was still reading about the experiment on that poor wretch."

"Well, I have told you all I am going to, so you can return the papers and leave. I have a lot of work to do."

Anice became aware for the first time of what he was holding.

"Is that the girl?" she asked in horrified tones.

"No, Anice, it is not," and he went on to tell her about what they had found. "However," he continued, "you may be interested to know that we also found the skull of a newly-born baby, from which you may deduce.... Anice." Oah rushed forward to catch her as she fell. Carefully he carried her to one of the couches and laid her down.

"Oah what is the matter with Anice? I have been searching for her." It was Eloni. Oah explained what had happened.

"You celibate man of medicine," she stormed. "You have no intelligence at all when it comes to handling living people. You are so impervious to warm, human feeling. You should have stayed behind." Oah said nothing but continued to attend to Anice. Finally he looked up and said to Eloni, "You had better help. She is starting to contract and will deliver some time this evening." Wordlessly Eloni went to help, her feelings wrenching at the sight of gay, outgoing Anice lying there in silent torment. Hours went by and still there was no sign of any delivery. Anice swayed between periods of pain-filled consciousness and blessed unconsciousness. Oah fretted back and forth. "She should be producing," he kept muttering.

"What are you going to do?" asked Eloni after yet another hour had gone by.

"I will have to deliver it by Caesarean section," said Oah authoritatively as though he had suddenly come to a decision. "Go and find Aqa. He can help. I don't think you will want to stay," he said. Eloni nodded and left.

Presently Aqa returned and together the two men formed a silent partnership. Meanwhile Eloni put Abeno to bed and then lay on her cot waiting for news. She could see the outlines of the two men as they crossed and recrossed in front of the windows. Surely it would soon be over. At last she fell into an uneasy doze when Aqa shook her awake.

"Eloni, can you come? It is Anice."

"What is it?"

"Just come. I have arranged for Uth to sleep here in case Abeno awakes."

Eloni grabbed him by the arm. "What has happened? Is Anice all right/"

'Yes, she is, but….," and his voice broke.

"What? What?"

"The babies."

"Babies, Aqa, what are you talking about?"

Aqa began to limp to the door. "Come on, Eloni, there is no time to waste."

As fast as they could they went to the ship. Stepping inside Eloni was struck by the silence. Advancing across the cabin she saw Anice lying still and pale on the operating table.

"Is she dead?" she cried.

"No, no, she is asleep, thank goodness, although she is very weak," spoke Oah, who emerged from the far end.

Noticing how flat her stomach was Eloni said, "And where is the baby?"

"Sit down, Eloni," he said firmly.

"But where is the baby?"

"Eloni, I don't know how to tell you," and Oah buried his head in his hands. "Anice's babies are dead, and I killed them."

"But why?"

"It was awful….." His voice trailed into silence and he began to sob.

"Aqa, tell me please."

Quietly and concisely Aqa told her. Anice had been a difficult patient, fighting the labor pains, and Oah had been forced to sedate her. The delivery followed quickly, neither of them realizing that there were two babies. When the first one appeared Oah and Aqa simultaneously realized that there was something awfully wrong. The baby's head was far too big for its body. "Monstrous, it was," shivered Aqa. On checking Anice, Oah had realized that there was another one to come and it too, was the same way. Swiftly and ruthlessly he had destroyed them and then put Anice into a deep sleep. Now explained Aqa, he was haunted that all the primitive women could possibly give birth to the similar beings. Eloni stared at him in widening horror as Aqa recounted the events of the evening. The conversation was halted by loud banging on the door.

"Oah, Oah, I want to see my next child," said the all too familiar voice of Arabus.

He must have heard the news somehow and was now waiting to gorge himself with the glory of being a father again. Eloni ran to the door and opened it. Arabus stood there as disheveled and dirty as ever, leering at her, eyes half glazed.

"Anice has had twins, dean, and they are not yours but bastard experiments of Oah's" she screamed and slammed the door shut.

The next few minutes of Eloni's life passed in a haze as Oah's predictions became nightmarishly true. One or two of the infants were apparently normal but most of them were creatures who were destroyed. What the primitive women thought she had no idea. Most of them gave her some sign of recognition and they all seemed to be fond of Abeno, who spent more and more time with them. She saw very little of Arabus during these times. His absences from the main camp were more pronounced as they became longer and longer. Matester was often left to amuse herself and Eloni watched as she began to show an increased interest in Oah. Eloni assumed that her imagination must have been stimulated by the discovery of the skull site. Eloni was increasingly concerned over Anice, who had lost most of her vigor and vitality. The only times she would show signs of her dominant personality was when another baby was due to be delivered. She would appear silently and watch, and when it had to be destroyed she would taunt Oah. The doctor became even more withdrawn and when he was not attending to his patients Eloni would find him hunched over piles of notes in his laboratory. At night Eloni would lie on her cot and alternatively watch Abeno and the night sky. Her thought would retrace the steps to the leaving of Capernica, and she would feel a surge of longing as she thought of Abello.

As she spent so much time at the primitive village she had begun to look upon it as her home. She noticed that the older children had apparently accepted Abeno without reservation and indeed seemed more than pleased to follow his lead. One of the huts in the center had apparently been left for her and Abeno and she had managed to bring a few personal possessions with her each time she came over. She noticed, too, that one of the men would shadow her. He was a shade taller than the rest and was obviously held in high esteem by the others. Once or twice as she stayed by a patient all night she would feel something whisper across her hair, but when she turned around there would be nothing there. Increasingly, however, she felt more secure in the little primitive compound than she did at the original camp.

One morning as she was nearing the end of the long trek from the primitive village to the camp she walked into Uth and Efa.

"Eloni, we have not seen you for a long time."

149

"I have been busy helping Oah with all the deliveries."

"We think it is terrible," blurted Efa. "We thing the doctor went too far. If he had left us all alone I am sure some of us would have made the primitive woman pregnant."

Eloni flinched.

"Well, it is probably true," said Uth. "Sit down a minute, please. We would like to talk with you."

Eloni moved to the side of the road in order to be under the shake of the trees. Uth thought how tired she looked. Gone was the happy relaxed woman who had arrived with them from Capernica. She looked many years older and her beautiful black hair was streaked with gray. We are all aging fast, he thought, shivering suddenly.

"What is it you want to talk about?" questioned Eloni.

"As Efa was saying, we are increasingly dissatisfied with our lives. We were banished from Capernica and we survived the trip, it would seem to no avail," said Uth.

"We are going away," said Efa.

"Away/" said Eloni.

"Yes," they chorused.

"We have been talking among ourselves for several days now. We are going to find another place and start afresh," said Uth.

"And we are to take, or rather negotiate for two primitive women each," said Efa.

"He has some seeds saved from the first crops we planted here and we feel we have enough knowledge to succeed."

Eloni nodded. "Will you come with us?" asked Uth.

She shook her head. "I cannot leave. I must stay and try to put right the many things that have gone wrong since we came. But why not stay here?"

"Because of Oah and Arabus. We feel that Oah would always be watching us and Arabus is too unpredictable nowadays."

"Well, I can understand, and I wish you two well. If you would like I will come to the village with you and see if I can help communicate your desires to the primitives."

"Thank you, we would appreciate that, wouldn't we, Efa?" said Uth. Efa nodded. "Come on," said Uth cheerily and pulled Eloni to her feet. Wearily she started back down the trail with the two men, not realizing that if she had only continued upon her way she might have forestalled the turn of events which were to have such a horrific effect upon the remaining survivors of the journey. But happily and innocently she did not, and continued walking between the two men but conscious, too, of the unseen watcher who looked after her. By the time darkness fell they were almost halfway to the primitive village. The two men were quite eager to continue but they realized that Eloni was tired. They found a small sheltered clearing and sat down. Neither of them had given any thought to eating, but Uth did manage to find some fruit for them to such on. Eloni was soon asleep, and silently Efa and Uth lay down either side of her and slept. Up early the next morning they were soon on their way to the primitive village.

"Hallo, hallo, hallo," greeted Oah as they emerged into the clearing. "What brings you two men here, and Eloni – I thought you had gone back to our base." She shook her head.

"These two wanted to see the village again and they were curious as to how you were faring with the results of your experiments," she added bitterly.

The two men said nothing but followed Eloni past the doctor and on towards the hut which she now considered hers. She found Abeno there playing a game with a couple of the primitive children and Aqa watching over them. She had a few words with Aqa and kissed Abeno fondly before leaving again.

"I am looking for a particular primitive," she told Uth and Efa, who nodded. "Did you have any particular women in mind?"

"No. No, we did not, but we would like them young," said Uth.

"Because we want children," said Efa, rather shyly.

"I see," said Eloni, and fell silent. Just then she caught a glimpse of Primo behind one of the huts and darted towards him. He stood there watching her approach with no apparent change of expression. Gently Eloni took him and pulled him towards the two men. He was obviously very doubtful as to her intentions but his hand remained firmly in hers. Eloni realized after a few minutes of heavily one-sided conversation that it was impossible to communicate Uth and Efa's request to Primo. She therefore again took Primo's hand and led him down the main path.

"Take a look at the women as we go by," she instructed them, "and when and if you see the ones you want, let me know." They nodded.

They must have walked about the village for about half an hour before suddenly the two men gave a cry. They had walked behind the huts and came upon a group of women laying an animal skin out to dry. Uth pointed to one and Efa to another.

"Go and bring them over here," suggested Eloni.

The women looked up at their approach, but the selected two offered no resistance. Probably conditioned by Oah's treatment, thought Eloni wryly. The four of them stood in front of Eloni and the primitive. Eloni tried to indicate by hand signals what they wanted. Not a flicker of enlightenment passed over Primo's face or over the two women's, as a matter of fact.

"What is going on here?" came the voice of Oah.

Efa and Uth looked at each other.

Eloni put up her hand. "Oah, have you not any patients to attend to?"

"No. All seems to be quiet for the moment."

"What are you going to do?"

"I was on my way for a short rest when I saw the six of you standing looking so serious, and I am naturally curious."

No one said anything for a moment.

"You had better explain to him, he is bound to find out," said Efa tonelessly.

"Are you sure?" said Eloni. They nodded.

"Why don't you four walk on ahead and I will explain to Oah," suggested Eloni. This they did. By the time she had watched them set off up the path Eloni realized that Primo had disappeared. She then turned to Oah and explained Uth and Efa's plan to him.

"Hm, I see. Fundamentally it is a good idea," said the doctor, rather surprisingly, "but there is one major problem."

"What now?"

"Well….." The doctor hesitated.

"Go on," insisted Eloni.

"These people are completely different from us. I know they have two arms, two legs, etc. but their blood type, molecular structure and other physical structures are different."

"So?"

"Well, they may have intercourse all they want but they will never impregnate the women. It just isn't possible. The two sets of people are different races. Just like you wouldn't have a treeclimbing animal copulating with an animal who lives on the ground."

Eloni looked at him, puzzled for a moment.

"But when you had all of the women imprisoned in your ship and you used to let them out so that the men could enjoy them and then they became pregnant, how do you account for that?"

"Because, my sweet Eloni, all that was just an exercise to keep the men happy. It was my experimentation with them that made them pregnant," he finished proudly.

Eloni looked at him in horror. She had always suspected this but secretly hoped she would never have it confirmed. "No wonder Anice is so bitter," she spat. "At least I had my children conceived naturally, although one was rather forced upon me. It is still better than carrying a bastard experiment of yours."

"Eloni, you condemn me too, but it was your Abello who brought us

152

here safely. We have survived the hazards of the journey and the landing, only to find we are dying slowly one by one and this will leave no trace of us for future generations to find. Surely as it is within my power to help, I must."

"But I have had Abeno."

"But who would Abeno mate with. He cannot have children by the children with whom he plays now. And after your skull has been laid out in the sun by the primitive people, what then of Abeno? An empty life and a welcome death. No. No. I had to experiment, and I will continue to do so. Naturally I did not expect such a high failure rate but next time I will do better." The doctor finished and strode purposefully off to catch up with the other four.

Eloni sank to the ground and started to weep silently. Gradually she was aware of strong hands around her and she knew instinctively it was Primo. This time it was she who allowed herself to be led to his hut, where he laid her on the floor and poured a cooling drink between her lips.

Meanwhile, Oah had caught up with Efa, Uth and the two women. "I must talk to you both," he said firmly.

Efa and Uth looked at each other. "Very well, let us hear what you have to say."

"Sit down over here in the shade and I will explain to you what I have just tried to explain to Eloni. All I ask is that you listen to me and then when I have finished you can comment."

The two men nodded. Oah then proceeded to tell them in precise details what he had just outlined to Eloni. The two men listened as requested, not showing either a positive or a negative attitude. At length the doctor sank back, worn out by his impassioned attempt to reach the two men's minds.

"Excuse us a minute," said Uth, and he motioned to Efa to follow him. The two of them stood talking and gesticulating to one side for quite a while. All this time the two women sat side by side and stared at Oah, who had by now dozed off. Finally Uth and Efa approached Oah.

"As you no doubt realize, Oah, we have been discussing the facts you have given us and drawing our conclusions."

"We are not at all pleased with the information but accept that you are telling the true facts," added Efa.

Oah nodded.

"We have decided," continued Uth, "that we will take four women between the two of us and return to the compound. There you will operate on two of them."

"Two?" queried Oah.

"Yes, two," repeated Uth.

"We will then continue with our plan and we will let you know in due course whether your experiments are successful or not. Depending upon this and the sexes of the children, if there are any, we will then consider our next moves. Agreed Efa?" Efa nodded.

"I see," said Oah. "Very well, we will start tomorrow for the compound."

He left, and Uth and Efa went to find Eloni. They explained their decision to her. She agreed with them that their suggestion was probably for the best, and added that she would return with them tomorrow leaving Abeno and Aqa with the primitives.

The eight of them made a silent group as they made the journey once again back to the compound. It took them two days to complete the trip because the four primitive women seemed reluctant to move very fast. Privately Eloni could not blame them as they probably remembered the previous trips. When at last they arrived at the clearing all appeared normal and quiet. Oah strode purposefully ahead of them to the ship. Eloni noticed that it had by now lost most of its layers of protective paint and looked worn and rusty. Hard to believe that once it had been their home. As they walked up the steps Anice appeared at the top with Matester by her side.

"The great doctor returns with more women for experiments," she mocked.

"Anice, please," said Oah.

"Well, it may interest you to know that Matester and I have been trying out our own experiments while you were gone."

"Oh, no," exclaimed Oah, and pushing the two of them aside rushed into the ship. Eloni could hear muffled exclamations. Uth, Efa and the four primitive women sat down on the steps and she ran on inside. A scene of chaos met her eyes. Anice and Matester must have taken out all Oah's notes and strew them around. In addition, most of the bottles were lying around, either empty or half empty. None of the livestock remained. All Oah's papers were strewn around the ship. Oah collapsed in a chair, his hands clasped to his head.

"Well, Matester, it looks as though you and I have achieved some effect with our experiments. The great doctor shows emotion at long last."

"I enjoyed cutting up the animals the best," added Matester.

"Dissecting is the correct word," said Anice.

"How could you Anice?" said Eloni.

"Don't tell me that you, dear sweet Eloni, are critical of what Matester and I have done. It is not as bad as what the doctor did to me. No. I enjoyed it all, and so did my helper here."

"You should not have encouraged Matester," said Eloni. "She has inherited the predominantly malevolent nature of her father and needs no encouragement."

At that moment a burst of raucous singing interrupted them. "It is my father," said Matester, and ran out to greet him.

Anice took another look around the cabin. "I am leaving now that you have returned, Oah, but I shall be back and she strode out.

Oah remained hunched in his chair while Eloni began clearing up the mess.

Presently Uth came over and asked, "Will Oah still carry out his experiments on our two women?"

"Ask him," retorted Eloni. Uth crossed over to talk to Oah. During this time Efa had remained seated with the four women at the back of the ship. After a while Uth walked over and discussed something with Efa. Their heads nodded in agreement and quietly all six of them left. Presently Oah stood up wearily.

"Thank you for your help, Eloni, but I can now manage. I must prepare this ship and myself for tomorrow's experiments. Yes," he said in answer to Eloni's quizzical look. "I shall operate. I still believe in what I am dong. Now, if you will go and leave me."

Eloni nodded and walked out of the ship, across the compound and into her little hut, which seemed strangely bare. Suddenly shivering she crawled into bed and lay there listening to Arabus' drunken murmurings and a low pitched laugh in reply, which could only belong to Anice. Quiet, suddenly she found herself longing for the primitive compound and the comparative serenity of her life there with Abeno, Aqa and the others. Next time I leave this place it will be may final move, she thought. I need nothing here and I shall make my life with the primitives. Reassured by this thought she fell asleep.

The next few days passed smoothly enough. Uth and Efa came to see her alternately to inform her of the progress of the operations. She say very little of Anice or Arabus and Matester, and nothing of Oah. She informed Uth and Efa of her decision not to return to the camp and they agreed with her. She would have liked to have told Anice but hesitated because of her relationship with Arabus. After a week Efa came to tell her that the two women had apparently recovered and that soon they would be on their journey. He also told her that Anice and Arabus had both been in and out of the ship, but had kept very quiet. He told Eloni that due to the unpredictability of Arabus' behavior they planned to slip away at night. Probably two nights from now, and if she would like to travel with them she would be welcome. Eloni readily agreed. She was impatient to leave. As she walked down to the river the following day Anice appeared beside her. She appeared fairly cheerful, although rather nervous.

At length she told Eloni. "You were quite right about Matester, she is now carrying out all sorts of experiments day and night with lots of encouragement from her father. In fact, the two of them often disappear into the jungle for the day, and I know they have been back to the primitives' graveyard as they appear with various bones."

Eloni grimaced.

"I know, I know, but I am an impatient woman and a vindictive one, too, and I wanted to revenge Oah for what he had done to me. I still will, but I wanted you to be warned about Matester. I know you often took her to the primitive village, and there is no telling what she will get up to there."

Having finished she disappeared before Eloni had a chance to say anything. Eloni turned back towards the camp, as she was suddenly apprehensive about straying any further on her own. When she returned she found Arabus and Matester sitting in the middle of the camp ground, taking turns to pull the legs off some eight legged creatures they had captured. They had other assorted insect-like creatures tied together, and would every once in a while give the strings sharp jerks, so as to almost maim the creatures.

"Stop it!" said Eloni. Neither of them took any notice of her.

"Stop it!" she repeated. Again there was no reaction. Eloni then picked up a stone and smashed it on the eight legged creature's head.

"You have spoilt my game," said Matester and burst into sobs.

"Arabus, you must stop her, teach her respect for living creatures," berated Eloni.

"Just like I do," replied Arabus, leering nastily at her.

Eloni ignored that remark, and kneeling down started to untie the strings.

"Be careful, Eloni," called Oah, "I know that some of them are poisonous."

Eloni jumped back, and Arabus laughed. "So much for your good intentions, woman," he mocked.

Oah appeared wearing gloves and carrying a surgical instrument. He came over and carefully removed the strings from the crawling insects. As the creatures began to scuttle away Matester who had been watching the proceedings, jumped forward and picked one up.

"Drop, Matester," they all cried.

"No, it is mine," she yelled.

She began to back away from the three of them as they advanced towards her. Unfortunately she did not realize that one of the creatures was behind her and she trod on it. Silence. Then she screamed.

"She has been bitten," said Arabus.

"Carry her to the ship immediately," said Oah as Arabus picked her up.

The three of them rushed her inside where Arabus laid her on one of the tables. Oah began to search frantically through his collection of medicines while Eloni and Arabus tried to calm the screaming child.

"Hurry up, you fool," ordered Arabus.

"Better that I take my time and find the right one," retorted Oah.

In the short time it had taken for them to bring her to the ship her foot had already swollen and now her leg was started to swell. Oah suddenly gave a grunt of approval and quickly filled a syringe with some orange fluid. He quickly turned Matester over on to her stomach and gave her a shot in her left buttock.

"What does that do?" enquired Arabus.

"I have given her a mixture of sedative and what I hope is an antibiotic for the bit."

"What do you mean, you hope?"

"Well, I am not certain because I do not know the type of poison."

"But you might have given her the wrong one."

Oah said nothing.

"You heard what I said."

"Yes, but I will tell you that I had all my medicines in neat, organized, labelled rows, but while I was over attending to the primitive women Anice and Matester came in here and upset everything."

"Anice and Matester?"

"Yes."

"Well, what are we going to do?"

"Arabus, I would like you to go and catch one of those creatures."

"Why?"

"Because, Arabus, if you can catch one and bring it here I can get it to bite something, then I can analyze the poison and maybe find an antidote for your daughter."

Arabus looked at him for a moment and then wordlessly he picked up one of the cages and disappeared out of the ship. Oah and Eloni sat on either side of the now sleeping Matester and watched and waited. Every so often Oah would check her pulse and Eloni would bathe her forehead with water. Darkness stole across the clearing and through the ship but neither of them moved to turn on the lights. The hours passed and the two of them sat motionless, waiting.

As dawn pushed back the dark Oah said, "Go to your hut, Eloni, and rest. I can manage. You should not take on any more burdens."

Eloni stood up wearily and left. As she crossed the clearing she met Anice who had obviously come back from a morning swim. She greeted Eloni cheerily but soon her happy mood dissipated.

"I will go and sit beside her," she said. "I feel that I am partly responsible as I encouraged that side of her nature while you and Oah were gone."

"Thank you," said Eloni, and watched her cross the clearing.

Soon she was lying on her cot and thankfully sleeping. When she woke up it was past noon. For a moment she lay there, luxuriating in the warm rays of the sun, but then the memory of the night flooded back and she rushed over to the ship. Inside all looked the same.

"Is she better?"

"No. No sign of improvement yet."

"Did Arabus return yet?"

"Yes, he brought several of the insects back and Oah is now trying frantically to find a solution. Arabus has disappeared again, I don't know where."

Eloni went over to see if she could help Oah but the doctor brushed her away. Eloni became aware of raised voices coming closer. Suddenly the door burst open and Arabus flung Anice inside.

"Here, doctor, I have brought you the meddler. Make her help you to find the correct solution. I want her to see Matester suffer."

Anice stood up and spat on Arabus. Arabus leapt forward but Eloni ran between the two of them.

"Stop it, the pair of you. Where is your compassion? Matester is the only being who matters at the moment."

Arabus looked at her for a moment and then went and sat down beside his daughter. Anice walked over the help Oah and calm was, for the time being, restored. The time that followed was long and silent. Matester's body was now all swollen and her face was flushed. At length Oah came across.

"I have found some antidotes, but I think I should first puncture her skin and see if I can draw any of the poison out. Have I your permission to do this, Arabus?"

"Yes," said Arabus almost inaudibly, and for the first time since she had known him Eloni felt a stab of sympathy for him.

"Very well, I will do it on her foot where the insect bit her."

All eyes followed Oah as he made the incision and soon the air was filled with the stench of poison as the liquid flowed out. After a while the doctor grunted and then expertly sewed up the hole. He quickly gave Matester another shot and then wearily sat down. "All we can do now is wait. You had all better have a rest now."

"I will stay here with Matester," said Anice.

"And so will I," said Arabus.

Eloni left again, walking slowly across the sun-filled clearing. She sat in the shade of her hut for a while. She could only hop at the outcome. Later that evening Oah emerged from the ship. Eloni looked up expectantly as he crossed the clearing. "She is better, but only time will tell if there is any permanent damage."

Eloni caught her breath. "You mean the poison was powerful."

"I really know so little about them. It is a marvel that none of us have been bitten before," said Oah. "From my tests I would say that it could leave her paralyzed or damage her brain." Eloni looked at him in horror and realized that they were both thinking of Arabus. How would he react if such a thing happened to his daughter?

"Come for a swim with me," said Oah, and Eloni agreed. "At least our bodies will feel better," Oah remarked drily.

When they returned all was apparently quiet. Eloni left Oah at the door of her hut. "Thank you for the swim. It was really refreshing." Oah nodded. She continued. "I am going to father the rest of my things together and tomorrow I leave permanently for the primitive village. I am telling you in case you should need me but I no longer wish to stay here." Indicating by the sweep of her hand the once proud site where she had set forth on a new life with Abello, she added, "I hope all goes well with you and Matester. Be careful of Arabus and Anice, especially the former is anything should happen to Matester." The doctor looked at her, and then swiftly embraced her before running across the clearing.

Next morning Eloni was gone early as she was anxious to be reunited with Abeno. Her journey was uneventful and she was soon happily resettled with Abeno, Aqa and the primitives. The weeks passed and she soon relaxed, feeling at long last free of the stresses and strains of the past months. The primitive village seemed comparatively undisturbed by past events and apparently normality had returned. One day she was surprised to see Uth enter the village. Upon seeing Eloni he came rushing up to her.

"One of my women, whom I call Uia, is pregnant. I know it is hardly just over the time but I had to tell you, and now I am on my way to tell Oah."

"That is wonderful news, but don't tell Oah."

"Why ever not? His experiment is successful and he certainly deserves to know."

"I realize that, but I am just uncertain as to what his reaction would be."

"Nonsense, Eloni, you worry too much. Anyway I must go. I must not leave my Uia alone too long. You must come and see us," he called over his shoulder as he left. Eloni stared after him, unaccountably afraid. She felt a strong arm around her and turning found Primo standing there. They smiled at each other before she went back to her hut.

Days passed and there was no sign of any react ion from the camp, so Eloni dismissed her fears and began to make plans for a journey to Uth's new home. She was anxious to see how he and Efa had succeeded. She sincerely hoped that all was going well with them. We must succeed here, she thought, my beloved Abello having brought us so far. She was explaining the idea of a visit to Abeno and Aqa when Oah and Arabus appeared in the clearing one afternoon. Both of them looked like wile men and were yelling and singing. "My experiments have succeeded," said Oah, and he and Arabus lurched down the pathway.

"Oah, what has come over you?" chided Eloni.

"My dear sweet Eloni, Oah's experiments have succeeded. My Matester can have the pick of men when she grows up instead of relying on your precious Abeno," sneered Arabus.

"But none of them are suitable," gasped Eloni.

"You thick-headed fool. Oah is going to round them up and redo his experiments – aren't you my friend," leered Arabus.

"Yes, yes," and Oah cracked the long whip he had in his hand.

"No, no."

"Oh yes, and no one, not even you, is going to stop us."

Eloni stepped forward to plead with Oah but before she could reach him Arabus hit her across the face and knocked her unconscious. Suddenly Primo I appeared and picking her up disappeared into one of the huts.

"She'll be all right," said Arabus.

"Maybe I had better check."

"No, no. Let's get on with the work in hand," grunted Arabus running his tongue over his lips.

Oah's eyes lit up, and the two men went to the end of the village. As they returned they stopped at each hut and systematically dragged out any women that were in them. At the end of the village Oah gave a large crack of the whip and Arabus gave them a shove and off they went again down the path. This time the women were markedly more reluctant to leave, and some of them had to be tied together and led by Oah. Aqa watched them go from a vantage point in one of the trees. He shook his head several times as he watched them disappear from view. When all was quiet he crept down and ran back to the hut where Eloni lay. She was actually unconscious for a day and somewhat delirious for a while after that. Arabus' blow had crashed her to the ground with such force that she had been concussed and was in fact barely conscious for a whole week. Aqa and Primo took turns in looking after her and Abeno, who remained calm and helpful throughout. As he explained to Aqa, his mother always seemed to recover no matter what she had been through. Aqa was very glad when she recovered. She evidently had trouble remembering what had caused the blow and he did not want to remind her. However, Abeno told her, and her face registered dismay.

"What can we do?" she cried.

"There is nothing. Nothing we can do," said Aqa as he held her hand. "These people are not advanced enough to rescue their women. We must only hope that some good becomes of these experiments." Eloni nodded wearily and nothing more was said. Several days later Uth came tearing into the camp. It was Aqa who saw him and brought him to Eloni's hut. Uth lay on the ground for several minutes, gasping for breath, while the others clustered around waiting anxiously for him to begin speaking. He sat for a while shaking his head from side to side.

"What is it?" asked Aqa, at length becoming impatient.

"It was ghastly," Uth repeated over and over again.

"What, what?" questioned both Eloni and Aqa.

"Well, we managed to get all but one of the women there. One of them sat down and refused to move. Eventually we had to leave her to her fate. All seemed well at the camp site and Oah and Arabus were soon busy in the surgery. Yes, Arabus as well. Soon the two of them were operating on one woman after another, apparently without encountering any problems. Many hours went by, and the smell of blood and urine was overpowering. I went outside into the dusk and walked about for a while."

"When I returned Anice and Matester were in the s hip. Anice was taunting Oah about his lack of success the last time he operated on these women. The doctor was trying to finish the penultimate primitive, and Arabus was standing beside him. Then Anice pointed to Matester. She told the doctor that he was a failure here, too. Arabus rushed over and grabbed her by the shoulders and shook her violently. 'What do you mean?' he asked. 'Well,' said Anice, 'it is obvious that in spite of her recovery from the bite she had retarded mentally.' Arabus then went over to Matester and in the first gesture of affection I have ever seen him do he cradled her in his arms. He then started to question her about various objects in the room but Matester did not respond to these or to his affectionate touches. Arabus then went over and began to berate the doctor. Oah tried in vain to take no notice, but finally he must have lost all self-control because be....." and here Uth's voice hesitated, "..... he took up a scalpel and drove it deep into Arabus' navel. Arabus gave him a funny look and sank to the floor. Matester seemed unable to understand what had happened, but Anice gave an angry shriek and rushed towards Oah. However, Oah stood his ground with the bloodstained scalpel in his hand. Anice paused and then ran up the steps into the surgery. She cast about for something, and then having obviously found what she wanted she took the syringe and filled it full of this liquid. She then walked calmly back down the steps, across to Oah, and plunged it into his buttock. The doctor leapt into the air and then grabbed hold of Anice. 'What have you given me?' he yelled to her. 'A s hot of your own medicine,' replied Anice nastily. Oah abruptly let go of her arm and finished attending to Arabus. He then continued to operate on the last primitive.

"Anice stood watching him and then went over and spoke to Matester, who was crooning softly on the floor. The two of them left. I did what I could to help and then went outside. Oah seemed very withdrawn and all the women were sleeping. I spent the night dozing fitfully by a small fire that I had built. There was no sign of human life at all, and I was glad to see dawn arrive. I returned to the ship partly to see if everything was all right and partly to see if Oah had any food. To my horror Arabus had the doctor pinned against the wall with one hand, while in the other he held a syringe. Whatever they had been doing it had reopened Arabus' wound and the blood was dripping onto the floor. Oah was alternatively screaming and begging him not to use whatever was in the syringe. I rushed over and tried to push Arabus away, but it was no use. He was beyond human understanding. We struggled for a while, and the he reached over me and stabbed Oah with the needle, several times. Oah opened his mouth but said nothing and slid to the floor. I went to help him but he too pushed me away. Meanwhile Arabus left, leaving a small trail of red spots as he went. I finally managed to pull Oah to his feet and led him over to a chair where I sat him down. There did not seem much more I could do, so I felt. I am anxious to go back to Efa and our two women now. I don't know what has happened to Arabus, Anice or Matester, or the primitive women. I wish I had never gone."

He stopped then, and Eloni gave him something to drink. They were all very silent after this. They could only wait and speculate upon the sorry story that Uth had related. At length Eloni said, "I think I should go back and see if all is all right. Arabus may be unconscious somewhere and Matester obviously needs more care than Anice may be willing to give her."

Aqa smiled at her. "Eloni, after all you have been through I would not return to the encampment for anything."

"I don't want to go," Eloni retorted, "but who else can go? It would take you too long, and after all there are all Primo's women to think about."

"What about Uth?" asked Aqa. "He is so distressed."

"But he does want to return to his new home", said Eloni. "Make him rest here for as long as you can before his journey. Someone ought to go with him."

"I will," piped up Abeno.

"You?"

"Yes, I can take care of him and I shall be all right on the return journey." Eloni gazed at her son as if realizing for the first time how mature he had become. She realized that she had still been thinking in terms of life on Capernica when it came to maturity. Here everything seemed to grow much faster, including people. her son was almost as tall as she was and except for his piping voice looked more like a young man than a child. She sighed inwardly. "Yes, you can go with Uth, Abeno. But please take care."

Abeno hugged her, and then left. "I will go now," she said abruptly.

"But you are hardly well enough, Eloni."

"I know, but I want to find out what is happening," she said impatiently.

Aqa gave a shrug of acquiescence and watched Eloni as she made ready for yet another trip to the compound. However, she had barely reached the end of the center path when she felt dizzy and had to sit down. After a while she continued, but soon the heat and the oppressive atmosphere of an approaching storm overcame her and she collapsed. She did not realize that Primo and two of his fellow primitives carried her back to the hut. Much fuss was made of her then and she was left to sleep away the day. As a result of her abortive attempt to return to the camp, Uth and Abeno left ahead of her and were not there to witness the return of the women with Oah. The women seemed well enough, but the doctor was obviously in a very alarming state. he was waving his arms around and dancing up and down and generally behaving in a most uncharacteristic way. He came prancing down the path and stopped in front of Eloni's hut.

"Eloni, my good woman, and how are you?" he sand out.

"I am much better," she replied in a puzzled tone of voice.

"Good, good. And in response to your unspoken question, I am marvelous. I have had a dose of my own medicine and I am feeling marvelous," he repeated. "Would you like to have sex with me?"

"Oah, what has come over you?" exclaimed Eloni.

"My own medicine," laughed Oah. "Would you believe I have had intercourse with all of these women, and I would still have intercourse with you. There is no limit to my capacity. Can you not see the difference in me/" he leered at Eloni, who was only too aware of the change in Oah.

Before she had a chance to reply to this Oah turned and grabbed one of the primitive women and dragged her behind the hut. The rest of the women filed past and entered their respective huts. Eloni went into hers and sat down. There was obviously no need for her to leave now, and her thoughts returned to Abeno and Uth. All through the day she could hear the sounds and the doctor enjoyed himself with one woman after another. Eloni could only speculate as to the long term results of the shots. She realized that Oah probably did not realize that she knew the full story, and as her thoughts returned to the scene that Uth had described Anice walked in.

"Greetings, Eloni," she said and sat down beside her. "Have you seen

Oah?" she asked.

Eloni nodded.

"I am sure Arabus never realized what he was doing or he wouldn't have been so generous," she said.

"Where are Arabus and Matester?"

"Matester is outside. She followed me, but Arabus has disappeared again."

"I wonder where he goes?"

"It does not matter, he will always return," Anice said confidently.

Eloni looked at her.

"I know what you are thinking," challenged Anice, "but he is the only man left here as far as I am concerned. I would rather have one of his children than another of Oah's experiments." She paused. "But no, I am not pregnant at all."

"I am surprised you did not try Oah while you have the chance," remarked Eloni drily.

"No. That I would not do. I hope he suffers in the end," she said bitterly, not realizing how prophetic her words were.

The two women and Matester spent several days together. Abeno returned to say that Uth was safely back at his new home with Efa and the two women. The small camp was neatly set out and Efa and Uth were busy attending the line of plants they hoped to grow. Uth's woman seemed happy enough and the four of them appeared to have settled in and formed their own language. When they returned to the compound Oah appeared to have recovered, or maybe was resting, after the first effects of the medicine. He asked many questions about Uth's woman, and was also seen playing close attention to Matester. Of Arabus there was still no sign, and Eloni privately began to hope that maybe they had seen the last of him.

Months passed and all was peaceful. Matester now lived permanently with Eloni. Some days she was more alert than others but spent the majority of them sitting on the ground playing endless games with bunches of sticks and twigs, or building different shapes with piles of earth Abeno gave to her. Of Arabus there had been no sign, and Eloni was content to stay in the primitive village. Oah spent quite a lot of time with the primitive women and then would try to encourage some signs of coherent speech from Matester. Eloni noticed that now he seemed even more subdued and she wondered if he was feeling the effects of the medicine. However Oah never referred to that fateful day and neither did she.

Anice divided her time between the two camps and Uth's new home. She seemed to be fascinated by his efforts to establish an independent life and would report all the details to Eloni. The women who belonged to Efa still did not show any signs of pregnancy, but Uth's Uia, as he called her, was now many months along. Abeno often went with Anice on these trips and was maturing rapidly. He was tall with dark hair like his mother but blue eyed like his father and Eloni was often filled with regret that Abello was not here to see him. She also noticed that Primo had appointed himself as her unofficial guardian and had taken to sleeping in the hut across from her, and none of his women ever appeared in this hut. Eloni was hoping that Uia's pregnancy would be successful as she feared Abeno's only other choice of female would be Matester.

She was sitting under her favorite tree one day, gently speculating on these line when Anice came running into the clearing.

"Arabus is coming," she panted, "and he has some syringes in his hands."

Eloni stiffened. What now, she thought. Shortly afterwards Arabus came striding into the clearing.

"Eloni, I am so glad to see you. I want you to be the first to know that I am leaving."

Eloni was speechless for a moment and could only echo his work. "Leaving?"

"Yes, I am leaving, and I am taking Matester with me. I am sure I will find a different world somewhere," waving his hand in a large arc, "a place more like Capernica."

Eloni stared at him disbelievingly. He must have left his senses, she thought.

"Have you nothing to say, woman?" Arabus demanded, grabbing hold of her and shaking her violently. "Leaving," he bellowed into her face.

"What are the syringes for?" she said, pointing to them where they had been flung carelessly on the ground.

"I have been checking over Oah's supplies and injecting myself with various compounds to see what effects they would have. As you can tell, I feel marvelous. Now I am going to see Matester," and he walked over to where Matester was playing on the ground. He squatted down beside her and Eloni watched as he tried to elicit some response from her. Time and again he tried without success. For Arabus, she thought, he is remarkably patient. Finally he shook his head and returned to Eloni. He passed no comment on Matester and merely said, "I will be back when I have completed my preparations. I leave her in your good hands."

Eloni went to find Anice and tell her of the events. She was halfway through when Oah came in, and she recounted the news to him as well. Anice seemed stunned and Oah of course was horrified to learn about the experiments and the syringes. He rushed off to return to the original clearing to check on the equipment. Anice went and sat close to Matester, occasionally reaching out to touch her. A general air of sadness and impending gloom seemed to stifle Eloni. Wearily she sat down and leaned against the tree.

Weeks passed and the air of tension lessened. All thought of Arabus' plans were banished one day when Abeno came racing in to announce that Uia had given birth – apparently without any trouble – to a perfectly formed little girl. Eloni immediately sent him to tell Oah and left herself with Anice to see the new miracle. Uth was overjoyed to see them and proudly showed off his little daughter. She was a tiny coffee-colored, plump little thing, and seemed to be perfectly normal. There was much good rejoicing throughout the day and during the evening. Efa produced a fine meal which was eaten around the fire amidst much merriment. Eloni wondered how Matester was faring with the primitives but soon put the thoughts behind as she relaxed in the first enjoyment she had felt in months. Oah arrived the next morning and soon was involved in weighing and measuring the new baby and checking the mother. He kept chuckling to himself and the three of them stayed with Uth for several days, reluctant to tear themselves away from this contented community. However, Oah said that he would have to leave because some of the primitive women were due to have their babies and he thought that the two women should not risk another journey by themselves through the jungle.

"We should not be complacent," he warned.

Sadly Eloni bade farewell and she and Anice followed Oah back to the primitive village. Abeno begged to stay as he was entranced with the as yet unnamed baby and Eloni agreed to him staying, on the condition that Efa brought him back.

As they neared the village Primo appeared looking very distressed. The three of them began to run in fearful haste. They found no sign of Matester or Aqa. "But Aqa cannot get very far with his leg," said Eloni. "Let us each go a different way and try to find him. I am sure he is near."

In fact it was quite a while before they found Aqa unconscious on the ground on a little-used path. Oah, arriving last, pronounced him alive but suggested they did not move him. Eloni went to fetch some water and Anice began to gather some branches to build a fire. They waited quite a while before Aqa's eyes eventually flickered open. At first he seemed terrified but on hearing Eloni's voice he relaxed. Gradually they discovered that Arabus had appeared soon after they had left and had swooped upon Matester, gathered her in his arms and left. Aqa had followed as best he could, but Arabus had apparently been aware of this, and leaving Matester in the patch had waited until Aqa rounded the corner and struck him on the back of his head. Aqa kept apologizing until Anice told him brusquely to shup up and stop fretting. The next day they returned to the primitive village and tried to decide what to do.

"I really can't believe he would just leave without saying a farewell, at least to you, an ice," said Eloni.

Anice shook her head sadly.

"We must go and find them," said Oah.

After talking it over it was agreed that this was the best thing to do. Wearily they decided to rest and then leave at the first sign of light in the morning. Eloni wished she could explain this to Primo, because she wondered what Abeno would think when and if he returned to the clearing before she did. It was useless to try, though, and she went to sleep. It did not seem very long before Oah was shaking her awake.

"Come on, come," he said urgently. "We do not know how far we have to travel."

Eloni was surprised to find Anice outside, all ready to leave.

"I could not rest," Anice said, and Eloni nodded.

By this time Oah was halfway across the clearing, and taking Anice by the hand Eloni set off after him. They had only the barest indication of the way to go. Poor Aqa had not gone very far before being attacked by Arabus. However, Oah plunged confidently into the bush while the two women tried to keep up. It seemed to Eloni a nightmare day of heat, insects and perpetually fighting for one more step. At long last they came to a small clearing and Oah indicated that they should take a rest. Nobody was very eager to speak and so for about twenty minutes the little group sat silently.

"Come on, we must keep going," said Oah.

"But where?" cried Eloni despairingly.

"I feel quite strongly that we should find the river. Arabus always seemed fascinated by the running water, perhaps because we never had any on Capernica. He has probably found another campsite on one of his sojourns into the trees and is setting up home there."

The two women had to agree with this, and so they followed Oah like the robots who used to do the work on Capernica. The rest of the day passed without any variation in the routine, and at nightfall they all lay down together, too tired to do anything else but huddle into fetal balls clutching at each other for warmth. Halfway through the next morning Oah suddenly put his hand up.

"Listen," he said excitedly. They all stopped and listened.

At first they could not distinguish any different sounds but gradually they became aware of a pounding noise which seemed to be coming from the left of them.

"That must be it," said Anice. "Come on you two, let's go and find out."

They all hurried forward, anxious to see for themselves if it was Arabus or not and to find out what the noise was. They could also hear the noise of water as they pushed forward.

It seemed to Eloni that the sounds of water would play tricks on her mind, one minute she would be nearly deafened by the sound and the next it would be fading away. She followed after Oah and Anice, hurrying along as she sensed that all of them were tense with fear at what they might find. Suddenly Oah gave an exclamation and stopped suddenly. The two women rushed to join him. They stared in amazement at the small, shiny, six-legged ship that perched in an ungainly fashion on the edge of the river bank. After their eyes had adjusted to the bright daylight they saw Arabus emerge, somewhat awkwardly, from the interior and disappear around the back. Slowly the trio walked across the open grassland to the ship. As they neared the vehicle Oah called out Arabus' name.

He came swaggering around the right-hand corner. "Come to see me leave, have you?" he called mockingly. "I thought you would not resist after you found Aqa, the lame fool."

"Where is Matester?" cried Anice.

"Ah, Matester, it is really for her sake you have come," Arabus said angrily. "I should have known you are not interested in me and my fine ship. I built this all myself from parts of the original craft. Thanks to you, Oah, with all those drugs in your medicine locker I have been able to work long and strenuous hours and now it is all done."

"What are you going to do now?" questioned Eloni.

"My dear, sainted Eloni, I thought you would be glad to see me go, or…" advancing upon her, "would you like another turn at having my baby? No?" he laughed, as Eloni backed away. "Well, sit down, all of you, and watch my departure. I have had enough here, and I am travelling on to other planets with my daughter. Anyone can join me."

Oah, Anice and Eloni looked at each other. Oah and Eloni shook their heads and turned and looked at Anice. She also shook her head negatively.

"I thought as much," sneered Arabus. "Too scared to take the risk, but it will work. I am almost ready, so you can wait and watch if you like."

"Matester, is she all right?" asked Anice again grabbing Arabus by the arm as he turned to walk away.

"Yes, yes. I have given her some of the pills that Oah had to make you sleep. She is all right, I tell you." He flung Anice's hand off his arm and ran back to the ship. Anice looked appealingly at the two others.

"She is probably fine," said Oah. "Those pills will do her no harm."

Anice continued to pace up and down as the others watched Arabus disappear inside the ship.

"It will never work," murmured Eloni to herself, and Oah laid a warning hand over her lips.

Suddenly there was a terrific roar from the ship and a spurt of flame. Anice stopped pacing and looked at it as though transfixed. The noise increased, and suddenly with a primeval cry Anice tore across the clearing and flung herself at one of the legs. Eloni and Oah rushed after her but slowly, irrevocably, the ship lifted off the ground, hovered for a moment, and seemed to shake, throwing Anice into the river below. Eloni and Oah watched in horrified fascination as it fathered speed and disappeared from view. Immediately they rushed along the river bank until they could find a place to get down to the water's edge. Oah pointed, and they ran to find Anice's body, or what remained of it, lying inert by the water's edge. Neither of them said anything but began to drag her body to safety. In silence they found some branches and sorrowfully set light to the pyre. Only then did Eloni give way to hacking sobs of grief. Oah did what he could to comfort her but they both stayed all night staring at the flames.

Several days passed before either of them made any effort to leave the ashes of Anice. On the fourth day Primo emerged from the trees and hurried over to them. He looked agitated and kept motioning for them to follow him. "We had better go with him," said Oah, and Eloni nodded her head in assent.

Primo took them back to his village where Eloni was horrified to discovery Abeno, lying, sobbing, on the ground with Uth's baby girl beside him. She gathered from the incoherent stream of words that tumbled from him that Uia's house had been torn about by huge gray animals. They had suddenly appeared and plunged through the house, crushing Efa and Uth, but he, Abeno, being a light sleeper, had woken in time to grab the baby and run out of the way. He had returned when all seemed safe but was unable to find Uia and so he had brought the baby back to the village. Eloni comforted him, and Aqa produced a little basked for the baby to sleep in.

The following weeks passed in a hurry. The primitive women began to give birth to normal children and Oah made certain that Eloni helped him with every birth. He also made sure that she recorded and understood all the information he gave her. For Eloni's part she felt quite detached about the w hole business. She longed for each night when she could sink into deep, oblivious sleep. Uia came back to the village one day, looking very thin but otherwise all right. No one could find what had happened to Efa's wife and Uia looked blank when questioned. The babies continued to arrive and Uia showed a great interest in all of them. At length the births were over and relative normality returned to the clearing.

"Well, Eloni, my work is finished now," said Oah, as the two of them sat beside a fire one evening.

"Over? But I thought you had more plans?" replied Eloni.

Oah shook his head. "No, I have achieved my success with the normal births. My experiments now mean that y our son's sperm is acceptable to the new generation and thus life will continue here. I have no doubt that this was what Abello would have wished and in time our descendants may return to Capernica. After all, we have achieved Abello's goals of finding a safe place to live and to adapt to the environment. We have, in fact, learned to live in a different climate, at a different temperature, and to eat different food. That is quite an achievement when you think how little physical work we did on Capernica. I feel we have succeeded beyond our most secret longings. I take little credit," he raised his hand to stop Eloni protesting. "I have made it physically possible for the generations to continue, but it will be you and Aqa and Abeno who will see the long term effects. You all will mold the new characteristics that the race will throw up. I realize that I am talking as though I shall not be here, and this is quite true. As a result of the injections that Arabus gave me and of my own neglect of my body while experimenting I am slowly dying of poisoning. I have no cure, but I do have something to put me out of my misery should the pain become unbearable. I am sorry to have to leave you, Eloni dear. I have long since admired you and wish very much that I could see the result of a union between your son and a primitive girl, but I am content now, which for me is a rarity."

Having finished this long speech, Oah left. It was a few days later that Aqa came to say that Oah was still in his bed. Eloni crossed over to see him and found him dead but looking more peaceful, she thought, than she had ever seen him before. They burned his body, and returned to the village.

CHAPTER VIII

For many, many days Eloni seemed to be in a trance-like state, sunk deep into herself seemingly unable to lift her mind and spirit above the tragedies which had struck her in such rapid succession. Her head ached abominably and her eyes felt as though they were starting out of her head. For the first time in her life she was aware of the nerve which ran from the back of the eye towards her brain by the overwhelming tension there. As for her brain, this seemed to be racing away, giving her no peace, for no sooner had one thought come into it than it vanished, pushed aside by an incoming thought totally disconnected with the previous one. At first she tried to concentrate, to hold a thought for a while, but it was all to no avail. It seemed that her whole body and personality was being fragmented, so she gave up the struggle and allowed herself to sink down into a semi-coma, allowing her mind to shut itself off in a manner of self-preservation, not thinking about anything, not even about the welfare of Abeno. Instead, as each new day came she allowed herself to be lifted from her sleeping couch and moved to the entrance of her shelter where she rested her back against one of the upright posts which supported the roof of leaves. Here, having covered her eyes with a thick piece of an old garment, she spent her days allowing the warm rays of Benu to penetrate her very bones. This gave her great comfort. The gentle soughing of the breeze through the leaves of the nearby trees and the soft buzzing of a variety of winged insects soon had soporific effect and the days passed without her being aware of events or movements. Thus Eloni lost all track of time but gradually her brain came to peace and the pain disappeared.

One day, she was suddenly aware that she could think coherently once more and able to pursue mental argument in a lucid manner. She gave a sigh of relief and a brief smile. A sudden grunt of satisfaction next to her caused her to start, and taking away the material from her eyes she was blinded momentarily by the brightness of the light, but after a few moments of squinting her eyes adjusted to the glare and she saw Primo crouched to the ground a pace away. As soon as he saw that she was able to see him his eyes lit up in obvious relief and pleasure at her recovery, his mouth opening into a broad grin. She suddenly understood that he knew that her crisis was over and his joy that this was so warmed her heart and mind and she was aware of the strength of the bond of mutual trust and affection which existed between them. She stretched out her hand towards him and Primo came to her side on his knees. She touched the hair on the top of his bowed head and then slid her fingers through it towards the back and then down to the bare skin below the hairline. His skin, though moist from his perspiration, was smooth to the touch and not nearly as rough as she had anticipated. She smiled warmly at him again with her eyes full of understanding and she knew that she had a faithful friend and ally who would protect her and hers against the frightening dangers of this still strange and alien world. Relief flooded through her and he found she was able to start thinking again about all that had befallen her without undue pain and distress.

She found that the conviction was gradually growing upon her that Oah had been right to concentrate upon the experiments of genetic adaptation but she wished that he could have approached the work in a different manner. She tried to rationalize on how this could have been achieved, but could only come to the conclusion that she meant in a kinder fashion. The thought that such an approach would have meant nothing to the primitives and very little to the other members of the expedition, including herself at the time, was disturbing. If only Oah had been able to explain matters from the beginning in terms which she could have understood ….. but it was too late now to speculate along those lines. What had been done was done. It was all in the past now and the past was fixed and immutable. Much better to concentrate upon the future, for here at least she might have the ability for influence. But try as she may, Oah and his work kept coming back into her mind and waves of compassion would sweep through her at these memories. What agonies of mind he had experienced in his scientific training, dedication to what had to be achieved had fought with the weaknesses of his own character she could not even begin to imagine and she wept for him. But there was admiration, too, that his dedication had finally triumphed and that he had lived just long enough to see the result of his effort. No doubt it was the intense satisfaction of his achievement which had permitted him to give up his life the way he had done. She felt that, in the totality of his work, there had been a nobleness of character and she felt proud that she had been privileged to know him.

In the end, she came to believe that Abello and Oah must have planned together this whole course of action. Just to have seen the possible necessity bespoke of minds beyond understanding. Thoughts of her beloved Abello, how he had anticipated the problems which would beset the expedition and how he had laid plans to overcome these, reduced her memories of him to a state of near adoration. He had foreseen nearly everything, everything, that is, except his own violent death. But that horrible event was now sufficiently far in the past that she could remember it and think about it without undue

172

mental distress. Only a sense of physical loneliness suffused her spirit but even this was counterbalanced by an inner conviction of some form of continuing mental communication.

From time to time, thoughts of Anice and poor misguided Matester intruded upon her reveries. But Matester had been but a child, one whose mind had been so easily led astray by personalities infinitely stronger than her own, personalities so selfish as not to care how they revealed themselves in her presence. Indeed, which had actively encouraged her to take the easy way out. Yes, Matester was much to be pities. And what of Arabus himself? It was strange how her thoughts and feelings had changed towards him and she was surprised to find herself actually feeling sorry for him. At first she was very angry with herself, for this feeling was totally irrational. Had he not murdered in the most savage fashion the very mainspring of her life and then compounded that crime by rape as the final indignity? But try as she might to prevent it her female sense of compassion for a poor, tortured mind finally overcame her original feelings of physical revulsion. If only he had not been subject to a blind, unthinking instinct. If only he had not given a greater priority to the immediate at the expense of the really important in a vain attempt to impress. If only, maybe, Abello had given a little more ruthless thought to his own outlook. If only….. but what did such thoughts achieve? Both were dead and could not be brought back again to life. They now only had a continued existence in her mind and in the minds of any of the others who might remember them from time to time.

Needless to say, she got no sympathetic understanding from Aqa when she voiced her changing feelings as they both sat by the dying embers of the cooking fire late one day. In fact, he snorted with derision and then scolded her roundly for being a fool with such irrational sentimentality, at least as far as Arabus was concerned. He was overwhelmingly arrogant and perverted in his madness and he, Aqa, was glad that he was no more. Their life was easier for his death and such morning was ludicrous. Eloni sighed inwardly and kept her further thoughts to herself, for she realized that Aqa would not and could not forgive Arabus his crimes. After all, Aqa loved her deeply with an understanding sort of love, a mental relationship which would not survive if any attempt were ever made to transfer it to the physical. She looked affectionately at Aqa in the soft light of the fire and smiled gently at him. She saw his bristling anger slowly flow out of his face and soon he was smiling back at her. "Old faithful friend and companion," she thought to herself, "you do not seem to enjoy many rewards in y our hard existence, with your innate shyness and particularly with your disability. I will have to see if something cannot be arranged for one of the young primitive females to take care of you."

"Sorry to interrupt your reverie," said Aqa, "but there is one important matter which I think we should discuss, and that is my increasing anxiety at the influence which Arabus has had on our people and also on the primitives. I see signs of irrationality and a degree of callousness creeping into the behavior of the young males in particular. I cannot be absolutely sure, of course, for I did not see them in their natural state before we arrived. Life must have been hard for them, maybe cruel and uncompromising by our standards, but they seemed to take a special care of the young children, whereas now….."

"Yes, I have felt these subtle changes, too," replied Eloni, "but they are very difficult to describe with any degree of accuracy. The best I can do is to say that it is as though an innocence has gone out of their way of life."

Both Eloni and Aqa became rather engrossed in their own gloomy thoughts at these words and no more of the subject was discussed at that time.

But a somewhat different aspect of the situation presented itself some time later during the middle of a particularly hot day, when very little was moving in the world of nature. Except, that is, for some of the young children whose energy and enthusiasm seemed boundless. The adults watched them in a kind of torpor. In particular, Eloni and Aqa noticed Uia's little child Uika, who was running around the compound in a world of her own. She was now a sturdy little child with a mind and character all of her own, full of innocent mischief and able to drive Abeno wild to the point of distraction with her teasing. She had but to see him to run to him, chattering constantly. It required all his guile and constant alertness to keep out of her sight, and he could only relax completely when she was asleep. He complained constantly to his mother asking that she keep Uika away from him, sounding very gruff and masculine as he did so.

But Eloni had a sneaking suspicion that this was merely a pose to disguise his true feelings of affection for the child, and so this hot day was to prove. Uika ran into the space between two of the sleeping quarters and Eloni could no longer see her. Quite suddenly Uika started to scream, screams that indicated pure terror. Abeno, who was on the opposite side of the clearing, immediately looked towards the sound and he could see Uika standing too petrified with fright to move, piercing cries and sobs coming from her opened mouth and her brown eyes starting from their sockets. Abeno sprang across the compound just as fast as he could, and as he got near to the screaming child he could see sliding over the ground one of the strange legless creatures, long, and a brilliant green in color, whose bite could kill within the space of but a few minutes. He had once seen the agonies of one of the primitives who had had the misfortune to be bitten by

174

one of these creatures and the sheer horror of helplessness had been with him ever since. He snatched Uika from the ground just as the vivid neck was retracting ready to strike at the unprotected ankle and leapt as high in the air as he could over the animal, beating a quick retreat around the rear of the sleeping hut. The animal, frustrated at the loss of its prey, turned towards its retreating victim and this proved its fate, for Primo, who by this time had nearly caught up with Abeno was able to decapitate the beast with one lightning blow from his sharp stone knife.

Abeno carried Uika around to the entrance of his mother's quarters and sat down with his back supported by one of the entrance posts. He cradled the hysterical child in his arms, making comforting noises which only Uika could hear, all the time gently stroking her hair and face. Gradually she quietened.

By this time, of course, Uia had joined Eloni, Aqa and the other primitives who had come over to see what the commotion was all about. They all stopped and watched. Uika was gazing up at Abeno with an unmistakable expression in her eyes while Abeno looked down at her, smiling gently all the while, marveling at the tender look framed by such, long blue-black lashes. He continued to caress her face and shoulder, wondering at the warmth and softness of her skin. She sighed contentedly and had no resistance to nature's own way of relieving tension in the young – her eyelids started to flutter and presently she fell into a deep sleep. Abeno held the sleeping child quite still for a long time, keeping his thoughts to himself. Presently he stirred, looking up to see the ring of faces around him. He felt and showed a twinge of embarrassment.

"She is only a little child and was very frightened," he explained needlessly, handing Uika over to her mother. Then, the too, closed his eyes and was soon dozing. Eloni moved away with Aqa. They looked at one another and nodded.

"Somehow I do not think this expedition has been in vain after all," said Aqa. "So much for my recent gloomy thoughts of futility. I think from what we have just seen that the future is in good hands."

And so the seasons passed, wet following upon dry and dry upon wet as Eloni and Aqa grew older and more feeble and all the children grew to a sturdy puberty. The original landing site was seldom visited by now but occasionally Eloni, although she hated the place, forced herself to make the trip as she felt some responsibility to the remaining crew members. After each visit she felt upset for many days after having seen the crew, the ship that had brought them all the way from Capernica, the general squalor and degradation to which all and everything had sunk. It was clearly seen that the gases, etc. in the atmosphere, the rain and the encroaching growth would soon obliterate all signs of their means of transportation and thus the last link with their original home would be finally broken.

Then came the time when one more visit was needed but on this occasion Aqa firmly forbade her to attempt the journey. Instead, he, Primo and two other primitives made the trip, which took them three weary days to achieve, and they found the situation even further deteriorated. The fabric of the ship could not be easily crumbled in the hand, which Aqa supposed had originally been caused by the radiation it had endured during its long journey through space and the strongly acidic nature of the atmosphere of the white planet on which they had been forced to make an emergency landing in order to repair the engine housings. Of course, Aqa could not tell Primo of these events for he would not be able to comprehend such places. He noticed that Primo and the other primitives kept very close to him while they were in the camp. At first, Aqa thought this was some sort of protective gesture but then he noticed how their eyes were rolling around in their sockets showing much of the white of the eyeball, which was a sure sign that they were very much afraid, although of what was not immediately apparent.

The food growing areas were sadly neglected with the thick jungle vegetation regrowing in the cleared spaces. His companions were grossly emaciated and obviously had not the strength or the willpower for the work of cultivation. Instead, they seemed to rely on the fermented fruit juices which they produced continuously and drank just as fast. These kept them in a state of continuous intoxication in which the awareness of their filthy naked bodies was obliterated. One effect of their reduced metabolism was that the rampant sexuality and license which Aqa had previously witnessed was not gone. The whole place reeked of death and decay but Aqa was excessively wearied from his journey on account of his disability and needed several days rest to gather his strength for the return journey. Thus, he slept quite a lot through the hot days, while Primo and his companions went into the forest to kill some of the wild animals. Several large carcasses were brought back which were crudely butchered and cooked over the fire. The smell of the roasting meat revived some degree of animation among the crew members and a few roused themselves sufficiently to partake of a small meal.

Due to their general neglect of themselves and the subsequent semi-starvation, their gastric juices had largely dried up, and after a short while the food rotted in their stomachs and they vomited before any nutriment had been absorbed. The strain of the vomiting left them lying on the ground in a state of exhaustion. Primo drew Aqa and the other primitives to one side and indicated that they should leave at once, but Aqa protested his own weakness and a compromise was reached, in as much as they would start back at first light the following day. After themselves partaking of the rest of the meat they lay down and Aqa immediately drifted into a deep, dreamless sleep. It seemed to him but a moment before he was aware of being violently shaken by the shoulders, and when he was at last able to force open his eyes he experienced a violent stabbing pain in his eyes as he had looked directly at the disc of Benu which was just showing above the horizon across the clearing. He turned over on to his other side before opening his eyes again. He sat up and found Primo and the other primitives around him, their eyes wide with terror.

As soon as Primo saw Aqa look at him he pointed towards one of the sleeping quarters to the right, shaking his head violently from side to side as he did so. They all got to their feet and shuffled towards the hut. Primo stopped Aqa well short of the entrance and pointed inside. Slowly as his eyes adjusted to the darker interior Aqa could just make out three bodies lying on the ground, their arms and legs twisted about them in grotesque designs. They were quite obviously very dead, and then Aqa could see that their bodies were bloated with large, weeping pustules, about which large flies were already gathering in increasing numbers, their angry buzzing filling the air. Their mouths were wide open in silent screams of agony and despair. Aqa felt sure that death had come with merciful speed but unfortunately not fast enough for the victims not to realize their fate and the attendant anguish.

The primitives pulled Aqa away from the scene by the arms, muttering to themselves and shaking their heads violently. They turned Aqa around and half pushing, half lifting, made him break into a run. They soon left the huts behind and entered the forest by the now well-worn track. The heat and humidity under the canopy of dense vegetation soon reduced Aqa to exhaustion. The pain in the stump of his leg and the friction between the bone end and the wooden foot which Abello had made so long ago caused him to stumble carelessly, and soon he tripped over a root of a tree flat onto his face. He could not move for quite a few minutes, his lungs moving violently in an effort to increase the supply of air. The primitives allowed him to lie for a few minutes and then lifted him to a sitting position and rested his back against the trunk of a large tree. They then withdrew a few paces, squatted on their haunches and talked quietly among themselves, glancing anxiously at Aqa from time to time. However, Aqa felt confident that, despite their obvious terror at what he could only conclude was some terrible, rapidly fatal disease, they would not desert him for their looks were compassionate and in no way hostile. Comforted with this thought Aqa closed his eyes and waited for the rapidity of is breathing to subside. When this happened, he heard the group moving about, and he got to his feet and they started walking along the trail away from the camp.

This time, although moving as rapidly as Aqa could keep up, there was no panic. By forced marches, they managed to reach the settlement in just over two days this time, although Aqa was completely spent when they finally staggered into the clearing. In fact, for the last day the primitives had been forced to almost carry Aqa, taking it in turns to do so. Primo was doing the carrying as they entered the settlement and he went straight to Aqa's sleeping quarters where he laid him gently on the ground. As he left the hut he grunted something at Eloni, who was entering at the same time, but she did not understand his meaning. She went over to Aqa and found him in a semicoma, his face and body beaded with stale perspiration. She wrinkled her nose with displeasure at the penetrating odor, went outside to collect a bowl of cool water, and proceeded to wash him all over. This treatment gave Aqa some comfort and he roused himself sufficiently to ask for something to drink. She gave him some of the milk from one of the large beasts which the primitives had domesticated. Having drunk it, Aqa fell back in a deep sleep and it would be many hours before he could tell her what they had found at the compound.

After seeing that Aqa was lying comfortably she went outside and sat down at the entrance. Across the clearing with the cooking fore in the center she could see Primo and all his people gathered together, talking among themselves very intently. Every once in a while, one of them would get up and look across to her. Although there was nothing menacing in the looks, Eloni suddenly felt very much afraid. Obviously something was very wrong, particularly as she became aware that even the children had stopped their chatter and constant running around. They stood in a little group to one side of their parents, anxiously watching their faces. A sense of grave crisis filled the whole clearing.

Eloni suddenly thought of Abeno – he would be down at the river swimming in the pool below the small waterfall with the older boys. Eloni liked this place too, for it was much cooler at the water's edge under the trees. The tumbling water produced some small air currents as well as cooling the atmosphere and the fell of the warm water on her naked body when she swam was most invigorating. She hurried down to the rock pool, the shouts of the boys getting louder in her ears as she approached. Abeno saw her coming as he prepared to dive into the pool from a high rock. One look at her face told him that all was not well, so he changed his mind about diving and clambered off the rock.

He walked briskly towards her while she approached him with short agitated steps. As he came towards her, even in her distress she could not but help notice the virility of his naked body, his brown skin still glistening with the drops of water from his previous dive. A warm feeling of maternal pride flowed through her. She quickly told him of Aqa's sudden return, of the way the primitives had gathered to themselves and the feeling of evil which seemed to pervade the encampment. She asked him if he would go immediately to Primo to find out exactly what the trouble was all about. The fact that Abeno had learned to communicate with the primitives sufficiently well to understand everyday matters had been apparent for some time now and had greatly reduced the gap between her and the primitives. Both she and Aqa had tried to make some sense of the complicated grunts and the clicking noises of the primitives but without any success at all. They guessed that they were just too old. But Abeno had grown through childhood with them and thus it was that much easier for him. This was obviously an occasion when they would all be very glad of that.

They hurried back to the clearing to find the conference still in progress. Abeno went straight across to the group of adults who grunted their greetings to him while make room for him in the circle. Eloni moved across to Aqa's hut, peeped in to find him still sound asleep and comfortable, and resumed her place at the entrance. The talking went on for a long time, in fact it was still going on some hours later when Aqa awoke and came to the entrance to join her. Once glance at the animated group told him of the gravity of the situation and Eloni quickly told him what had happened since his return. He then told Eloni about the trip to the camp site and what had been found there. He played down to a degree the discovery of the diseased bodies and what his instincts told him of its significance. He did so in order not to cause Eloni unnecessary anxiety but in this he was a little late. Eventually Abeno got to his feet and came across to his mother, smiling at her briefly, then asking Aqa if he would step across to the primitives with him. Aqa did so and the customary greetings were exchanged as the group made room for the newcomer and he sat down next to Abeno who immediately confirmed his worst fears concerning the virulence of the disease.

"Obviously this little colony must take every step for its own preservation," said Abeno, "and what has been decided is this. Because Primo and yourself with the other two primitives have experienced the greatest exposure to the contamination and the fact that my mother has been in contact with you since your return, Primo will immediately take all of you to a refuge some three days' march from here. There you will all stay in isolation from the rest of us for at least twentyone days, more probably, about twenty-eight days just to make sure. If none of you get the disease then it will be safe for you to return to the rest of us. Primo will decide what is to be done after that time."

"Of course," replied Aqa, "that is all that we can do as we are without medicines, and Oah is long since gone. I will go and explain this to your mother."

"Just before you do that," said Abeno, "there is one more thing that you have to know and more particularly understand and approve. You must realize that the old camp is now the center of pestilence and must be destroyed. The only way that this can be done with any degree of reliability is by fire. Everything, and I also mean everyone, must be burned, whether they be alive or dead. Personally I doubt if any of them will be alive after the next few days."

Abeno looked hard at Aqa who wilted under the horror of what had just been decided. That his own companions and friends should have to suffer in such a manner made him feel sick to his stomach. He looked helplessly at Abeno and then at the others.

"You have to understand," said Abeno with pity in his voice, "that this harsh decision has been made for the sake of the children – the next generation who will carry out my father's plans, yours and Oah's too. Just look behind you at the children."

Aqa turned slowly as he was bid to see the group of the little ones standing so forlornly a little way away, their large brown eyes fixed upon him with the mixture of innocence and trust that is childhood. Tears filled Aqa's eyes and he could only nod his agreement as the enormity of the decision filled his brain.

"There is a little more that you should know," continued Abeno, "and that is that two of the old males here have volunteered to carry out the task. Their words were that their constructive lives were past and they are too old to but sit in the warm and eat. Should they catch the disease then they will have done a great good for the rest of the community and can die happy in this knowledge that they will be remembered for a long time for their sacrifice. Should they survive, then they will live in honor for the rest of their days. I think that this piece of information should be kept from my mother, at least for the present. The men will slip away from here after dark and she will not know of their going."

"Yes, your mother must not know of this," agreed Aqa.

So Aqa went across to Eloni and told her what they had to do. Although she did not like the fact that she could not embrace her son before she left, she made no audible complaint. She wrapped a few necessities into an animal skin for herself and for Aqa and went outside where they both waited a short while for Primo and his two companions to join them. As soon as the five were assembled they moved off into the forest in complete silence watched similarly by the rest of the community. At the edge of the forest none looked back except for Eloni, her eyes seeking those of her son. Despite the distance was aware immediately of the other and a jumble of emotions of

180

love and hope passed between them in a flash. Abeno raised his right arm in a gesture of salute and Eloni turned back towards the path and in a few more strides was lost to view in the jungle. It was as Abeno had explained to Aqa, three days of quiet walking towards the place where Benu set each evening brought the party to a small outcrop of rock at the base of which was a small cave. Here the party settled in for the long wait. For Eloni the waiting was particularly tedious, as she remained close by, but Aqa seemed more capable of amusing himself as he studied both the plant life nearby as well as spending many hours on his knees or stomach watching an insect busy about its work. It never ceased to surprise him how each individual insect had its place within its community, and Aqa often wondered if such an organization was purely instinctive or if there would be some sort of rudimentary communication.

Primo and the other two spent their time in more practical pursuits such as hunting for fresh supplies of meat. Fruits were easily obtainable from a considerable variety of trees and shrubs growing nearby. Thus the days slowly passed, and each morning and evening everyone would carefully examine his companions for any signs of the dreaded disease. Aqa kept a record of the passage of the days by making notches in the trunk of a tree – the numbers grew to eighteen, then nineteen and twenty. By this time Primo had lost his anxious looks, and Aqa realized that he had forgotten to mark up the three days of their journey and also the two days which the men had spent on the trip from the infected area to the settlement. Hope and confidence now rose rapidly but they forced themselves to be patient until the number notches counted at twenty eight. That day Primo indicated that they would start the return journey the next day, and this they did.

They walked steadily for two whole days and were well into the third and almost back to the settlement when Primo, who was leading the party, suddenly stopped in his tracks indicating with his hands that they should be silent. They froze. Above the constant noise of the wild life in the jungle was suddenly borne to their ears a faint sound of confused shouting. The primitives listened carefully for a few moments, then motioned Eloni and Aqa to the side of the track. They dropped the loads they were carrying, and taking only their wooden clubs, spears and stone knives, ran off down the track towards the shouting. Eloni and Aqa watched them disappear and then quickly moved themselves off the track into the concealing undergrowth. Here they remained quiet and motionless. The shouting grew louder, and then softer as the wind changed direction, and then there was no more noise except the natural ones. They stayed where they were until they heard footsteps on the pathway and Abeno's voice calling them. They stepped out from their place of concealment and ran towards Abeno, who flung his arms around his mother and hugged her tight to his chest. There were tears of joy and gratitude in his eyes when he looked at Aqa over the top of his mother's head.

"What was all the shouting about, and why did Primo and his men run off like that?" enquired Aqa.

"There is no time to explain that just now," was the response. "We must get back to the settlement just as fast as we can."

Be broke away from his mother and Aqa observed to his consternation that the stone dagger which Abeno carried in his belt was coated with blood, already congealing. He made no mention of it, and his mother had already turned to pick up their belongings.

"You both walk on," said Abeno. "I can manage all of these things and I will be right behind you. But hurry as fast as you can."

A little while later and slightly out of breath from their exertions they cleared the forest into the settlement clearing. A very gruesome sight met Aqa's gaze who was leading the procession. Nine bodies of small, dark men were laid out in a row to one side of the area. They were completely naked with irregular daubs of colored paint on their bodies. Eloni could not suppress a shudder of horror when she spotted them, then quickly averting her gaze she passed rapidly into her sleeping quarters from where the corpses could not be seen. Aqa, meanwhile, had passed the gruesome line without a great deal of curiosity and joined Primo who was talking excitedly with his own people while Abeno listened carefully. After a while, the group dispersed and Abeno drew Aqa well away from his mother's hut and together they sat down.

Abeno told Aqa what had happened. "We were all scattered around the area, each one of us with one eye on the forest, for each day for the last several days your return had been expected. In fact, some little doubts as to your safety were beginning to enter our thoughts, although the time to give up hope had not arrived. I was over by the fire in the center facing the path when suddenly behind me there was a great screeching and shouting. I turned around to see some eleven of these little painted men come out of the forest brandishing long spears. They were bunched together ready to throw these, when they suddenly saw me standing there. As you well know, both you and mother are taller than Primo and I am almost as tall. Well, these little men would scarcely have reached Primo's shoulder. They were so surprised at seeing a giant of a boy that they stopped in their tracks. This gave our men just that amount of time," continued Abeno, "to gather up their own weapons and mount a counter-attack. The fight was brief but bloody. The little men regained their senses and threw their spears, but they fell short of our charging warriors but unfortunately one of our little boys in his fright ran into the spears and was killed. I three my stone knife at one of the attackers and he died immediately. Our men killed nine of the invaders but two of them managed to escape back to the forest, taking with them one of our pubescent girls."

"Will Primo organize a party to go after them and rescue the girl?" asked Aqa.

"Apparently not," replied Abeno. "Primo says that the little men can move through the forest much more quickly than he can."

"Will the girl be killed and maybe eaten?" Aqa asked somewhat nervously.

"Well, according to Primo," replied Abeno, "that seems very unlikely. The purpose of the raids is not primarily that of killing. The target seems to be the capture of women of child-bearing age and all the younger girls down to babies. They will also take the very young boys and baby boys. As these will eventually grow to be men of a physical stature greater that the little men they will be employed as slaves to do those physical tasks which are rather beyond the strength of these people. The function of the females will be to be kept in an almost continuous state of pregnancy, which, after all, is very little different from their function here. Primo says that this is only the second time he has seen such people in his life, the first time being a similar raid when he was an adolescent. Apparently, their life deeper in the forest is very precarious and survival demands any sacrifice. They seem to know the minimum number of both males and females they need to survive as a group, knowledge that they must have gained over a very long period of time and after many hardships. Because they are very often close to the point of starvation infant mortality is very high and the females very quickly exhausted by the continual pregnancies. Thus the overall wastage rate is severe and when they find that their numbers are down to the minimum they make these raids. Of course, some on both sides are killed because the raided fight back, but the little men are quite content just to drive the protecting groups away in order to take the females. They know that the larger species are no match for the little people in the densest part of the jungle where they dwell. Being nomadic they move around the forest every few days and do not have permanent camps. While you can sometimes stumble across evidence of them it is always where they have been and never where they are."

"The two that seem to have escaped with the girl?" enquired Aqa.

"Probably well away by now," said Abeno. "But their very escape has caused Primo a lot of anxiety. He feels that having killed so many of their men and their curiosity about me – for my capture would bring much honor to my captor – they will return with a much greater force. It is remarkable that Primo seems to have some understanding of what Oah was doing, for he says we must all leave this place in no later than two days in order to avoid further conflict. Now, as you know, Primo and his warriors are no cowards so I was surprised at his decision. His reply was that he would not just to protect the three of us, but more to protect Uika and those other children who are the result of Oah's work."

"Not surprising, really," retorted Aqa. "You are confusing intelligence with knowledge."

Abeno digested this for a few moments and then agreed that this was the case.

"One last question for you. Has anything been see of the two old men who went to destroy our landing site?"

"They have not reappeared up to the present moment," was the reply, "but four nights after they left I managed to climb to the top of that tall tree over there," said Abeno, waving his hand across the compound. It was a tree which Aqa had often stopped to admire, its graceful shape and immense height never failing to impress. "It took me a long time to get to the top," continued Abeno, "particularly as I soon lost the benefit of the firelight because of the dense foliage. However, that thinned out as I got to the top and the going became easier. It was surprisingly light up there with the stars so bright they seemed almost to be dropping out of the sky. On the horizon, in the direction of the landing site, there was a faint flickering red glow in the sky. I climbed up again early the following morning and there was a blue haze of smoke in the same place, so we all suppose that the job was successful."

"But should they not have been back by now, that is if they did not catch the disease themselves?" asked Aqa.

Abeno was silent for a few moments, and then he said, "Primo does not talk very much about what the two men were told to do but I rather suspect that they would have killed themselves rather than endanger the rest of their people."

Aqa stared at Abeno in some disbelief and then gave a small shudder of horror. This emotion then gave way to one of adoration. "And we thought when we first came to this place that these people were little more than animals with no emotions, only instincts," he said.

"No, I think they are much more than that. I have talked with some of the young boys about the customs and beliefs of these people and I have been quite surprised by what I have learned. As I said a little while ago, killing one another is not their prime object. In fact they go out of their way to avoid it. The two old men, for instance, once they had reached the landing site would have given any still alive an infusion of the root of a poisonous plant, which causes almost instant unconsciousness and then paralysis of the heart muscles. Thus, our people would have felt no pain and would have been quite dead before their bodies were burned."

"How would the old men then make sure that their bodies would have been similarly destroyed?" asked Aqa.

"It seems that the stronger of the two would have given the weaker an infusion and then burnt his body. He would then have built a fire under one of the trees, climbed up into it himself, drunk the infusion and then would have fallen off in to the fire or the tree itself would have caught alight and he would have been burnt that way."

The thought of this horror drove Aqa to seek his own company for a while, and he wandered around the compound vaguely aware of a lot of bustle around him as the few personal belongings, the cooking utensils, were packed into bundles so that an early start could be made the next day. Where they would be going he had no idea. Later, after they had all eaten and were lying down to rest, he questioned Abeno, who thought they would be going in the direction where Benu rose each morning, up on to the higher ground and out of the dense forest. There they could not be taken by surprise so easily should the little men come back after them.

Next day dawned and the whole party set off into the jungle. Leading were six of the younger men, armed with stone tipped spears, stone hammers and daggers. Next came the primitive females with their offspring, each loaded down with those of their possessions which were easily moved. In this group were Eloni and Aqa, although they were not heavily loaded. Bringing up the rear were Primo and the remainder of the fighting and hunting males, including those young males who had almost reached adulthood. Included in this group was Abeno. Looking over her shoulder, Eloni noted with pride how he stood so much taller than all the other males, and that included Primo. Every now and again they would march into a small clearing where the light from Benu shone down. She noticed that the rays from Benu had turned his skin a dull red-brown color, as distinct from the almost black color of the primitives.

"No wonder the little men were stopped in their tracks when they caught sight of my son," she thought to herself.

All that day they marched in the direction where Benu had risen above the horizon that morning. A little before the setting of Benu the procession came to a halt and just sand down upon the ground. Aqa in particular felt the fatigue of the all-day march which had been carried out at quite a fast pace. Eloni lay stretched out beside him, too tired to speak.

Presently Abeno came to where they were lying. "We will be staying here for the night," he said, "but you must be ready to resume the journey as soon as it gets light tomorrow. In the meantime, we must not light any fires to cook our food, as Primo says it will guide any parties of vengeful little people to us while we sleep. That is if any are yet following."

The following day was a repeat of the first, except that Aqa felt more dead than alive when a halt was finally called. The pain in the stump of his leg was very bad due to the continual movement against the unyielding surface of the wooden foot which Oah had made for him. He undid the straps and Eloni saw that the end of the stump had been rubbed red raw and was bleeding. She soaked a spongy leaf in a little cold water and gently bathed the stump clean. She also carefully cleaned the dried blood from the hollow in the wooden foot where the stump fitted. One of the primitive females happened to have watched this, and she went across to a thorny bush which was growing nearby. She carefully picked some of the spiky leaves and crushed them in a bowl with a small amount of water. She came across to Eloni and taking the cloth from Eloni's hand soaked this in the milky solution in the bowl. She then gently dabbed the stump with it and finally bound the cloth right around the inflamed part. Aqa watched this without the slightest fear and presently he became aware that the discomfort was going away, and soon he could feel no pain whatsoever.

"There must be some form of local anesthetic in that plant's leaves," he remarked to Eloni. "I wonder how they first came to realize that?"

"Probably generations ago," replied Eloni. "I think these must be a very ancient people as they seem to have developed quite an astonishing degree of culture."

The third day promised to be a mere repetition of the previous two. At least it was until about the middle of the day when Eloni happened to look back along the way, looking for Abeno's bright hair marching along behind her. She was horrified to find that he was missing, as was Primo and six of the strongest males. Her alarm at this communicated itself to Aqa.

"Well, it is true that they are missing, " said Aqa after Eloni had told him of her discovery. "I wonder what they can be doing?"

"Do you think that they are waiting to see if we are being followed?"

"No good asking me that," replied Aqa. "If only we could speak with these people we could find out, but I can only interpret a few of their grunts, certainly not sufficient to translate a reply even if I could make them understand my question."

Just then the rear guard caught up with them and by impatient gestures made Eloni and Aqa clearly understand that the whole group must press on. That night Eloni spent in an anguish of mind, not knowing what had happened. She fell into a fitful dreamless sleep of exhaustion, finally waking a little before dawn, but Abeno and the rest had still not reappeared. For two more days they continued the march without the others, much to Eloni's rapidly increasing alarm. Aqa did his best to keep her from worrying during the day with talk of the old days, but he found his spirits flagging towards the end of each march as his strength was giving out and it required all his concentration to prevent himself from stumbling over the smallest of obstacles.

Suddenly he said to her, "Have you noticed that the forest is getting less dense now and that we seem to be gaining height?"

"No, I had not seen that," said Eloni, looking all around her, "but you are right, and the air seems to be a little less humid now."

About the middle of the morning of the third day the leaders of the party suddenly sank down to the ground and the rest did likewise as they caught up, including Aqa and Eloni. The grass here was quite high and they could not see more than a very little way in front of them. The whole group remained still and silent and Aqa and Eloni assumed that there must be an unknown danger ahead of them so they remained equally still and silent. Benu advanced to the overhead position but as they were all in the shade they did not suffer from the burning rays. They ate a little and Eloni and Aqa lay back and went into a sound sleep. They woke later feeling very stiff and not a little chilly. Benu was well towards the horizon and soon it would be night again. Presently one of the warriors arose and silently melted away into the long grass back along the way they had some earlier that day. Aqa noted with a slight degree of apprehension that the warrior was fully armed, but he resisted calling Eloni's attention to this fact.

A little while later, Abeno, Primo and the rest of the warriors slipped quietly back into the camp. Abeno came straight across to his mother and embraced her – there were tears of thankfulness in her eyes. Aqa slapped him affectionately on the shoulder and Abeno turned his head to smile at him. Still later that night Abeno explained to them both that he, Primo and some other warriors had, on Primo's signal, stepped off the trail to the right when they were both not looking. Once the faint sounds of the procession had faded and the forest was completely still they had set off up a faint side trail which increasingly led them away from the main group until that night they were actually travelling in the opposite direction. They had paused for two hours to eat and refresh themselves with a little sleep and then they were up again, marching back by the light of the moon. A little before dawn they had rested again for several hours and did not move again until the middle of that day, when they did start again and swung slowly again to the right. By the middle of the next day they were back on the original trail, a good day's march behind the place where they had left the main party. Just before they broke cover on to the main trail Primo had made them all crouch down, perfectly still and in complete silence. They stayed like that for quite some time, ears straining for the slightest untoward sound. But nothing other than the normal noises of the forest could be heard. Primo gave a little grunt, then he alone broke cover onto the main trail. Abeno could just see him through the undergrowth, carefully examining the ground. He went slowly back towards the original camp, the retraced his steps and went forward an equal distance. He came back, examining the tree trunks with equal care, even gazing steadily upwards as far as he could see. He came back to where the rest of them were waiting. He conveyed to Abeno that he could find no signs of any raiding parties following them and so they should be safe from now on. They quickly gathered up their weapons and caught up with the rest of the party by a series of forced marches. Young and vigorous though he was, Abeno was very tired after his exertions and after eating a little and taking a long drink of water he curled up on the ground beside his mother and was very quickly in a sound sleep. Eloni and Aqa soon took the hint and slept soundly also.

The next morning in a blaze of golden light they broke out of the trees into a sea of tall grass. As they marched forward the ground rose steadily and as it did so the grass became shorter. The air became clearer and the light brighter, and although the rays of Benu still burnt upon their skins they did not feel the enervating effect of the high humidity of the forest region. Rather their skins became pleasantly dry and they were able to move about without breaking into a saturating sweat. Their length of vision steadily increased and they began to see many strange animals. One yellow striped animal had an enormously elongated neck which enabled the beast to reach to the top of the now stunted trees in order to eat the fresh green leaves which were out of reach of the smaller animals. The creature had a peculiar loping style of running which caused them all much amusement, the children particularly jumping up and down with excitement. There were also large numbers of very large and ponderous animals flapping ears and noses nearly as long as their tails. These creatures turned to face the group each time they came upon them. They threatened by flapping these giant ears and gave out ear-splitting trumpeting noises. The party came to a standstill when this happened and made no sound or sudden movement. After a few heart-stopping moments the animals grew bored with their own aggression and with one final blast of defiance moved slowly away so that the march could continue.

After several more days of marching Primo suddenly gave a signal and immediately everybody lay down. Primo, who was leading, quietly called to Abeno to bring his mother and Aqa to him, but not to stand up at all. So they crept forward, keeping as low to the ground as they could, consistent with making forward progress at all. When they reached him he made them lie flat on their stomachs and slide forward very carefully. They went forward in this manner for a few minutes, when Primo made them stop. He indicated that they could slowly lift their heads, and the sight which greeted their eyes was totally beyond anything they had ever imagined, even in their wildest dreams. Within two or three arms' length from them the ground suddenly dropped away from them very steeply indeed. Looking both to the right and to the left they could see the continuation of the wall of rock dropping way down to the valley below them. Looking straight ahead through the haze they could just distinguish what seemed to be a near vertical wall of rock rising out of the flat plaint.

They gazed at this in awe for many minutes until Aqa suddenly exclaimed, "Do you know what I think this place is?" He look Eloni, who replied with a shake of her head. "Do you remember when we were examining each of the planets as we approached Benu? In particular the giant yellow one with the contra-rotating bands of colored clouds and the little red planet which was the next one in towards Benu?" Eloni wrinkled her brow with the effort of remembrance.

"Very vaguely," she finally admitted.

"Probably I did not let you look through the telescope at what I discovered at that time, but certainly I showed Abello. Well, one of the innermost satellites of the large planet had a large area of its surface where hot molten rock from deep within its interior was flowing out on to the surface. Sometimes as we watched the rock would be thrown out explosively. I suppose the heat was being generated by the enormous tidal forces being generated by the very large mass of the primary, which in astronomical terms was very close. Then, I found three very lofty mountains on the red planet which were really very large indeed considering the comparative smallness of the planet. These mountains had large circular basins towards their summits, but there was no sign of any continuing activity although I could see evidence on the flanks of the mountain that there had been activity in the past by the river-like appearance of the rock formations. I think that we are looking at the same sort of thing except that here the effects of the atmosphere and the water have eroded the sides of the crater and softened the whole appearance. The last activity was probably many millions of years ago and the whole scene is modified by the vegetation down there as well as the grassy slopes up here." Aqa pointed to his right. "If you look over there you can just see a break in the mountain wall where the molten rock must have burst through or the rock was blown out in an explosion."

Primo saw that Aqa was pointing that way and he told Abeno, who was lying next to him, that that was where they would all be going. Primo then directed their attention to the valley floor so far beneath them. The whole atmosphere seemed to be weaving about and the changes in refraction made the outlines of the trees very hazy. Suddenly the conditions altered and the atmosphere acted as though it was a magnifying lens and they were able to see large animals of all sorts of animals grazing on the grass and the leaves of the trees. Some were running about seemingly being chased by much smaller creatures which they were unable to distinguish from this distance. For a moment more the atmosphere remained comparatively clear and they could see animals in every direction. Although there was some random movement, they were aware that the whole mass of creatures was steadily moving away to their right, but towards what they could not distinguish. Then just as suddenly as it had cleared, the air started to move again and vision was lost. Eloni, Aqa and Abeno sat back and gazed at one another, speechless for a few minutes.

"Why, there must be millions of creatures down there," said Abeno, "and if we are going to settle down around here then there will never be any shortage of food, provided we can catch them."

Primo stood up and led them back to where the rest of the group were crouching. He glanced up at the sky and assessed how long it would be before they had to make a camp before nightfall. Apparently satisfied with his calculations, he picked up his weapons and started off parallel to the rim of the crater, leaving the rest to pick up their belongings and follow after him. They slept that night under one of the stunted thorn trees which were dotted about the landscape and early the next morning started marching once more. By now the mood of the people was relaxed and joyful and the very young children were laughing and shouting and running about, glad to be free from the restrictions of silence which danger had forced them into for all the days following their hurried flight from the settlement. Soon they come to the edge of the steep-sided valley which they had seen from the rim of the crater and with great care and in single file wended their way carefully down the side going twenty or thirty paces to their right and then a similar number to their left, but always descending.

By the time all had reached the bottom of the gorge, Aqa's face was gray with pain and fatigue and he could do no more than sink down onto a rock by the side of a small stream which bounded down the valley towards the crater center, although there was a mass of tumbled hills between them and the crater which prevented clear visions. The party decided that they would proceed no further that day, and before settling down for the night Primo sent three of his young warriors back up to the top of the little valley, three more a distance towards the head of the little stream, whilst the last three were sent across the water and up to the top of the opposite side of the valley.

Abeno explained to Eloni that this was a precautionary measure although he thought it very doubtful that they would be attacked during the night.

The next morning was spent in cleaning off the dirt of the journey in the small stream – Aqa felt tremendously invigorated after lying in the warm water for a long time, and the pain of the descent was forgotten. The rest of the day was spent in a short march further down towards the crater – they rounded a small hill on their left to be greeted by the sight of the mouth of a large cave. Primo indicated that this was to be their new home. From the bright sunlit position outside the cave, the interior was terrifyingly black to Eloni and Aqa but the rest of the party, particularly the children, trooped in with shrieks of delight. The adults followed at a more dignified pace and once their eyes were accustomed to the lower intensity of light they set about the exploration of the place. Although quite large at the actual mouth, they found that just inside the cave opened out much wider. The main chamber seemed roughly semi-circular with the roof well above the level which would give a claustrophobic feeling to the Capernicans. At the very back of the cave was a small opening in the rock, which in turn opened into another much smaller cavern at the back of which there percolated a small flow of water. This ran through the entire cave system and over the outside lip of the floor. Primo indicated that this was a very easily defensible position and that they would be safe from both two-legged and four-legged predators.

Abeno soon discovered that by continuing beyond the cave for a short distance he could see through a gap in the low hills right into the crater bottom. This was now much closer to him and he found himself only a little way above the floor. He could see the main stream of water issued from the other side of the hill directly in front of the cave mouth, very quickly entering into a marshy area. Beyond this he could see a comparatively narrow neck of dry and slightly higher ground running across the marsh in front of him but not away from him. There then seemed to be another strip of march before the ground rose again slightly and was dry. Here he could see a very small fraction of the enormous number of animals which they had been watching from the lip of the crater. Here, too, he could see the whorls of dust raised by their innumerable feet as they walked and occasionally galloped away to his right, pausing every once in a while to graze on the coarse brown-green grass. He could also appreciate the noise of the continual bellowing and roaring, interspersed with the occasional scream of pain as one of the grazing animals was brought down and killed by the swift running orange and striped predators. Eloni did not like to see these things and would cover her eyes and ears when such an event seemed imminent. But despite this, she, together with Aqa and her son, sat on the ground watching the spectacle during late afternoon, nor did they tire of it as the days succeeded one another in rapid succession. Primo and his older warriors were out hunting the large animals each day and they always returned with a heavy kill.

In the meantime the younger men had been out collecting long wooden poles from a species of straight-growing trees and they gradually assembled a wooden frame by lashing the poles together. A series of upright poles had been planted into the ground and others lashed to these to form an open roof. With much finer ropes which the females made from the coarse fibers from another leafy plant, the men hung strips of meat from the butchered carcasses which slowly dried in the hot sun. the children were out before Benu rose each morning and played noisily under this framework all day, thus keeping away the large predatory birds which constantly circled in the bright blue sky overhead. Primo explained to Abeno that if they did not do this, those birds would swoop down and devour everything within a very short space of time. Gradually the number of animals passing in front of them dwindled until there were none to speak of. Many a day the hunters would return to the cave without a kill, which explained why there had been so much trouble taken in drying the meat and laying in such a stock. By care, their supplies would carry them through without too much deprivation until the time when, after the rains when the grass grew again, the animals would return.

While they waited for this to happen, the men gathered some large rocks together which they placed on each side of the strip of land between the two marshy areas. These were built up so that several men could hide behind them as well as effectively narrowing the gap between the two swamps. Further back, to the left of the cave, a small natural dip in the dry bridge was deepened so that several men could lie down here and be hidden until they were almost looking into the trench. Another two large rocks were placed just in front of this trench, one to each side, and large enough to conceal a man crouching down behind them.

After all this activity, when the preparations had been finished, a relatively slack period ensued and Aqa took advantage of this to tell Abeno the story of his home planet and all that had happened since leaving Capernica. At night, when the stars were so bright that it seemed as though one could reach up and touch them, he would point out the faint yellow star which was home. From this distance it looked quite insignificant. But Aqa pointed out that, bright and hot that Benu seemed, from Capernica it was equally insignificant. He passed on all these things which he could remember and which he thought would be of use to Abeno when, inevitably, he would be left on his own.

"It is quite obvious that sooner or later you will be the sole survivor of the expedition," said Aqa, "and I can quite imagine that after Primo's death y you will be the leader of this little group. So learn as much as you can from us, including Primo, while we are still here, and in your turn pass onto the others as much as they can understand. I can quite see that this knowledge, couple with their own experiences, will help them to start their own culture and technology which eventually will lead to the ordered civilization we had on Capernica."

"I wonder if that will eventually mean that our descendants will find it necessary to leave this place and find homes on planets encircling other suns?" enquired Abeno.

"Who can tell what sort of civilization they will eventually create," countered Aqa. "There may be disasters visited upon them that will destroy the threads of culture and all that will be left will be vague collective memories of an idealized people and existence and faith that eventually they will triumph over these adversities."

One morning, much later, when the camp arose and went outside they saw that the otherwise cloudless blue sky was full of high black clouds, while away opposite them an especially black mass hovered over the opposite rim of the crater and from time to time bright flashes of light could be seen in the cloud. This gradually approached them until presently Benu was blotted out. When this happened the cloud lost some of its blackness and they could see a wall of water descending from the cloud rapidly approaching. For a while just before this reached them there was frantic activity to collect everything moveable from the outside and bring it into the cave. It grew suddenly colder, and then the storm hit them. The rain descended in torrents and the lightning flashes and crashing thunder was almost continuous. This lasted for several hours and then seemed to stop just as suddenly as it had started. After the torrents of water had stopped running over the mouth of the cave it grew suddenly light as the clouds rolled away and Benu shone out in all his brilliance. Soon steam was rising from the wet rocks, and then from the hot ground, and the whole crater was filled with a light mist which swirled around and then evaporated in the hot sunlight. This seemed to happen day after day for a long time, so long in fact that they lost count of just how many days had passed. But, just as Primo had said, they woke up one morning to find the sky a deep blue once more without a trace of cloud anywhere. Within a few more days, the floor of the crater was covered with a brilliant green luxuriant grass with the brightly colored heads of flowers scattered throughout. Primo indicated that it would not be long before the animals started to pass, and sure enough only another two days passed before the first of the vast herds arrived. Their numbers grew steadily over the next few days until the untold millions could be seen once more. Back, too, were the ferocious predators who pestered and killed continuously. Once more the air was filled with cries and the intermittent rumbling thunder of hundreds of hooves, as first one part and then another part of the vast herd tried to evade the murderous chase of the predators.

A few days later, Primo roused Abeno from his sleep well before Benu rose into the sky and in the darkness they carefully made their way down to the near edge of the swamp. There, they concealed themselves and watched the sky as it grew steadily lighter, passing from a deep purple, through a green color to a pale yellow and finally a steely blue as Benu lifted clear of the horizon. Very carefully, Primo parted slightly the tall grasses in front of them so that he had a clear vision of the length of dry ground in front of them across the swamp. From the on as the day wore on they kept a careful tally of the number of animals which passed between the first two rocks and grazed their way forward finally passing the last two rocks with a small leap over the small ditch. Primo noted with satisfaction that the animals did not hesitate in the passage and that quite obviously the older beasts had no recollection of their previous visits to this part and no recognition that there had been various alterations.

That night Primo explained to Aqa and Eloni through Abeno that the next day they would start to kill the animals to start the stockpiling of fired meat in preparation for the scarcities until the next rainy season. He said that he and Abeno would be stationed in the small ditch and two other hunters would be hidden behind each of the first two rocks. These would signal to Primo and Abeno as soon as suitable animals had passed the first rocks. These hunters would then startle the beasts by shouts and waving of arms and as they galloped towards the ditch they would be further frightened by Abeno and himself who would rise up from the ditch. This would cause the animals to check their headlong flight which would give the hunters just a split-second chance to throw their spears and hopefully would bring down at least one of the beasts. The carcass would then be carried out of sight where others would carry out the butchering – they would return to their hiding places and if they were very lucky they might make two hills before the middle of the day. After that it would be hopeless to wait for the wind direction change during the afternoon and the animals would small them and keep well away from the trap. They would rcpcat these operations until the animals started their return journey.

Abeno was tense with excitement when they arose the next morning well before daylight and after they had eaten they took their places behind the rocks and in the ditch. He noticed that Primo had closed his eyes when they first crouched in the ditch, but he could not rest likewise. However, it was not long before he became aware of distant snorting and sounds of the grass being torn up. Primo opened his eyes immediately and clutched the shaft of his spear in the throwing grip. Abeno did similarly. Otherwise he remained motionless carefully watching Primo who was very carefully looking out through the underside of his rock where it curved down into the long grass. Presently he heard the shouts from the front two hunters which were immediately followed by a thunder of hooves. Both he and Primo leapt to their feet and Abeno was horrified to see an enormous animal bearing down on him at full gallop. He could see one red eye staring out of its socket in absolute terror and saliva cascading from its jaws as it shook its head from side to side. In four strides it reached him and during that time Abeno had taken his eye slightly away from the animal to watch Primo take a small step towards him and as the animal on his side drew level thrust his spear deep into the beast's neck just above the shoulder. But before Abeno could raise his weapon his animal was upon him and Abeno was struck by its hind quarters as it turned slightly away from him without a pause in its pace. Abeno hardly knew what had hit him as he was flung violently onto his back, hitting his head so heavily on the ground that he was knocked unconscious. The next thing he knew was that he was back in the cave and his head, which ached abominably, was cradled in his mother's lap. He opened his eyes a fraction but even in the dim light there was an immediate stab of pain behind each eyeball and he quickly closed them again very tightly. He cautiously moved first each finger, then his arms and legs, and finally twisted his trunk from side to side. Apart from feeling very bruised it did not seem that any bones had been broken. So he just rested and seemed to drift away into a profound sleep, for when he became aware of noises again Eloni told him that he had slept all through the rest of the previous day and night. He got to his feet and hobbled to the entrance of the cave and every movement of his muscles was sheer agony. He was glad to find that the light no longer hurt his eyes and the pain in his head had retreated to a slight fuzziness.

Primo greeted him somewhat anxiously, but as soon as he saw that no real harm had been done he eagerly showed Abeno the two large animals which the others had killed and which were now being skinned, butchered and then hung in strips to dry. After watching this for a while he went with Eloni back to the spot where they could watch the animals passing through the neck of dry land. Abeno showed his mother where he had been hiding and explained what he was supposed to do. Eloni was anxious for his safety and told him he must be more careful in the future.

"Yes, of course, I will take every care possible," he reassured her, "and if I get into a bad situation the large rocks are there so that we can take refuge. The rocks are not there to hide us and that is all. I think why I was so slow was because I did not quite know what to expect when I first stood up. It was quite frightening to see this large beast, many times heavier than myself, running straight at me at a full gallop and only four paces away. I shall never forget the look of terror in the animal's eye, nor the fear. But I shall be all right next time, for I know just what to expect."

He put his hand on his mother's shoulder in a reassuring fashion. Three days later Abeno had recovered himself sufficiently to take up his position behind the rock once more. When the signal was given he straightened up, moved slightly to his right and plunged his knife into the neck of the animal as it thundered past him. The blade entered the neck between the extended vertebrae as the beast reached forward for its next stride over the little ditch. The spinal cord was immediately severed and the animal barely made another two paces before sliding down in a heap. Primo and the other warriors came up to Abeno and started dancing around him. This puzzled Abeno for a while, but when he looked around him he saw that he had made the only kill that morning. Primo lifted him up on his shoulders in one swift effortless movement, and with the other warriors shrieking and dancing around him made his way back to the cave. They passed other warriors on the way who went down to bring the animal back to the camp. The fire was immediately replenished and when really hot and glowing large slices of his kill were thrown on. In a little while the outside of the meat was scorched deep brown, the meat was taken from the fire and cut into small slices with flint knives. Everybody, both the very youngest and the very oldest, sat down and gorged themselves on Abeno's kill.

On this occasions Abeno was made to sit between Primo and his second in command, and not with Aqa and Eloni. Aqa rightly surmised that the celebration was some sort of initiation rite and Abeno had reached adulthood within the tribe. The whole camp was asleep that night even before Benu had set and the blackness of night descended. But the very next day the killing began in earnest and continued relentlessly until the animals disappeared once more. In due season, the rains came again and each day was a misery, to be followed by the return of blue skies and deep green grass, and then the animals.

Several seasons passed in this fashion with Eloni and Aqa becoming more enfeebled but despite their infirmities they were revered by the whole tribe as Elders. Primo, too, began to show the strain of the hard physical life he had always had to live and gradually more and more of the daily routines were left to Abeno. Even the warriors of the tribe who were older than he looked to Abeno more and more as the next leader of the tribe. In the meantime Uika had been progressing from a sturdy childhood full of fun and teasing, to a giggling adolescence and then to a shy womanhood. Although Abeno pretended not to notice her too much he was well aware of her wellformed breasts, her wide hips and graceful carriage when she walked. She was not so shy that she was unaware of the surreptitious looks which Abeno cast in her direction from time to time and she was keenly sensitive to the purpose in his eyes when she happened to look at him as he looked at her. When this happened, they seemed to understand one another completely although there was no word spoken. One day, during a discussion about many things, with Aqa and Eloni, the subject of Uika came up.

"Both Aqa and I think that the time has arrived when you should make your own home with Uika," said Eloni, "and for myself I would like to see at least one of your children before I die. I feel that I shall not see many more rainy seasons and Aqa feels the same way about himself. Would the idea of taking Uika as your mate please you?"

To his surprise Abeno found himself squirming with embarrassment that his mother, of all people, had raised such a matter. But as he thought about the idea he calmed down somewhat and recognized the force of her argument. He gazed out across the crater floor for a little while, remembering the pleasure he took of Uika.

Eloni, accurately following the drift of his mind from the expressions which flitted across his face, and smiling to herself, said, "I think that Uika herself would not be adverse to such a union."

Abeno gave a little grunt but in the end had to admit that his mother was right. And so Primo was called to the little group for his opinion to the proposal. His reaction was immediate and very positive. He told Abeno that the whole settlement had been watching both of them for some time past being very well aware of the final outcome and watching the young people find themselves and become aware of their need for each other.

Abeno stood up and said, "So be it." Primo leapt to his feet in turn and let out a great bellow of delight. Everybody stopped what they were doing immediately and all eyes turned expectantly to Primo and Abeno. Quickly he told the whole tribe that what they all had hoped for had been agreed and that Abeno and Uika were to live together. Abeno hesitated a little and muttered to his mother something about consulting Uika first, but before Eloni could reply Abeno was aware of a soft, warm body pressing up against him and two arms eagerly wrapping themselves around his chest. He looked down into those beautiful brown eyes looking up into his and he knew that he did not have to ask for her consent.

So, once again, a great feast was prepared and the celebrations and dancing went far into the night. Eloni in the meantime had gathered a large quantity of sweet smelling dried grass which she spread over the frame of light poles which were used as a frame to raise the sleepers off the hard, cold, rocky floor of the cave. Over this she spread the soft skins which were taken from the animals which they had been killing since they had arrived at this place. Eventually the enthusiasm began to wane with first the children falling asleep where they sat, followed by the adults, one by one. At the end there was only Primo, Aqa and Eloni and the t wo young people sitting quietly warmed and lit by the dying embers of the fire. Soon Eloni and Aqa retired to their couches. Primo grunted and gathered the fire together and made sure that there would be embers in the morning to cook the first meal of the day. Then he too lay down by the fire, and Abeno and Uika sought the warmth and comfort of their special bed.

Both were a little shy as they lay down together, but presently Abeno turned on his side towards Uika and putting his left arm under her neck gently drew her to him. She turned on to her side to face him and they lay quite still for some time with their bodies touching all the way down from the chest to feet. It was not very long before this close contact had the desired effect on Abeno, and he started to twitch between his thighs, his penis grew rigid between them and Uika gurgled with pleasure as she felt him pressed against her abdomen. Instinctively she turned onto her back and opened her thighs wide, pulling him on top of her as she did so. Gently, cautiously, he entered her and then very slowly started to move rhythmically within her. For a while his mind remained in charge of his body and he was able to maintain this slow movement, to the intense gratification of them both. But then their youth and instinct began to take control and they both moved faster and faster until they reached a mutually exhausting climax with Abeno planting his seed deep within her body. They then lay quite still, panting a little, holding one another very tightly. Abeno felt that he had found someone to whom he belonged, for she had given herself freely to him and she belonged to him. He had always felt a very close affinity for his mother, for she had given him life itself. But this was something very different, for Uika belonged to him in a way in which his mother could not. They separated and fell into a light doze. But not for long, because Abeno's manhood was aroused again and Uika instinctively realized this. Once more this happened before the sky began to lighten and the less brilliant stars appeared. Abeno now felt exhausted and fell into a very deep sleep. How long he slept he had no idea, for when he opened his eyes the females of the colony were about their business and the warriors had obviously gone down to the kill. He arose somewhat sheepishly as the women, when they saw he was awake, teased him about his night's activities. He fled the cave and went around the corner of the hill to the little river where he plunged into the warm water of a small pool in the rocks. After splashing around for a while, he lay down on a sun-warmed slab in the center of the stream. He quickly dried off, and then Uika joined him.

"We will have many sons," she said softly, "and we will be very proud of them."

"I shall be equally proud of them if they are daughters," he replied.

But Uika made no further comment and Abeno realized that she had been brought up in the belief that the production of male children was all that really mattered. He wondered how these people would answer the question of what would happen if every child should be male, but he did not pursue the matter as he knew that the question would be dismissed with a shrug of the shoulders and observation that some children born were always female. Soon could be heard the shouts of the returning hunters with another kill, and Abeno suddenly realized just how hungry he was. So they both returned to the cave to be greeted by the menfolk with knowing grins. However this banter soon passed, particularly when Abeno started to give back as good as he was getting. After the meal, Primo took him to one side and asked him to restrain his appetite for Uika each night as he was needed each morning for the hunting, which was dangerous to say the least. Abeno needed his wits about him at the moment of the kill and he could suffer grievous harm if he was befuddled with sleep as a result of his sexual activities. Abeno had to admit the wisdom of this for as each season passed there were more and more mouths to fed as the colony was prospering and multiplying. He was a little put out when later he saw Primo talking quietly with Uika, but he refrained from comment.

Much later another rainy season started, by which time Uika had lost her slender shape and had become fatter round hips and waist. Soon it became unwise for them to take pleasure from one another's bodies and, although this caused Abeno some anguish it obviously did not bother Uika, for her mind was full of the preparations for the coming birth. So, temporarily, Abeno resumed his sleeping place among the warriors and the lighthearted companionship soon dispelled his ill humor. He was awakened in the predawn darkness one day by the noise of women moving about and chattering among themselves. When he sat up, Eloni came to his side and sat with him.

"What is all the fuss about?" he asked.

Eloni smiled at him and said, "Your child is being born."

Abeno started to his feet as though to go to Uika but Eloni pulled him down again.

"It is better that you stay away for the moment," she said kindly. "Uika has quite enough to attend to without you fussing around."

"How long will it take?" he asked. But before Eloni could give him a reply his question was answered from the back of the cave by a thin, piercing cry. He rose to his feet trying to see through the gloom exactly what was going on, but all he could vaguely distinguish were the backs of the a number of the females bending over what he presumed was Uika and her new baby. The yells continued and presently one of the females came over to him with the casual announcement that he had a daughter. Abeno was beside himself with joy, embracing his mother in a bear hug and then throwing his arms around the shoulders of Aqa. The rest of the tribe shuffled back to their sleeping places and dropped to the ground. Abeno and his mother raced across to where Uika was lying to find her cradling the babe in her arms while tears of remorse were streaming down her face. When she saw Abeno she cried even harder, and for some time he could not understand what was wrong, so he quietly lay down by her side and took her and the baby into his arms. He gently stroked her face and arms muttering small comforting sounds which gradually had the desired effect and she quieted. Eventually she was able to speak to him.

"I did so want to give you a son," she told him, "but instead I could only manage a daughter. I am sorry."

"But it does not matter to me whether we had a son or a daughter," he replied. "All that matters to me is that you are both well." The baby was sleeping now, lulled by the warmth of her mother's body. "Just look how beautiful she is with her chubby golden body. She is an absolute picture of health, and we should be thankful."

Uika gazed at her child for a few moments. "If you are not truly disappointed then I will be content. After all, there will be plenty more opportunities to have sons." They grinned at one another roguishly. Then it was Eloni's turn to admire the new arrival which she did with great joy in her heart. She patted Abeno's shoulder and said that she looked forward to greeting a son next time, at which Abeno promised to do his best. They left Uika to rest and regather her strength.

Life for all the colony quickly resumed its normal pattern built around the successive wet and dry seasons. The next year Uika produced twin boys, a phenomenon which was very rare, indeed almost unknown among the primitives. This produced a profound effect on the whole tribe and Abeno found himself being treated almost reverently. Eloni was afraid that this might give Abeno an exaggerated view of his own importance, but Aqa kept reminding him that the main reward of leadership of others was responsibility to others. After that, Uika produced no more twins but in successive years they had another daughter, then another one, and then a son.

The rainy season that year was particularly miserable for the whole group. It rained and rained without cessation and it was so cold. They kept as large a fire going as they possibly could bearing in mind the cramped conditions under which they were all living. A consequence of this was that before the rains departed they completely exhausted the dry wood they had collected for warmth. They reduced the fire to a minimum just for cooking purposes but even this was at an increased rate to normal for they found that they were eating more to generate body warmth. Food now began to run low but still the rains came down. They could see from the cave entrance that the quiet little stream was now a raging torrent carrying down mud and rocks from the higher ground. The air was so full of rain and mist that they could not see down into the crater bottom but Primo speculated that the hunting ground of the last few seasons would be destroyed and they would have to devise a new scheme. Abeno suggested that now that their numbers had grown so large they had obviously outrun the resources of the immediate neighborhood and when the dry season eventually arrived it would be better if they divided the colony in two, and one party should see new shelter a day or so's march away. After some debate it was agreed that this is what they would have to do if they were all to survive. Abeno said that his people would form the nucleus of the new settlement and that the next day he would set out to find a suitable place, whether the rains had stopped or not.

Consequently the next morning at first light he stepped out from the cave wrapped in skins against the cold and carrying his spear, hunting knife and food for twenty days' travel. He had not walked more than a few dozen paces before he was soaked to the skin and regretting his foresight. He turned his face towards the cave and raised his arm in a final salute. He could just see the faces of those he loved at the cave entrance. They raised their arms in salutation but he could not hear their voices for the noise of the rain. The first problem he met with was the crossing of the torrent of water now flowing down the small valley to the right of the cave entrance. He gazed at it in some consternation for a long time and came to the conclusion that it was impossible to cross it low down with any degree of safety. The only way to success would be much higher up the valley where the flow of water would be much less. So, bracing his shoulders, he put his face into the wind and rain and started the slow climb up.

This proved far more difficult than he first imagined as the track had been churned to a thin mud by the sheer force of both the wind and the rain. Consequently, he kept slipping back and on one occasion he actually fell on to his face, which did not please him at all. But he could not solve his problems and ensure the survival of the group by sitting in the mud and cursing. So he picked himself up and resume the climb. Some hours later and near to the head of the stream he came to a place where the rocks in the water were so placed that he could scramble from one to another and by this means he reached the other side. He started the downward descent and a little while later reached a large rock which had an overhanging portion. He scrambled under this and to his relief found the space to be fairly dry. Being worn out by his exertions he decided to stop for the night, which was now rapidly approaching. He ate a little of the dried meat he had brought with him and then wrapping the damp skins more closely around him to keep out the cold air he soon fell into an exhausted though disturbed sleep.

When he awoke the next morning it was already light but still raining heavily. He wearily eased his aching muscles by stretching and then reluctantly stepped out into the rain once more. He soon reached the point of the track immediately opposite the level of the cave site but he could see nothing through the rain nor could he hear any voices. The track bore around the base of the hill to his right and he passed beyond the vision of the cave dwellers if they could have seen him. All day he marched and saw neither animal nor bird. That night he could not find a rock under which to shelter and so he slept beneath a thorn bush which did little to keep off the weather. Two more days passed thus and on the third day when he woke he found that the rain had lessened to a thin drizzle. To his disgust he found that the drizzle was just as uncomfortable as the driving rain although he felt a little less cold now that the wind had dropped considerably. The following day dawned with practically no drizzle but instead there was a thick fog. He groped his way forward slowly, his instinct telling him that he was keeping to roughly the same altitude, thereby avoiding any swampy complications by inadvertently wandering down on to the floor of the crater. By now he had lost count of how many detours he had had to make up side valleys in order to cross streams rushing down to the bottom. As he walked slowly forward he became aware that the light of the fog ahead was slowly dimming. He wondered what could be the cause of this when suddenly the ground rose sharply in front of him and he was forced to turn to his left. The angle of the ground increased considerably and he found some difficulty in keeping his balance. His ankles began to ache with the strain the sharp angle placed on them but he pushed on as rapidly as caution permitted. He realized with a sudden sense of foreboding that there were not very many hours of daylight left, and as he could not camp for the night on such an angle he would have to descent to the crater floor or hope he would stumble on a flat area fairly soon. But the angle did not lessen, and just as he was about to decide that the time had come to descend he stumbled into the entrance of a moderate sized cave. He shouted loudly at the entrance but there was no answering roar from any animal inhabitants. With a sigh of relief he entered the cave and found in the gloom that there was a small shelf of rock on one side. There were large deposits of animal droppings on the floor from which he concluded that the cave had been occupied at one time but as these were bone dry it was obvious that the owners had left some time ago. He regretted that he had no dry wood with him for he could have made a fire with the droppings and warmed himself as well as cook some of the dried meat. At the thought of that his stomach positively crawled with hunger and he realized that he had not eaten properly for days. He felt himself slowly drying off and so he was able to eat more heartily than he had done for a long time. By this time it was quite dark outside and feeling exhausted he curled up in his skins on the shelf and slept dreamless the whole night.

In the morning light he was able to carry out a thorough inspection of the cave which he found to be entirely satisfactory for his purposes. It was a little smaller than the one in which his mother was even now awaiting his return but in general aspect was very similar. It would certainly house for many seasons to come the small number of persons who would come with him. He decided that he would rest in his new home for the rest of that day and start the journey back at first light the next morning. When he awoke the next day he found to his annoyance that it had started to rain again, and as there was no wind to alter the angle of the rain it descended vertically, driving heavily onto the saturated ground.

However, buoyed up by the thoughts of seeing his loved ones again, he decided to accept the discomforts and started to walk. In a short while he reached the part where the hillside rose much more sharply from the crater floor and he took the greatest care in negotiating this part of the journey. His progress was painfully slow when he stopped for a short while to ease the strain in his legs. He turned half right so that he was facing directly down the steep slope. He stood there for a few minutes, when he suddenly felt his feet give a small slip beneath him. It was not enough to throw him off balance but he looked further to his left and could see that the moving mud was rap idly filling up the footmarks he had previously made. He turned to face the way home and became aware that the whole hillside in front of him was moving down towards the crater bottom, very slowly at the moment and then visibly increasing in speed. He turned around and saw that the same thing was happening behind him. He hesitated for a few moments, not sure what was the best course of action. Should he go forward round the base of the hill? He decided that that was too risky for he did not remember just how far he would have to walk to get to the place where the ground sloped less steeply. No, the best thing to do was to go back to the cave. He turned around once more and took a few paces. The mud beneath his feet slid faster and faster at the same time gradually getting deeper. He realized that very soon the force of the mud would force him to lose his footing. He began to feel that he would not make the safety of the cave and he began to be afraid. But he could see no alternative but to keep going on just as fast as he could. The volume of sliding mud steadily increased and suddenly he became aware of a roaring nose coming from the hillside above him. At that moment he lost his balance and fell onto his side, the sliding mud rapidly built up behind him rapidly accelerating his downhill movement. Faster and faster he slid forward and downward until he was moving so rapidly that he could no longer regain his feet. The bulky pack on his back was his main downfall as the weight of mud built up rapidly behind this. The roaring nose grew rapidly louder but he was unable to turn his head sufficiently to see what was causing it. He suddenly saw the trunk of a small tree right in his path and he hoped for the moment that he would be able to arrest his slide by clutching hold of it. He hit it a few moments later with such a blow in the middle of his chest as to knock the breath right out of him. At least the downward slide was halted. He waited a few moments for the pain in his chest to subside and then struggled up on to his hands and knees. The roaring noise was now deafening and he looked up the hill. He experienced a moment of total horror as he saw just a few paces away from him a great wall of mud rushing towards him. He realized that the whole hillside was sliding down into the crater, the topsoil having become waterlogged by the very heavy rains of many days. Then the mud hit him. His head was brought into violent contact with the trunk of the tree, there was a fraction of time when he felt his ears, eye sockets, mouth and lungs filing with mud, a great explosion of sparks in his brain, and blackness. Abeno was no longer in this world.

The mud roared on past the little tree which help fast for but a few seconds more and then it too was overwhelmed, sliding with the irresistible mud down to the crater bottom. Presently all was still, the fog broke to reveal a hot sun shining from a cloudless blue sky. There remained no trace that Abeno had been on the hillside but a few moments before.

Uika had been sitting in the dry cave, idly watching the fog swirl around the entrance as she suckled the latest addition to her family. Suddenly she sat up straight, uttered a shriek of despair and fell back unconscious. Eloni rushed over to where Uika lay and cradled her head in her lap. After a while Uika opened her eyes to discovery the whole group gathered anxiously around her.

"Abeno is dead," she said, in response to the unspoken question in their eyes. She turned her face to the cold wall of the cave and wept. Later she recovered herself and went to the entrance. She could fell the warmth of Benu on her body, for the clouds had parted and the sky was the familiar deep blue. She turned her face up to Benu and finished her previous remark, this time only to herself, "but life must go on." She turned again to go back into the cave while her children silently came to her side, vaguely aware that something was wrong but not comprehending anything of the tragedy which had befallen the family.

Several days later Primo and some of the warriors returned to the camp, dejection written on their faces. Primo reported that they had found the cave where Abeno had spent two nights and from whence he had obviously left on the return journey, but that there was no sign of Abeno and they presumed that they would see him no more. Eloni and Uika silently mourned their mutual loss and seemed to draw ever closer in their misery. Aqa felt that he would not long survive this blow to all their hopes. Primo sat by himself one evening, thinking over all that had happened since the strangers had come down from the sky together. He realized that the two survivors would not live for very much longer, and in a flash of intuition realized that it was his destiny to train Abeno's children so that in due course they could assume their rightful places as leaders and teachers of his little flock. At this thought he was content.

FINALE

During the 1960's reports were coming out of East Africa concerning the discovery of a broken skull with a cranial capacity in excess of those hominids also being discovered of similar age. Associated with this skull were finely worked stone tools of a quality superior to those made and used by man a million years later. The original skull was dated at about 2.5 million year old.

Well………………………..